THE CURSE OF CAIN

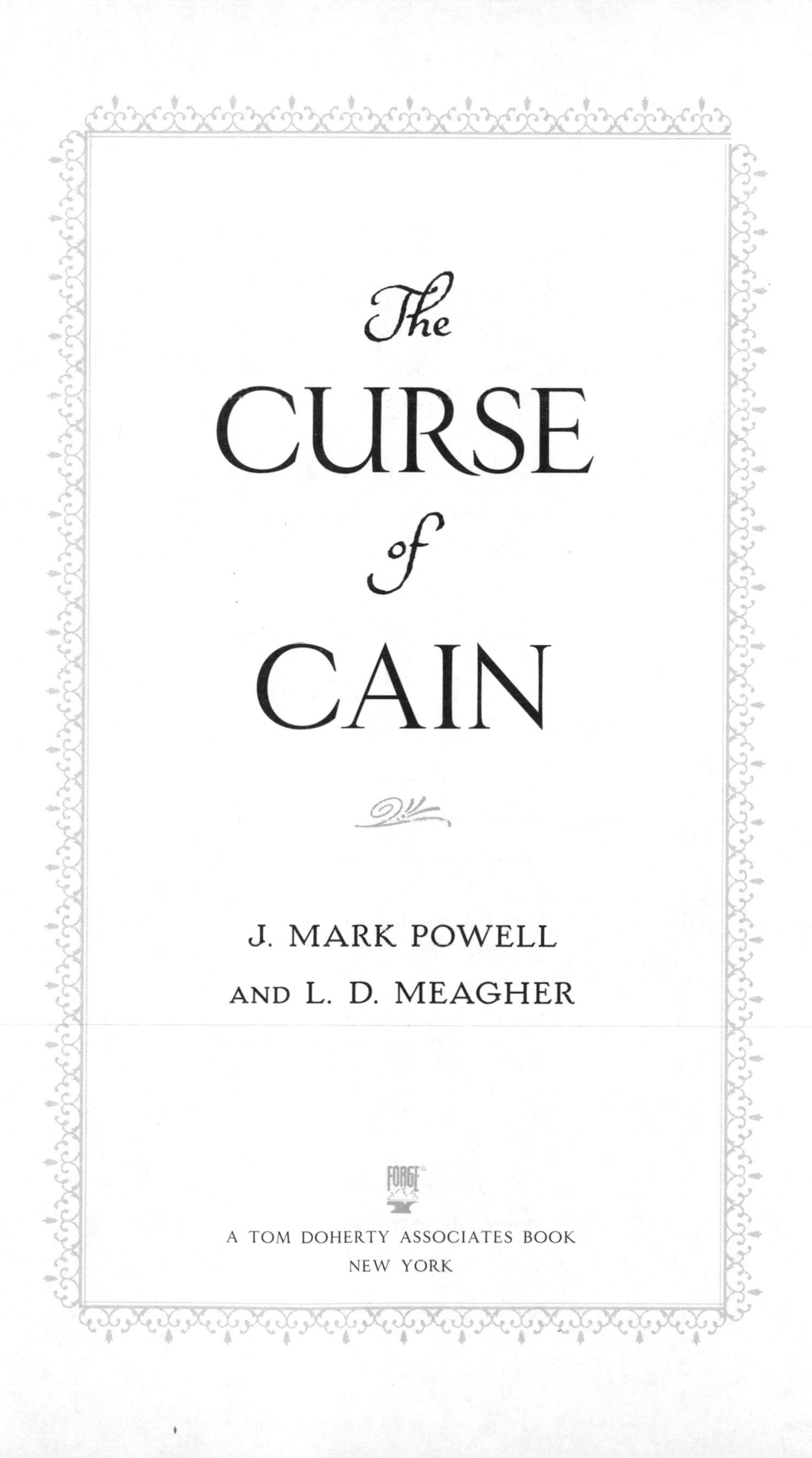

The CURSE of CAIN

J. MARK POWELL
AND L. D. MEAGHER

A TOM DOHERTY ASSOCIATES BOOK
NEW YORK

This is a work of fiction. All the characters and events portrayed in this novel are either fictitious or are used fictitiously.

THE CURSE OF CAIN

This book is printed on acid-free paper.

Edited by Brian M. Thomsen

Photos from the private collection of J. Mark Powell

A Forge Book
Published by Tom Doherty Associates, LLC
175 Fifth Avenue
New York, NY 10010

www.tor.com

Forge® is a registered trademark of Tom Doherty Associates, LLC.

Library of Congress Cataloging-in-Publication Data

Powell, J. Mark.
The curse of Cain / J. Mark Powell and L. D. Meagher.—1st ed.
p. cm.
"A Tom Doherty Associates book."
ISBN 0-765-31088-0 (acid-free paper)
EAN 978-0765-31088-0
1. Lincoln, Abraham, 1809–1865—Assassination—Fiction. 2. United States—History—Civil War, 1861–1865—Fiction. 3. Government investigators—Fiction. 4. Washington (D.C.)—Fiction. 5. Assassins—Fiction. I. Meagher, L. D. (Larry Dale) II. Title.

PS3616.O8795C87 2005
813'.6—dc22

2004054118

First Edition: April 2005

Printed in the United States of America

0 9 8 7 6 5 4 3 2 1

This book is dedicated to

JOHN RONALD *and* SHIRLEY POWELL

and to

VIRGINIA MEAGHER

and the memory of DONALD G. MEAGHER.

ACKNOWLEDGMENTS

It takes much work to transform an idea into a finished book, and a great many people play important roles along the way. Without the support of our literary agent, Frank Weimann, who refused to stop believing in us, this novel would never have reached publication. His editor, Karen Haas, showed us how to trim a manuscript and still like it. At Forge Books, our editor, Brian Thomsen, has been unflaggingly supportive and his editorial assistant, Natasha Panza, has been unfailingly helpful.

From the January day during Louisville, Kentucky's, Great Blizzard of 1994, when the first line of this story was typed, through the day the final pages were typeset, countless people have offered counsel and encouragement. In the early days, Neil and Anita Kuvin, Laurie Bruffey, Matt Williams, Kevan Ramer, Rosalie Mainous, and Melanie Onnen kept hope alive. Our Atlanta colleagues Brad Johnson, Cameron Baird, John DeDakis, and Martin Hill, as well as Diane Lore, offered helpful insights. The support of curator Retha Stephens and Kennesaw Mountain National Battlefield Park's staff is too valuable to describe. This book would not exist without the perpetual friendship of Michael Graham, Don Holmes, Tim Chew, and Ed Seiz, who read the original manuscript while recovering from heart surgery. Dana and David McCallum opened their Washington, D.C., home to us during an eventful week at their mutual place of employment, the United States Senate.

Countless people freely shared their historical expertise. Foremost is Michael Kauffman, who never hesitated to dip into his amazing well of knowledge. Laurie Vergie of the Surratt Society was generous with her time, and Betty Owensby acquainted us with wartime Richmond. The late Michael Maione, historian at Ford's Theatre National Historic Site, graciously welcomed us during a very stressful day, and Park Ranger Roger Powell assisted us with much-needed research. Colonel J. A. Barton Campbell and John Coski of Richmond's Museum of the Confederacy opened their doors with the warmest Southern hospitality. Mark Greenough of Living History Associates, Ltd., fleshed out important details about the Confederate capital. Gary O'Neill of Rochester, New York, introduced us to Chatham Street. Special thanks go to Capitol Police Officer Jeff Burnside, of the Shreveport, Louisiana, Burnsides.

Any faults, historical or literary, are ours alone.

I am abandoned,
with the curse of Cain upon me,
when, if the world knew my heart,
that one blow would have made me great . . .

—FROM THE DIARY OF
JOHN WILKES BOOTH, APRIL 1865

THE CURSE OF CAIN

PROLOGUE

Near Port Royal, Virginia
April 26, 1865

"You've got two minutes to make up your mind. Then we're opening fire."

John Wilkes Booth didn't need two minutes. He didn't need two seconds. His mind was made up.

He leaned forward and squinted. A sharp stab of pain shot through his broken leg. He gritted his teeth and peered through a crack in the barn wall. In the predawn gloom, he could make out a dozen or so Federal soldiers milling around outside.

"What are we going to do?" The young man in the barn with him was pale and drawn.

Booth gave a grim smile. He pulled a pencil and small leather-bound appointment book from his coat pocket and began scribbling. "What's wrong, Davey? Afraid of a little fight?"

David Herold was pacing around the small barn, dodging sheaves of tobacco hanging from the ceiling. "This is insane. They've got us licked."

"Are you turning coward on me?"

Herold looked through an opening in the barn wall. "Call it what you like. If we stay in here, they'll kill us for sure. I'll take my chances out there."

Anger flooded Booth's features. "You're a damned coward!" He resumed scribbling furiously.

Herold crept over to the door. "They're pointing their rifles at us."

Booth called out without looking up, "There's a man in here who wants to surrender awful bad."

"Tell him to come out," was the shouted reply.

Herold gave Booth a long look. The actor's eyes were trained on his writing. Herold shoved open the barn door. Blue-coated arms grabbed him and dragged him away.

Booth's pencil raced over the page. *"I don't wish to shed a drop of blood, but it's all that's left."* He quickly reviewed the passage he considered his final testament, deciding it was a fitting farewell.

"Now what about you, Booth?" the voice called again.

"I'll never surrender!" he shouted. Booth closed the cover on the appointment book and stuffed it back into his pocket. Then he smelled smoke.

It was coming from the back of the barn. He pulled himself to his feet, teeth grinding against the pain. He placed his hand against a wall to steady himself. He heard the sharp report of a gunshot; before he could react, Booth felt a lance of pain burn into his neck. All sensation in his body vanished as he toppled to the floor.

Soldiers swarmed into the barn, coughing and waving their hands to ward off the thickening smoke. Grabbing Booth by the shoulders, they dragged him outside. Detective Everton Conger rushed forward and began patting down Booth's pockets. He found nothing but the appointment book.

"Have your men check the barn," he told the officer in charge of the detail. "Quickly, before we lose evidence in the fire." As the detail sprang into action, Conger walked back toward the farmhouse. A young army officer was standing in the shadows. He took the appointment book from Conger and opened it.

The cramped scrawl was hard to make out in the flickering light of the burning barn. *"For six months we worked only to capture; but with our Cause now lost, something decisive and great must be done."* The young officer glanced toward Conger. "It's some kind of diary," he said. He looked toward the barn. "Did they find any weapons?"

"I'll see," Conger said and set off toward the barn.

The officer returned his attention to the diary. The rambling account began with Booth's reasons for plotting against President Lincoln. The officer flipped forward and saw that two pages had been torn out of the book. When the writing resumed, Booth was recounting the plans he had made to kidnap Lincoln the month before. The diary named all Booth's accomplices and described the role each was to play in the abduction.

He flipped ahead, giving each page a passing glance. They had been written in obvious haste over the course of several days. Finally, the name he was searching for leapt from the page. The young officer quickly scanned the passage. *"I am betrayed by a man I trusted, the man who struck the blow I had intended to strike myself."*

The officer glanced toward the burning barn. Flames silhouetted the figure of Conger marching toward him. He turned his back and quickly began tearing pages out of the diary, stuffing them in his jacket pocket.

"Anything of interest?" Conger's voice was close behind him.

He turned and held up the diary. "The nearest thing we're going to get to a full confession." He handed the book to Conger, who eagerly pulled it open.

"I did notice one thing," the young officer added. "There seem to be a few pages missing."

Richmond, Virginia
February 1865

A muffled drumbeat rolled down the street. It echoed off brick buildings in counterpoint to the patter of rain. Matching bay horses draped in soggy black crepe stomped their hooves and sent impatient clouds of steam from their noses. People lining the street bowed their heads as a squad of soldiers filed out of St. Paul's Church carrying a coffin through the steady drizzle.

An old man watched from the sidewalk in front of the church's massive portico as the funeral procession pulled away. To his right, an Irishman scratched absently at his thick, black beard. To his left, a minister from a nearby church silently recited the Twenty-third Psalm.

The hearse shed a stream of rainwater as it turned south onto Ninth Street. The old man passed a hand over his wet, flowing locks. He shifted his gaze across the street to the statue of George Washington, which dominated the high ground of Capitol Square. He looked up through a latticework of barren tree branches to the flagpole atop the Capitol building. The Confederate national flag hung limp in the rain. There was no sign of the St. Andrew's Cross in its upper left-hand corner. On this day, only its field of white was visible.

The old man sighed as he put on his tall black hat. "Anyone going out to the cemetery?"

"Not I," the Irishman muttered, looking up into the leaden sky dripping cold drizzle. "Not on a day like this."

"I can't go either," the minister added. "I have to perform a funeral at my own church."

"There's been more than enough of those lately," the old man noted. His eyes followed the funeral procession on its stately trip down Ninth Street. "Just ask poor General Pegram there."

The minister shook his head. "We are losing the bravest men of the Confederacy."

"Don't worry yourself." A grin spread through the Irishman's whiskers. "Soon we'll have the Negroes armed and in the trenches alongside our white soldier boys. That will teach the Yankees a thing or two, eh, Ruffin?"

"You sound more and more like a walking editorial from that newspaper of yours," the old man answered.

"Just doing me bit for the noble Cause," the Irishman sneered.

The minister tugged at his frayed black velvet waistcoat. "If ever there was a time for Christian charity . . ."

"Charity won't bring poor Pegram back," the old man observed as the drums died away in the distance. "Nor will it produce a new commander to lead our troops."

"It isn't officers we're needing." The Irishman snorted. "It's a commander in chief who knows how to fight a war."

The minister's eyes widened. "How dare you disparage the man who stands between us and the vile Yankees! Why, if the president were here—"

"He is, Reverend Hoge." The old man nodded toward the church steps. The President of the Confederate States of America stood bareheaded in the rain with the late general's family. Drizzle collected on the small tuft of beard at the bottom of his long face. His crown of gray hair gave him an air of distinction. He started to speak, then coughed. A racking spasm seized him. Two army officers rushed to his side and helped him back into the church.

"There's your savior of the Southern Cause," the Irishman spat. "Can't even take care of himself, much less look out for the rest of us."

The minister peered down his long nose at the Irishman. "All the more reason for us to give him every ounce of support."

"The Yankees are already at the city's back door, man. Are we to follow him like lemmings off the side of a cliff?" The Irishman's voice rose. "Are we to allow that fool to destroy the very last hope of our independence? Why, if there was a single member of Congress with an ounce of spine, Davis would be hauled before an impeachment proceeding."

The old man spotted a familiar figure emerging from the church. He caught the man's eye and smiled. "Here's the very sort of man you described. Hello, Congressman."

The newcomer offered a wan smile. His ashen face and bloodshot eyes contrasted sharply with the rich green brocade of his vest. His finely cut black coat, like everything else in the Confederate capital, had been patched often. He mumbled a greeting.

"Perhaps you can settle an argument," the old man went on, nodding to the Irishman. "My passionate friend from the newspaper says our country needs a new president." He tipped his head toward the minister. "My compassionate friend from the clergy says our country needs more prayer. What do you think?"

The congressman shrugged. "What we really need is a way through that damned Yankee blockade. With Fort Fisher fallen and Wilmington in a vise grip, we're cut off from our lifeline to England and France. The hard times of this winter will seem a fond memory come spring."

The old man frowned. "That's a particularly harsh assessment."

"Reality is harsh, Ruffin," the congressman replied. "We're already hard-pressed to feed the people of Richmond, not to mention the army. In another few weeks, there won't be a shop in the city with anything to sell."

"My point exactly," the Irishman thundered. "The mismanagement of this government is criminal." He wheeled on the old man. "Is this what you planters saw in our future when you raised the banner of secession? Is this the vision that filled your mind when you pulled the lanyard on that cannon aimed at Fort Sumter?"

"Don't browbeat him, Mitchel," the minister objected.

"He is entitled to his anger, Reverend." The old man squared his shoulders, then glanced at the Irishman. "Even if it is misdirected."

"What do you mean?"

"The source of our troubles is not to be found over there." The old man gestured toward the Capitol. "Were Thomas Jefferson himself to walk among us again, I have no doubt he would find the task of protecting the South every bit as daunting as President

Davis does. No, my friends, the true problem is not in the Confederacy." He lowered his voice to a menacing whisper. "It's our enemy. Our implacable, tyrannical foe who will not rest until he has crushed the skeleton of every Southern man to dust."

"We must pray for deliverance," the minister intoned.

"Pray if you like," the old man growled. "But the Good Lord helps those who help themselves."

The Irishman threw up his hands. "What more can we do? We hurl our armies at them, but the Yankees keep coming."

The old man stroked his chin. "We must find a more effective strategy. Something that would strike at the very heart of the matter."

"And slice it out," the congressman added.

Ruffin cocked an eyebrow. "Yes. If there were only some way to remove the offending organ."

A look of resolution settled on the face of the congressman. "That would require the services of a surgeon." A grim smile tugged at the corners of his mouth. "A gifted specialist. If only there were such a man . . ."

She was snoring. The flare of a match sent light dancing across her naked form. Her hair was a dark waterfall cascading over her shoulder into the pool that was her breast.

Beautiful girl, he thought.

She snored again.

Pity, he told himself as he drew the smoke from a long Havana. Unbecoming in one so lovely. And so talented. Slowly, he exhaled and closed his eyes. He recalled her laughter as he'd unbuttoned her dress, how eager she had seemed for him to take her, like so few women of her calling.

He tried to remember her name as he pulled on his trousers. Annie? Amanda? Adelaide? Did it matter? Soon she would be a memory. Basil Tarleton seldom bothered to catalogue such memories by name.

He cracked open the door, allowing a sliver of gaslight to slip into the room. This woman might be worth remembering. She had kissed and caressed him with a passion he had seldom experienced. As he buttoned his fly, he thought of her hands. They seemed drawn to his body, eager to touch, to explore.

Amy, he remembered at last. Her name was Amy.

Tarleton reached into the pocket of his overcoat draped across a chair. His fingers slid quickly past an envelope and a pair of gloves to settle on what he needed. He gripped it in his palm as he walked back to the bed and stood over her.

She shifted to one side. Her breasts jiggled lightly. He smiled, remembering their soft texture. Her mouth fell open and another snore blasted across the room.

In a single lightning movement, his left hand clamped down on her mouth as the knife in his right neatly sliced her throat. Her eyes bulged open. He pressed harder to suppress her scream, ducking to avoid a stream of blood.

Her frantic kicking quickly subsided to a feeble twitch. With a final gurgle, she fell limp, her brown eyes staring up at him.

Tarleton wiped the knife on the sheet and returned it to his coat pocket. Then he finished dressing.

There was a faint tap on the door. "Mr. Tarleton?"

He walked over and opened the door. "Miss Rosalie," he said warmly.

"I trust everything was to your liking?" The owner of the highest-priced brothel on Cary Street stood with one hand on her ample hip. The other hand, heavily decorated with gold and silver rings, delicately held a smoldering cheroot.

"As always." He smiled.

"A fella showed up at the front door and asked me to give you this." She passed him a calling card.

MAJOR ROBERT MORTON was printed in bold black script. Flipping it over, Tarleton found a note written in a crabbed hand: *"Will you please call upon me at one o'clock tomorrow afternoon in Room 46 of the Spotswood Hotel? It concerns a matter of the most serious nature. R.M."*

He mulled over the message as he tucked the card into his vest pocket. The phrasing suggested this Major Morton was a man of substance. Tarleton smiled. That meant money. As he shrugged on his overcoat, he felt the comforting pressure of the loaded revolver he kept inside.

"Tell me about the gentleman who delivered it."

"He was no gentleman." Miss Rosalie puffed on her cigar. "A squat, dumpy little thing," she continued. "He was long past his last shave, and longer past his last bath."

Tarleton rubbed a thumb along his sharp jaw. He revised his image of Major Robert Morton, and his calculations of the man's net worth, sharply downward. "Did you tell him I was here?"

Miss Rosalie smiled. "I hope you know me better than that, Mr. Tarleton."

He returned the smile as he reached into his pants pocket and removed a wad of currency. He flipped through the bills, bypassing the green Yankee notes. "I know I can trust you." He handed her two red Confederate fifties. "And you know I appreciate the trouble you go to for me."

Miss Rosalie folded the bills into her palm. "It's no trouble at all, Mr. Tarleton."

He stepped back into the room and picked up the carpetbag he'd concealed behind the armchair. Miss Rosalie advanced a step into the room and looked in puzzlement at the stain spreading across the bed. Tarleton produced a Confederate hundred-dollar bill.

"That should cover the cost of cleaning this up," he said, dropping the note on the foot of the bed. He retrieved his flat-brimmed hat from the side table, tipped it toward his hostess, and strode out the door.

At precisely one o'clock the next afternoon, Tarleton stood outside Room 46 in the Spotswood Hotel. He passed his hand through his carefully trimmed dark blond hair and gave the waistcoat of his suit a quick tug. Then he rapped smartly on the door.

It opened to reveal a fat, shabbily dressed runt who smelled of foul beer. Tarleton narrowed his eyes. "Are you the one who sent for me?"

"I sent for you," a voice called from within the room. The disheveled troll stepped aside and allowed Tarleton to enter.

He let his eyes dart quickly around the room. The wallpaper was peeling, the drapes were frayed, and there was a musty odor in the air. Tarleton remembered when the Spotswood had been the pearl of the Confederacy, playing host to glittering Southern ladies and their dapper escorts. The best Richmond society could produce these days was the occasional "starvation party," full of false bravado but sorely lacking in amenities. Such as food.

Tarleton's gaze fell on the other man in the room. He looked more like a "Major Morton" than the lout who had admitted him. The man's dark green brocade vest may have seen better days, but it was freshly pressed and matched the cravat knotted at his throat.

He spoke in a rich baritone with a pronounced drawl. "I appreciate your punctuality, sir. May I offer you a drink?"

Tarleton's smile did not touch his icy blue eyes. "Perhaps later."

"Please make yourself comfortable." The man waved toward two faded armchairs. Tarleton glanced at the short, fat man still standing at the door. "Harry does odd jobs for me," his host explained, "when he's not fleecing some poor soul with a deck of cards. Harry, take Mr. Tarleton's hat and coat."

Tarleton glowered at Harry. "That won't be necessary." The unkempt gambler remained frozen where he stood. Tarleton turned back to the other man. "Your message suggested we have important business to discuss. You must know that all my business is conducted in strictest confidence." He glanced again toward the man at the door.

"I assure you, Harry is very discreet."

Tarleton eyed Harry, who seemed to shrink under his gaze. "I certainly hope so."

"Come sit down." The man placed his hand lightly on Tarleton's arm and steered him toward a chair. "I'd like to offer you a proposition I believe you'll find quite rewarding."

Tarleton settled into the chair and placed his hat on his lap. "By all means, Major." He smiled again. "Or should I say 'Congressman'?"

His host lifted an eyebrow. "You know who I am?"

The smile stayed fixed to Tarleton's face. "Robert Standiford is your name. You represent Georgia in the Confederate Congress."

Standiford returned the smile. "I'm impressed."

"I also know that you once served in the United States Congress, but quit Washington to return to Georgia and agitate in favor of secession." Tarleton's smile dimmed. "Perhaps that's why General Sherman paid special attention to your holdings south of Atlanta, and why your son Adam, when he was wounded at Peachtree Creek, was left unattended by Yankee doctors." He shook his head. "A belly wound, I am told, is a most unpleasant way to die."

Standiford's face lost its color. His mouth was hanging agape as he stared at the expressionless man before him. Tarleton held his gaze and waited.

"Why," Standiford finally sputtered, "why, sir, I must say . . ." He cleared his throat. "I must say, Mr. Tarleton, you seem to know quite a lot about me."

Tarleton bowed his head slightly in acknowledgment. "And may I return the compliment, Congressman? It's not everyone who would know to leave a message for me at Madame Rosalie's."

"That was Harry's doing." Standiford had regained some of his composure and offered Tarleton a small smile. "He has his uses." He cleared his throat again. "To business, then?"

Tarleton nodded.

"I would be willing to engage your services," the Congressman began, "for the sum of five thousand dollars."

Tarleton regarded him coolly. "Not interested."

"I assure you, five thousand dollars is a respectable amount of money."

Tarleton cast a dismissive gaze at the bare floor planks, discolored in the shape of a missing carpet. "Perhaps to the denizens of this hovel. I would suggest you engage one of them to do your bidding."

"I am a man of some standing, you know." Standiford sniffed. "I could hardly be seen trafficking with riffraff from the streets of Richmond."

Tarleton glanced toward Harry and snorted derisively. Standiford pressed on. "This is a most delicate matter. I require the services of a professional."

"Then allow me to offer a professional opinion." Tarleton picked idly at unseen lint on his hat. "For five thousand dollars, you could perhaps rid yourself of a wealthy maiden aunt who had outlived her usefulness or a sticky-fingered underling at a small retail establishment. I judge neither example describes your present circumstances."

"Certainly not."

Tarleton's gaze swept across Standiford's face. "Just who is it you wish to be rid of?"

"Abraham Lincoln."

Tarleton's eyes widened in surprise, then narrowed in contemplation. He absently tapped his finger against his pursed lips.

"Don't you wish to know why I want Lincoln dead?" Standiford asked.

"Not particularly."

"That vile man has supervised the unjust, illegal, systematic destruction of the Southern people," Standiford hissed, his face growing flushed. "Lincoln has made it his personal mission to—"

"Enough," Tarleton said sharply. "My relationship with my clients is strictly a business matter. Whether it's a wayward wife, a crooked partner, or someone the client just plain doesn't like, it's all the same to me."

"Even when the target is the President of the United States?"

"Well, there is that." Tarleton idly rubbed his finger along the brim of the hat on his lap. At last, he said, "Not for a mere five thousand. You'll have to do better than that. Much better."

Standiford frowned. "How much do you want?"

"Twenty-five thousand dollars."

"What?" Standiford exploded.

"In gold."

"Dear God! You have nerve, sir!"

"*I* have nerve?" Tarleton gave a quiet laugh. "You ask me to kill the President of the United States and you say *I* have nerve? No, Congressman Standiford, it is not I who has nerve."

They stared at each other.

"Ten thousand, cash," Standiford countered.

"Twenty. Ten in gold, ten in Yankee greenbacks. That is my final offer."

"That amount can be secured." Standiford swallowed in defeat. "I'll have to talk to some people." He gestured his minion toward him. "Harry has already secured a mount for your trip north."

"Tell him to have it ready at dusk."

Impressed, Standiford arched his eyebrows. "You do not waste time, sir."

"A great deal of money is at stake."

"The horse will be at a livery stable near here." The congressman smirked. "With the cavalry rounding up every piece of horseflesh they lay their eyes on, it's the last place they'd look for one."

"And the money?" Tarleton prompted.

"You will receive five thousand tonight."

"And you will deliver the rest after I complete the job."

"Agreed." They shook hands solemnly.

"Now," Tarleton said, "I believe I'll take you up on that drink."

A string of ambulances slowly groaned past. Jack Tanner stepped to one side so he could see around their tall canvas coverings and keep his eyes fixed on the hotel entrance across the street. The wind hit him full in the face, making him clutch his threadbare gray uniform jacket tight at the collar and huddle against a brick wall.

Two years in the Confederate Provost Guard had taught him patience was even more important than cunning when trying to capture a suspect. For three hours he had stood on this busy corner, eyes focused on the Spotswood Hotel. He stomped his feet to fight the cold, aggravating the shrapnel wound in his thigh.

As Jack rubbed the sore spot, he finally caught sight of the prize he had so patiently sought. A stump of a man in a coat more ragged than his own exited the Spotswood, turned the corner, and headed down Eighth Street toward the James River.

Jack ignored the complaints from his throbbing leg and set off after him. The man passed the door of the oyster bar on the side of the hotel, then paused at the next corner to let a horse-drawn artillery piece rattle past. By the time he crossed the street Jack was on his heels.

When they reached an alley farther down the block, Jack lunged forward and shoved his quarry into it. He slammed the little man against a wall and wedged a forearm against his throat.

"If it isn't Harry Kincaid." Jack leaned forward until his nose was nearly touching Kincaid's. "Remember me? I ran you out of town three months ago. I broke up your crooked little card game three months before that. I told you never to set foot in Richmond again four months before that. Remember, Harry?"

The gambler's piggish eyes blinked rapidly. "Sure, I remember." Beer-laced breath puffed out of his mouth.

Jack grabbed Harry's lapels and jerked him upright. "A lot of folks want to talk to you. First in line is that young fella you cheated at cards last week. You remember him, don't you?"

"Sure, whatever you say."

A grin cut across Jack's face. "It's not what I say. It's what the attorney general's nephew has to say. You picked the wrong pigeon this time."

Harry panted.

"The attorney general has been on my back all week to nail you. Confess and maybe he'll go easy on you." The only response was the man's stale breath. Jack again pressed his forearm against the man's throat. "I'm tired of chasing your sorry ass all over town. I can throw you back inside that hellhole of a stockade and make you so miserable you'll wish you'd died as a child. Or maybe I'll just march you down to Petersburg and let you starve in the trenches with the army."

Harry shook his head, his eyes bulging, lower lip trembling.

"What's it gonna be?"

"How's about . . ." Harry gagged on the words. Jack eased the pressure on his throat. The gambler coughed and sputtered. "How's about, maybe, you and me making a little deal?"

"What could I possibly want from you?"

Harry's eyes narrowed. "Maybe I know about something that's coming up, see? Maybe I tip you to it in time to stop it."

"What are you going to do? Squeal on some poker players you owe money to? Have me bust up their game for you?"

Rivulets of sweat streamed down the little man's face. "Nothing like that. Honest. This ain't no small-potatoes card game." Harry lowered his voice and leaned toward Jack. "It's big."

"How big?"

"Biggest thing I ever heard of."

Jack gazed evenly at the gambler while his mind sorted through his options. Harry Kincaid was the worst sort of gutter trash and couldn't be trusted. On the other hand, he did socialize with the sort of people who might have information useful to the Provost Guard. "I'll give you one minute to convince me."

"Not here." Harry nodded toward a vacant building a few paces down the alley. "In there." Jack led the way, dragging Harry by the collar. He stepped inside and cautiously looked around. The building was a deserted shop, one of the many driven out of business by the Union naval blockade and the wildly inflated Confederate money.

Jack backed Harry against a wall. "All right, talk. What have you got that's worth saving your filthy neck?"

Harry took a deep breath and said in a low tone, "Some men in this city are planning murder."

That was the last thing Jack expected to hear. He was ready for Harry to describe a swindle or maybe a robbery. But murder? "Who's the target?"

"You ain't gonna believe it."

"You're probably right."

Harry drew himself up to his full, if insignificant, height. "Abe Lincoln."

Jack paused, then threw back his head and let loose a roaring laugh. Harry blinked rapidly, then halfheartedly joined in.

"You're one funny man, Harry," Jack said as he gasped for breath. "That's the best one I ever heard. You expecting me to save your sorry hide for a wild story like that!" There was more laughter. This time, Jack laughed alone.

"It's the truth," Harry insisted. "I was there when they planned it."

The laughter subsided, but a smile still creased Jack's cheeks. "Who? Jeff Davis and General Beauregard?"

"No, no." Harry reached up to clutch Jack's sleeve. "I'm telling you straight. I was there in the hotel this afternoon when they set it all up. I even arranged the meeting between Congressman Standiford and that fellow Tarleton."

The smile evaporated from Jack's face. "Who did you say?"

"Robert Standiford. Congressman from Georgia."

Jack waved the name aside. "The other one."

"Tarleton. Got himself some fancy first name."

"Basil Tarleton," Jack muttered.

"That's the one."

"What do you know about this Tarleton?"

Harry shrugged. "Got himself a reputation for solving other people's problems, if you know what I mean." He tilted his head back and scraped his forefinger across his throat. "I heard about him when I was working the Mississippi riverboats."

"I've heard about him, too." Jack recalled the case of a wealthy planter killed the previous summer. There were no witnesses, no suspects, just a name whispered in dark corners—Basil Tarleton. When he had tried to track the man down, he'd learned Tarleton disappeared even before the body was cold, apparently aboard a blockade runner bound for Europe. "And you say you've seen him?" Harry nodded. "What does he look like?"

"Tall." Harry lifted his hand well above his head. "Thin as a rail. Dressed to the nines. A real pretty boy. Blond hair. And those eyes." He shook his head. "Those blue, blue eyes."

"Lots of people have blue eyes."

Harry shook his head. "Not like these. They're cold as a lizard's belly. Makes your skin feel tingly just looking at 'em."

Jack finally released his grip. "You think he could kill Lincoln?"

Harry's gaze was unblinking. "Sure as I'm standin' here."

Jack scratched his head. His instincts told him to believe Harry Kincaid. His brain screamed a thousand reasons why he shouldn't. He eyed a wooden chair and kicked it toward the toady little man. "Sit down and tell me everything you know."

"I've got a horse hidden at Green's old livery stable on Tenth Street. Place has been empty for months. I'm supposed to give this Tarleton feller the horse, and a big pile of money, at dusk."

Jack examined Harry's features closely, looking for any telltale sign the man was lying. He found none.

"You'll be there, Harry. And I will be, too."

A dark figure slipped through the rapidly fading sunlight. He was dressed entirely in black from his battered felt hat to his unpolished boots. One hand clutched a blanket roll, also dyed black. He hurried unnoticed down Main Street, then turned into an alley behind Tenth Street.

He followed a soft yellow glow through the open doorway of an abandoned stable. A lantern cast a pallid light on a swaybacked knock-kneed gelding. He dropped his bags and regarded the nag. "You call that a horse?"

"Get the hell away from him." Harry emerged from the shadows and moved protectively in front of the animal. "What's your business here?" He jutted out his stubbled jaw and glared at the man before him. "Mr. Tarleton? Is that you?"

"Who else would come to this godforsaken shamble?"

"For a minute there, I thought you was a preacher."

"That is exactly what I wanted you to think."

A nervous smile twitched across Harry's mouth. "Kinda early, ain't you?"

"I'm ready to go now." Tarleton strode to the horse, took its head between his hands and carefully examined its eyes and teeth. "Where's the money?"

"It's all packed up for you over in the corner." Harry grabbed a currying brush and hurried toward the horse. "I'll have him ready in just a minute, Mr. Tarleton."

Tarleton slapped the brush out of Harry's hand. "He's ready enough. Fetch me that blanket."

"But Mr. Tarleton—"

The tall man took one step forward and leveled his cold eyes on Harry. "The blanket, you insignificant cur. Now."

"Yes, sir," Harry said as he groped behind him for the blanket draped over the wall of the stall.

Tarleton jerked his head toward his mount. "Step lively. I'm in a hurry."

Harry sidled to the horse and tossed the blanket over its back. "Mighty fine idea, Mr. Tarleton." He busied himself arranging the blanket. "No sense wasting the last bit of sunlight. After all, you got a lot of miles—"

The wooden stock of a revolver smashed into the base of Harry's skull, stopping his words in midsentence. He reeled forward, blood flowing freely from the open wound. He seemed to catch himself for a moment before tumbling backward, crumpling to the floor. His head came to rest on a pile of dried manure.

Tarleton allowed himself a satisfied smile as he slipped the revolver back into his pocket. He stepped over Harry's body and finished saddling the horse. Then he scanned the corners of the stall until he found two saddlebags. Inside were wads of crisp

Federal currency. He grabbed a handful and started counting the assorted tens, twenties, and fifties, even the occasional hundred-dollar bill. It was here, all five thousand dollars of his deposit.

He flung the bags onto the horse, then strapped his blanket roll behind the saddle. Tarleton made a final check of the rigging, mounted the animal and rode off.

The sound of hoofbeats caught Jack's attention. One didn't often hear a lone horse in Richmond anymore. He checked his pocket watch. Quarter to six. Though the last fingers of twilight were still falling through bare tree branches, he hurried the last two blocks to the stable.

From the doorway, he saw a lantern's faint glow. He stepped toward it. "Harry," he called in a low voice. No response. A furrow cut across his brow. He took another step forward. "Harry, you in there?" Jack drew his revolver and crept toward the light coming from an empty stall. "Harry?"

Something caught at his foot. It was all his bad leg could do to hold him upright. He staggered a few steps before turning to see what had tripped him.

One look told Jack that Harry's luck had finally run out. The little gambler seemed even smaller and more pathetic in death than he had in life.

"Damn it to hell!" Jack returned his revolver to its holster and bent down to lay the back of his hand against the dead man's cheek. The body was already getting cold. He crouched over Harry Kincaid and cursed the day he had first set eyes on the miserable little man. Cursed him for telling him about Tarleton. Cursed him for getting himself killed. Cursed him for leaving Jack empty-handed. He cursed Harry for forcing him to figure out what to do next, for leaving him with nothing more than a vague description of the killer.

He lowered himself stiffly to his knees and bent over the dead man. "What do I do now, Harry?" He stared into the lifeless eyes of the shabby little gambler. He cupped Harry's chin in his hand. Jack felt the stubble of his beard and the clammy chill of death on his skin. He looked again into Harry's eyes, then reached up and pushed his eyelids closed.

Jack walked outside and lifted his eyes to the gray clouds rolling across the darkening sky. By the time he reached the Spotswood Hotel, Standiford would be gone. And Basil Tarleton was on his way to Washington City.

Jack knew there was only one thing he could do. He jammed his hands into the pockets of his coat and started walking.

It was fully dark as he began climbing Capitol Hill on Twelfth Street. The cold air was ripe with the odor of coal and wood smoke. Candlelight flickered in the windows of the fashionable houses on his right. The street was lost in shadow. The gas supply for the street lamps must be out again, he decided.

Jack hunched his shoulders against the sharp wind blowing up from the river against his back. He chided himself for dithering over gas and candles when he had more important matters to consider.

Such as what he was going to say when he reached the house at the corner of Twelfth and Clay.

Such as whether this long, cold walk was a fool's errand.

He had almost decided to turn around when he spotted the imposing mansion that was his destination. Chandeliers glittered in the top-floor windows, framed by pairs of ornate columns rising along the formal façade.

A sentry stood near the southwest corner of the President's House. As Jack approached, he snapped to attention and called for the countersign.

"Vigilance," Jack responded.

The man waved him forward and shouldered his rifle. Jack could hear the sentry's teeth chatter.

The sentry box at the Clay Street corner was empty. Jack turned right and saw another soldier walking his post in front of the house. Jack called out to him and again was waved on.

He stopped at the front steps. This side of the house was much less ornate than the other. Rows of windows rose three stories, framed by gray stucco walls. A single pair of slender columns guarded the dark double doors. A dim light illuminated the fan-shaped glass panel above them. Jack took off his hat and passed his hand through his thick brown hair. He tucked his hat under his left arm and straightened his jacket. Then he climbed the marble steps, pressed the doorbell and waited.

After a few moments, the doors opened. A black servant in a long dark coat stood before him. Jack explained he had a message for the president. The servant stepped aside and allowed him to enter.

Jack walked into an oval-shaped foyer. The man asked Jack to wait as he backed out of the room and disappeared through a doorway on the left.

Jack glanced around. He'd never been inside the President's House before and probably never would be again. He had little time to study the elegant surroundings.

A dark-haired young man in a black suit strode into the foyer. He extended his hand. "I'll take it, Captain."

Jack looked from the man's hand to his face. "Take what?"

"The message." The man snapped his fingers. "Give it to me."

"It's for the president."

The man's eyes narrowed. The edges of his luxurious mustache turned downward as he pursed his lips. "The president is very busy. Now, give me the message."

"You don't understand," Jack said evenly. "I need to deliver this message to the president personally."

"Who sent you?"

"No one, sir. I—"

"I don't have time for this," the man said wearily. "I'm the president's secretary. Give me your message and be on your way."

Jack now realized he was speaking with Burton Harrison, a close confidant of Jefferson Davis's who had once lived here in the President's House. Jack swallowed a lump in his throat. "I have information about a criminal conspiracy that could strike at the heart of the Confederacy. It requires the president's personal attention."

"What sort of conspiracy?"

"As I said, this matter demands the president's personal attention."

Harrison crossed his arms across his chest and gave Jack an appraising gaze. "Do you have any idea what the president is doing right now? He's in there." Harrison cocked his head toward the doorway. "With General Lee and General Bragg. They're trying to figure out how to stop Sherman from marching through North Carolina and joining up with Grant at Petersburg. And you want me to interrupt them?"

"Yes, sir," Jack replied evenly.

"And you won't tell me why."

"I can't, sir."

Harrison shook his head and brushed his mustache with his forefinger. "What's your name and unit, Captain?"

"Jack Tanner, Provost Guard."

"I'll give you credit, Tanner." A small smile twitched through Harrison's mustache. "You have brass. Wait here." He turned and disappeared through the doorway.

Jack wiped his forehead and wasn't surprised to find it damp with sweat. He stood still and locked his eyes on the yellow wall of the foyer. He was certain Harrison would be back any second to order him away. His mind was racing, trying to organize the information he had gathered in a way that would convince Harrison he wasn't a lunatic. He fought down a creeping sense of despair. Even if he had to argue with Harrison all night, he simply must tell the president about the plot he had uncovered.

Harrison was suddenly before him again, wearing an expression of exasperation and bemusement. "I'll admit, I never thought I'd be saying this," Harrison told him. "But the president will see you."

Jack followed as Harrison opened a carved wooden door leading into an ornate formal dining room. Jack took one step inside and froze.

He was face-to-face with the most powerful men in the Confederacy. His eyes were drawn immediately to one of the figures seated at a long oval table. There was an aura of quiet confidence about him. A mane of white hair, a carefully trimmed white beard, deep creases around clear black eyes that were trained on a map spread out before him. He looked up and Jack found himself staring at the man who commanded the movements and the loyalties of every soldier who wore a gray uniform.

Robert E. Lee.

Jack couldn't move. He could scarcely breathe. He might have stood in that spot all night had the moment not been broken by a guttural cough. Across the table, General Braxton Bragg sat stooped and scowling. His gaze, hooded by the crag of his eyebrows, pierced Jack to the core. He coughed again, then brushed his grizzled beard with his fingers and turned toward the third man at the table.

President Jefferson Davis sat between his generals, intently reading a document laid out before him. He flipped through the pages, seeming not to notice Jack or Harrison as his eyes raced over the papers. He sat erect, completely focused on his reading. Jack stole a glance around the room, noting the rich red wallpaper, the carved marble fireplace with its glowing coals, the portrait of George Washington on the opposite wall, the fine golden chandelier. The president looked up.

Jack was shocked to see the ravages carved into his face. His gaunt features were pale and deeply creased. Lines radiated from around his eyes. His formal bearing seemed to mask physical frailty. For the first time, Jack wondered if the president would be able to bear up under the strain of the war.

"This is Captain Tanner," Harrison announced.

Jack gave the sharpest salute of his life.

"Harrison tells me you have an extraordinary message, Captain," Davis said.

"Yes, sir." Jack waited for further instructions, but none came. The men looked at him. He realized they were waiting to hear his story. "I have reason to believe a serious effort is afoot to murder the President of the United States."

He summoned his resolve as he began to talk. Step by step, he recounted how his search for a small-time card cheat led him to a member of the Confederate Congress, a notorious hired killer, and a plot to kill Abraham Lincoln. He continued without interruption until he had detailed the discovery of Harry Kincaid's body.

"Mr. President," he concluded, "Basil Tarleton is on his way to Washington City at this very moment. Unless he's stopped, he may well commit the most outrageous crime of the age. Whether he succeeds or fails, his actions could be laid at the foot of this government. In fact, the Yankees might blame you personally, sir."

Out of words at last, Jack stood rigidly at attention. His posture masked his relief. No matter what happened now, his conscience was clear. He had done his duty.

"This is most irregular, Captain," the president said quietly. "Most irregular."

"You should have gone through the proper channels," Bragg growled.

"Begging the general's pardon, but there wasn't time, sir."

Bragg brushed aside the objection. "I hardly think a junior officer can be expected to make that kind of decision."

"You don't believe the report, General Bragg?" Davis asked.

Bragg knitted his thick eyebrows. "There are crackpots and hotheads capable of anything. But a single report from a small-time criminal is insufficient cause for action."

Davis nodded thoughtfully. "General Lee?"

The white-haired warrior gave Jack a thoughtful look, then turned toward Davis. "I have served with a great many officers in my time, Mr. President. I have learned a very important lesson. No officer, junior or ranking, would risk his commission unless he was absolutely convinced he is right."

Jack watched as the president reached for a white ceramic container holding a half dozen black cigars. "These gentlemen do not share my taste for tobacco, Captain." Davis handed a cigar across the table. "Care to indulge with me?"

"Thank you, sir," Jack said as he accepted the president's offer. "If you don't mind, I will save this for later."

"As you wish." Davis took another cigar and held it up. Harrison stepped forward and clipped the end, then struck a match for the president before retreating from the table. "Now let us consider this report of yours," Davis said as the first wisp of smoke swirled around his head.

Bragg wrinkled his face and leaned away from the offensive smell. Lee sat motionless, his dark eyes taking Jack's measure.

Davis sat back in his chair, puffed deeply and stared into the thin white cloud he had created. "This is not the first such plot we've heard of."

"And you can be assured it won't be the last," Bragg quickly added. "Desperate times make for desperate men. Those whose faith in the Cause has been weakened by our recent reversals are liable to attempt any manner of foolishness."

Davis frowned. "I hardly think flagging patriotism is grounds for lunatic actions, General."

"Lunatics don't need much more."

Davis studied a smoke ring as it floated across the table. "Perhaps."

Lee shifted slightly in his chair. "This situation is not unique to us, Mr. President. Our adversaries must also contend with the mentally unhinged running loose with wild schemes. You will recall the unpleasant Dahlgren matter last winter."

Davis exhaled another long finger of smoke. "Dahlgren." He spoke the name softly, almost tenderly, as if recalling a lost friend.

But Dahlgren was no friend. Jack knew the name all too well. Ulric Dahlgren, a young Union officer, had been killed almost a year earlier while leading a cavalry raid just outside the capital. He carried papers indicating he was under orders to kill Jefferson

Davis and his cabinet officers. The North had repudiated the orders, but Southern skepticism lingered.

Bragg snorted. "After what they tried to do to you, why not let this killer . . ." He cocked an eyebrow at Jack. "What's his name?"

"Tarleton, sir."

"Right. Why not let this Tarleton go after Lincoln?"

Lee stiffened. "A government founded on Christian values would never condone such a thoroughly evil act, General."

Davis shook his head. "I cannot be responsible for how the United States conducts its affairs. But I will not permit the Confederate States to overlook something so fundamentally vile, so horrendously wrong as this."

Bragg rubbed a patch of boils that covered the back of his left hand. Jack wondered how much the pain was driving his words. "If Lincoln is stopped, the entire Federal war machine is stopped. That means independence."

"That means certain defeat!" The voice was so forceful, every head in the room swung to see if it was actually coming from Lee's mouth. He was leaning forward, his cheeks flushed above his immaculately trimmed beard, his eyes angry black diamonds glimmering with restrained rage. "The men of my army have not sacrificed everything to defend a government that would sanction wanton murder."

Bragg also leaned forward, his face equally aflame. "Unless decisive action is taken, there may not *be* any government in a few weeks."

Jack looked across the room at Harrison, who had drawn himself so tightly against the wall he almost seemed part of the wallpaper.

"The government, indeed our very country, survives, General Bragg, because my thin line of brave men is keeping *those people* from entering this city. When my soldiers lose faith in the principles that guide and sustain this nation, there will be no more army. And that will mean . . ." Lee's words trailed off, their implication too clear to require explanation.

Smoke climbed from Davis's cigar, erecting a thin barrier between the two generals who glowered at each other across the table. The president leaned forward, tapped his cigar on an ashtray, then stubbed it out. A ribbon of smoke rose from the stump. His eyes followed it upward, then shifted to the portrait of the first American president on the wall. He sat motionless, contemplating Washington's face for a long moment.

At last, Davis shot a sidelong glance at Lee, who gave a barely perceptible nod. "There is no doubt about which course we must take," the president announced.

Bragg slumped in surrender.

Jefferson Davis looked Jack squarely in the eye. "Do you know this man Tarleton?"

"I have some familiarity with him, Mr. President."

Davis stood up and clasped his hands behind his back. "This government disapproves in the strongest possible terms of the sordid crime in which he is apparently engaged. Nor can we stand idly by as he prepares to carry it out." His voice deepened as he spoke slowly and deliberately. "I charge you, Captain, with finding Basil Tarleton and stopping him. Use whatever means it takes to . . ."—Davis groped for the right word—"assure that he never poses a threat to the Federal president. Do I make myself clear, Captain?"

"Very clear, sir."

Davis bent down, dipped a pen in a bottle of black ink, and began hurriedly writing. "Proceed to Washington immediately. This order relieves you of your duties. Give it to your commanding officer." He waved the paper dry and held it out. Jack stepped quickly toward the table and took the order. Davis began writing again. "This document will guarantee your safe passage through our lines." He passed it to Jack, who nodded and folded the papers into his jacket pocket.

"When you have completed your mission, you will report to me, here, in person. Understood?"

"Yes, sir."

Davis drew himself up to his full height and set his jaw as he studied Jack's face. "Your country is counting on you."

Jack swallowed hard. "I understand, sir."

The President of the Confederate States nodded slowly. "Good luck, Captain."

As Jack walked out the door, he realized he was still holding the cigar.

"It's going to be a long night," he said to himself as he tucked it in his pocket and stepped out into the biting cold of Clay Street.

Two

THE CROSSINGS

Jack hadn't expected to see a light in the office of his commanding officer. It was getting late, and Colonel Isaac Carrington seldom worked after sundown. Jack limped down the darkened corridor of the building across from the Capitol and peered into the open door.

A slight man in uniform sat perched on the colonel's desk. He was absorbed by the sheaf of papers in his hand. Jack didn't recognize him but found something oddly familiar about his face. With his regular features and rounded jaw, Jack decided the man could be just about anyone.

"Excuse me," Jack began. The man shifted his eyes toward the doorway. "Is Colonel Carrington in?"

" 'Fraid not."

Jack pulled a document from his pocket. "I have some orders to deliver. Know where I can find him?"

The man shook his head. "Haven't seen him this evening."

Jack's shoulders sagged. "I guess I'll have to wait until morning."

The man stood up. He was a bit shorter than Jack and tilted his head slightly to fix a gaze on him. "I can see he gets them."

Jack hesitated, unsure about handing an order signed by President Davis to a stranger, even one with a star on his collar. "I don't know, Major . . ."

"Matt Johnson." The man offered his hand. As Jack shook it, he looked more closely at the major. He had heard of Matt Johnson, of course. Everyone in Richmond knew about the exploits of the Confederate operative—his daring missions in Union territory, his knack for prying secrets out of unwitting Yankee businessmen, his ability to slip effortlessly through the lines.

"It's an honor," Jack said as he continued pumping Johnson's hand. "I never expected to find you here, sir."

Johnson carefully pried free of Jack's grasp. "Just catching up on paperwork between assignments." He eyed Jack's rumpled uniform. "You work for the provost marshal?"

"Yes, sir. Well, I did." Jack held up the presidential order. "I have a new assignment now."

Johnson reached for the document. "Mind if I have a look?"

Jack handed it over. "Not at all, sir."

"Let's put the formalities aside, shall we?" Johnson scanned the order. "First mission behind enemy lines?"

Jack nodded.

A friendly smile lit up the major's bland features. "Your belly must be busting with butterflies."

Jack shrugged. "I really haven't had time to get nervous."

"I know better than to ask what your assignment is. But maybe you can tell me where you're going."

Jack silently debated how much he could say. His mission was as secret as it could be. He didn't want to compromise it before it began. On the other hand, Matt Johnson was one of the South's most experienced operatives. Maybe he could help. "Washington City," he said at last.

"Straight into the lion's den, eh?" Johnson grinned. "Hell of a way to get your feet wet. Ever been there before?" Jack shook his head. "It's a town pretty much like any other," Johnson assured him. "A lot like Richmond, in fact. Same kind of riverfront, full of scallywags and gutbucket saloons. It's also a snake pit, crowded with men who'd as soon slit your throat as shake your hand. Especially a Confederate hand."

Solemn lines formed around Johnson's eyes. "Let me give you a piece of advice. When you get there, start looking for someone named George Webb."

"Is he one of ours?"

"Let's just say George Webb is a very useful person to know, and let it go at that." Johnson fixed Jack with a steady gaze. "Mention my name. That may grease the wheels for you."

"I'll do that."

Johnson leaned back and gave Jack an appraising glance. "You're not going like that, are you?"

Jack looked down at his uniform. "I hadn't really thought much about it."

"And how were you planning on getting to Washington City?"

"I was on my way to the quartermaster to see about a horse."

Johnson sighed. "By the time those folks finally come up with a horse, Grant will be lighting a cigar in Capitol Square." He placed his hand on Jack's shoulder. "I have a mare I won't be needing for a while. Take her."

"That's very generous."

Johnson waved the thanks aside. "I can also set you up with

some clothes that won't mark you as a rebel after you cross the lines. You'll need some money, too." A sly grin slid across his lips. "I know where to find a stash of Yankee greenbacks."

"I don't know how to thank you."

Johnson settled a steady gaze on Jack's eyes. "Just do your job, and do it right."

Dying flames slithered along a dwindling stack of dry twigs. Tarleton rubbed his palms over the fire, letting its warmth slide into his skin. In the few minutes since sundown, the temperature had plunged toward freezing. In another few minutes, when darkness completely enshrouded the countryside, he would stomp out what was left of the fire and hit the road again.

He had moved by night since leaving Richmond, cautiously making his way along dirt lanes and cowpaths. Wider, straighter roads would have made for a quicker trip. They also could place him in the path of Union patrols, renegade guerrillas, or roving bands of deserters from both armies.

He took a bite of salt pork and ground it with his back teeth.

"Hello!" a voice called behind him.

Tarleton's breath caught in his chest.

"That fire sure is a welcome sight." The voice, with its clipped Northern accent, drew closer. "Almost didn't see it. Would have ridden right on by if I hadn't smelled the smoke."

Tarleton forced his breathing to resume. He wiped his hands on his trousers and rose. "Praise the Lord!" He turned a beaming smile toward the newcomer. He wrapped a thick delta drawl around his words. "Another weary wayfarer on this bleak and cold night. Come, friend, warm yourself."

The man stepped into the fire's fading light. He wore a thick woolen coat turned up at the collar. He led a horse with one hand and carried a blanket roll in the other. "Much obliged." He tethered the horse to a nearby tree and sprawled next to the fire. Sparks glinted off his round spectacles and highlighted his ruddy cheeks. "What brings you out on a night like this, friend?"

Tarleton bowed his head. "We who toil in the Lord's vineyard are out on all sorts of nights, brother."

The man eyed Tarleton's black garb. "You're a preacher?"

"Reverend Israel T. Harris. Your humble servant, sir."

"I know a good many ministers. I'm an undertaker myself. Josiah Alton from Scranton, Pennsylvania." He reached across the fire to shake Tarleton's hand. "A pleasure to meet you. Say, do you have anything to eat?"

Tarleton held up the remaining salt pork. "I am afraid this is the last of my sustenance. However, He who fed the multitude with the fishes and the loaves can do wonders."

Alton screwed up his face. "No, thanks, parson." He reached inside his brown overcoat and produced a small silver flask. "With your permission, a shot or two of this will suit my belly just as well."

Tarleton gave a benign smile as he dropped to his haunches on the far side of the fire. "Our Heavenly Father would understand an indulgence on a night such as this."

"To your health." The undertaker wrapped his lips around the spout and drank liberally.

"And what brings you out at this hour, friend?"

Alton wiped his mouth on his sleeve. "Same thing I've been doing these past three years now. Coming down here to Dixie, finding Pennsylvania's brave, fallen sons and returning them for a decent Union burial." The man's face paled. "Begging your pardon, Parson. I don't mean to suggest there's anything wrong with a Southern funeral."

Tarleton's peaceful countenance could have come from a stained-glass window. "No offense taken. I find it commendable that you so unselfishly make the long trip to bring comfort to the families of the slain."

The undertaker drained the flask with a final deep swig and let out a satisfied sigh. "This is no charity, Parson. The families pay me quite handsomely for my trouble. You might not know it, being a man of the cloth and all, but it's a mighty hard scrabble for a dollar these days."

"The Good Book tells us, 'God helps them that help themselves.'"

The undertaker leaned forward and stared at Tarleton across the dying fire. His eyes seemed to grow larger through the lenses of his glasses. "Just what denomination of minister might you be?"

Tarleton kept a gentle smile pasted to his face. "I am ordained in the Methodist Episcopal Church, South."

"You have read the whole Bible, cover to cover?"

"Many a time."

Alton's gaze fastened on Tarleton's face. "Then you have read the Book of Lamentations?"

"Certainly."

"Ezekiel?"

"Of course."

"Hezekiah?"

"Often."

The undertaker frowned as he stuffed the empty flask back inside his coat.

Tarleton held his hands over the trickle of flames. "Something troubles you, brother."

"Just two things," the man answered. "First, there is no Book of Hezekiah." The soft click of metal falling into place came from inside the coat. The undertaker's hand reappeared with a revolver pointed at Tarleton. "And second, you're no Methodist minister. Now get those hands up."

Tarleton smiled broadly while doing as ordered. "Well, you caught me." All traces of Southern dialect evaporated from his voice. "I've been using this minister dodge for a long stretch now. You are the first man who has ever seen through it."

"Then just what are you up to?" Alton gestured with his revolver. "Dressed in that getup?"

"Same as you, friend. Making a profit traversing the Mason-Dixon line. I sell medicine to Southern families."

"Trading with Rebels!" the undertaker said with naked contempt.

"Would you believe I clear more than five hundred dollars per trip?"

Alton's eyes widened. "Go on!"

"It's true. More after a big battle, when chloroform and sedatives are in greater demand."

The man maintained a tight grip on his gun as he lowered the barrel a few inches. "Do you know how many stiffs I have to dig up and haul home to clear that kind of money?"

"The profits don't end there, friend. Let me show you my order book. It's in my saddlebag over yonder." He pointed to a dark outline near the tree where Alton had lashed his horse.

The undertaker nodded and followed behind Tarleton. "How many trips do you make in a month?"

"Two, three if the weather permits." Tarleton lifted the bag and opened the flap.

"That's fifteen hundred dollars! Why, for that kind of money I'd have to work—"

Tarleton swung around.

With a fluid motion, he thrust a knife into the man's chest.

A scream melted into a whimper as the blade plunged into him again and again. He crumpled to the ground. As the last sound of life left him, his midsection was a bloody mass of hacked flesh intermingled with the shreds of his coat.

Tarleton bent down and slowly drove the knife into the ground, removing the red stains from the blade. Then he wiped his hands on the dead winter grass, returned the knife to the saddlebag, and went back to the fire.

He calmly looked around for the last bit of salt pork, picked it up, and put it into his mouth. Tarleton was still chewing as he lashed his belongings to the dead man's horse, mounted, and rode northward into the night.

A shiver rattled through Jack. He burrowed his hands into the pockets of his thin suit coat. Under it, he wore every piece of nonmilitary clothing he owned. His hasty exit from the Confederate capital had given him little time to prepare for the long ride, nor for the brittle cold, which seeped into his bones. The pale sun, when it shone at all, offered no respite from the winter chill.

The days passed slowly as he picked his way through ancient forests. He dined on the occasional rabbit or squirrel he caught along the way. They were rare treats at this time of year.

The wooded trails of central Virginia reminded Jack of the rustic region around his family's farm. Only flatter. He had grown up in the foothills of the Blue Ridge Mountains. Any time he could escape his father's gaze, he would light out for the tall trees, exploring ravines and creekbeds, dreaming of the day he would have adventures like the legendary frontiersmen of Virginia's past.

He had never dreamed of an adventure like this one. Once beyond the protective perimeter of Richmond, Jack kept to the backcountry. His pass from Jefferson Davis would do him little good—and a great deal of harm—if he came across a Federal patrol. He avoided anything that looked like a farm, a settlement, or even a proper road.

Jack tried to find the sun in the small patches of sky that peeked between the tree branches intertwined over his head. He caught a brief glimpse, off to his left, of the small, milky disc. He checked the pale shadows stretching past him. Late afternoon, he concluded. Another day almost behind him, another day of covering too few miles far too slowly. He fought down his impatience. As much as he wanted to hurry, to kick his horse into a gallop, he knew speed would be folly. He might make better time, but he couldn't use that time if he was in a Yankee prison.

The trees thinned out before him. He spotted a tiny cabin tucked into a small clearing. The rough-hewn dwelling might once have been whitewashed, but its walls had grayed from exposure to the elements. There were no windows, only a weathered door. A rusted wagon slumped next to the building, ensnared in a bramble bush. The place had an air of abandonment. Perhaps,

Jack thought, he might shelter there for the night.

He dismounted and tied the horse to a sprawling elm tree, then hunkered down and watched. As shadows thickened around him, he saw no sign of activity. He stole forward, moving as silently as he could through the wizened grass of the clearing. A twig snapped sharply beneath his foot and he froze.

He caught a blur of motion in the corner of his eye. A scrawny yellow cat stood poised, ears at attention, over a wooden bucket by the cabin door. The animal spotted him and scampered off, leaving a trail of white liquid. Jack bent over the bucket, dipped a finger into its contents, and touched it to his lips. Fresh milk. Maybe the cabin was not abandoned after all.

Nearby, a half-dozen brightly painted toy soldiers lay scattered on the grass. That was all the evidence Jack needed to convince him he should move on.

"What do you want?"

Jack spun around. A tall man stood behind him. He wore dark pants and a dirt-crusted muslin shirt. One sleeve was ripped. A long-handled axe was slung over his shoulder.

"I was hoping you might let me sit a spell by your fire," Jack answered.

The man scratched his long, ragged brown beard. "Where'd you come from?"

Jack pointed toward the woods. "I've been on the road for a while."

The man nodded, his scraggly hair dropping over his face. "I'm chopping wood out back. Give me a hand." Jack fell in step beside him. "You look to be traveling light." The man glanced back toward the woods. "Got no horse?"

Something in the man's tone put Jack on guard. "No, but I sure could use one. You don't happen to have a horse for sale, do you?"

The man's eyes lit up. "You got money?"

Jack shrugged. He looked around the clearing. There was no sign of firewood. But there was something behind the cabin. He squinted and could just make out a figure lying on the ground. Another, much smaller, was nearby. "What the—?"

Jack turned just in time to see the axe handle swinging at his head. He ducked a split second too late and took the brunt of the blow on his neck. It sent him sprawling in the crinkly grass. He rolled onto his back and tried to blink his vision clear. A sharp ache was climbing up the back of his skull.

The man stood over him, raising the axe again. Jack's head was swimming. He couldn't focus his eyes. He felt consciousness slipping away.

The axe was slicing an arc through the twilight. Jack tried to dig his heels into the ground and scoot out of its path, but his legs would not cooperate. He clawed at the grass. The brittle growth snapped in his hands. The exertion left him light-headed.

The axe stopped in midswing. Jack could just make out the side of the blade smashing into his assailant's head, sending him tumbling to the ground.

Another figure swam into Jack's blurred vision. "You all right?" it asked.

Before he could answer, Jack fell into a pit of darkness.

When a pearly glow lit the eastern horizon, Tarleton reined the dead undertaker's horse off the path he had followed through the night. He found a dry creekbed, tethered the animal, and built a small fire. Once he had rubbed some feeling back into his hands, he unsaddled the horse and sorted through the man's belongings.

Tarleton snarled in disgust at the meager haul. He found a notebook listing the corpses the undertaker had recovered and shipped north, but there was no money, no food, nothing useful. Tarleton squatted by the fire and tossed the notebook into the flames.

The pages fluttered as they curled in the heat. An entry on the last page prompted Tarleton to plunge his hand into the fire and pull the notebook out again. He dropped it on the ground and kicked dirt on the burning pages. When the flames were out, he picked up the book and scanned the note that had caught his attention.

"Sandy Point Ferry," it read. "Cyrus Bingham. Ten dollars U.S. No questions asked."

Tarleton stuffed the charred notebook into his saddlebag. As he stretched out by the fire, propped his hat over his eyes, and drifted off to sleep, a small smile found its way to his lips.

"How's the head?"

Jack pressed two fingers gingerly on the back of his skull as he peered up at a towheaded young man bending over him. "Still attached," he muttered.

The young fellow let out a snort. "It wouldn't have been if that Yankee bastard had had his way."

"Yankee?" Jack looked around. He was on a dirt floor, apparently inside the cabin. A fire roared in the hearth. "A Yankee lives here?"

"Naw. Looks like he just came across this place. Killed a woman and a little boy. Found their bodies out back."

Jack propped himself on his elbow. "What makes you think he was a Yankee?"

"These." The young man held up a pair of pants.

Jack looked closely at the grimy garment and made out yellow stripes running down blue legs. He frowned. "Did you kill him?"

The young man shook his head. "He's tied to a tree out back." He tossed the pants into the fire. "He'll be fine, if somebody finds him before sundown. Otherwise . . ." He shrugged. "I should introduce myself. Sam Jenkins." He held out a hand.

"Jack Tanner." He let Sam help him to his feet. "Nice to meet you." He regarded his young savior. Sam wore a battered calfskin jacket and yellowish-brown trousers. "What's your unit?" Jack asked.

Sam shrank back from the question. "What do you mean?"

"I've seen enough of those butternut britches to know they come from the Confederate Army."

Sam dropped his eyes and shuffled his feet. "I reckon I ain't in no unit anymore." He let out a long breath. "By last week the whole regiment was down to fourteen men. We hadn't had a colonel since Christmas. So we talked it over one night and decided the war was over for us."

Jack studied Sam's face. "How old are you?"

"Eighteen," he replied, then mumbled, "Come August."

On principle, Jack hated deserters. But he couldn't bring himself to have any ill will toward this teenager. After all, he had saved his life. "Your accent sounds Tidewater, say, South Carolina? Is that where you're headed?"

The boy barked a bitter laugh. "You ain't seen South Carolina lately, have you? Not much left. Not after Sherman finished with it." He shook his head. "Reckon I'll head off somewhere new. I've got people in Maryland. What about you?"

"More or less the same direction."

A smile brightened Sam's face. "That's great! We can ride together."

"We'll see," Jack replied.

Tarleton stood on a bluff and stared across the Potomac River, more than a mile wide and running swiftly. He could see low-hanging trees hugging the far bank. His goal was almost in reach. If all went well, he would ride into Washington City by midday tomorrow.

Grime clung to his black suit the way fatigue clung to his flesh. He ran the back of his hand over his stubbled jaw. One more night, he told himself, and he'd be back between clean sheets on a downy featherbed in a respectable hotel. One more night.

Footsteps approached. He knew without turning around it was the man he had come here to meet, an old river rat who knew the Potomac like the back of his hand. Tarleton fixed his most sincere smile to his lips, shook off his weariness, and turned to greet him. "Brother Bingham." He offered his hand. "It's good of you to assist me."

Bingham squinted at the outstretched hand, then ran his gaze up to Tarleton's face. "What kinda preacher are you?"

"A mere laborer in the fields of the Lord, Brother Bingham." Tarleton caught a whiff of corn whiskey from the stooped, potbellied man. "He will bless you indeed for the kindness you show me."

Bingham spat over the bluff. "Ain't blessings I'm lookin' for. You bring the money?"

Tarleton patted his jacket pocket. "Rest assured, my friend. I have everything you need right here."

"Hand it over, then."

Tarleton shook his head. "Once we're safely on the other side of the river, you'll get everything you deserve."

"I'd better." Bingham squinted into Tarleton's face. "The Yankees are thick as bees in a hive on this river. Not many people left around here that can get you across."

"I am certain you will perform your task admirably." Tarleton looked down at the water. "How soon can we start?"

Bingham spat again. "Soon as it's dark."

Jack had been wary about traveling on a main road heading north, but Sam assured him he had passed that way only a few days earlier and seen no sign of Federal patrols. It was a much easier ride than Jack had been accustomed to since leaving Richmond. He did not admit that to Sam. He still wasn't sure if he could trust the young deserter.

They passed the morning in desultory conversation. Sam acknowledged he had seen lots of action, including the long march to and longer retreat from Pennsylvania. After answering questions about the battle, Sam asked Jack if he had been in the army as well. Jack gave a terse account of his service up through the fighting at Chancellorsville, where he had taken shrapnel in his leg. He let the boy assume he had mustered out after his injury.

At midday, Jack pulled to an abrupt halt. "Look there." He pointed at fresh tracks in the road ahead of them.

Sam studied them intently. "Yankee supply train?"

"I don't think so. It's only a wagon with one outrider." Jack looked up the road, which rose gently before them. "Whatever it is, it's close."

Sam took a final look at the tracks before nudging his horse to a steady walk. "Whatever it is, we had better stay on our toes."

They topped the rise and spotted the source of their concern. A brightly painted wagon had run off the road and was stuck in a ditch. A tall man in a shiny stovepipe hat sat on a horse, cursing as other men pushed, pulled, and pried at the stranded wagon. "Confound your everlasting souls! Push harder, Williams! Damn you, Ramer! If you'd been paying attention we wouldn't be in this fix."

"I was doing the best I could," a short man growled between clenched teeth as he threw his weight against a motionless wheel.

"Your best is pretty piss poor."

"Damn it, Perfesser, if you hadn't sold the other wagon . . ."

The man on the horse straightened himself and bellowed, "If I hadn't sold the other wagon you'd have stopped eating last week. Now, put your backs into it! Push!"

The men gave a collective moan, then heaved with all their strength. The wagon rocked forward a few inches, only to slip back into the mud with a loud squish. The man in the top hat unleashed another fusillade of oaths as the others sank to their knees in the mire.

"Perfesser," a man clutching the wagon wheel said sharply, nodding toward the approaching riders.

The mounted man turned toward Jack and Sam. He doffed his hat in a grand sweeping motion. "Good day, gentlemen," he called.

Jack tipped his hat. "Looks like you've had a little bad luck here."

"Ill fortune indeed. An all too common curse these days, I regret to say." The man settled the top hat on his snowy mass of curls. "Professor Marcus Beeler, at your service."

Sam's eyes lit up. "Are you all Beeler's Minstrels?"

The professor gave a courtly nod. "The very same."

"I'll be hanged," Sam laughed. "I saw your show when I was a kid!"

"It is always a pleasure to meet our appreciative public."

Jack surveyed the scene. "You fellows seem to be in a tight fix." The wagon had bogged down nearly to its axle in mud. "Maybe if we hitched up a couple of more horses, we could pull you free."

"Capital suggestion, good sir."

Jack and Sam dismounted and tied their horses to the wagon. Men and animals grunted and strained together until the wheels gradually started giving way, slowly emerging from the mud with a sucking sound. When it finally rested on dry ground, the group gave a cheer, smiling and shaking hands with each other.

Beeler leapt from his horse with surprising agility for a man of his years. He rubbed his hands in delight. "We are indebted to you, friends. I was beginning to despair we would be stuck here until the road dries in the spring. But we did it!"

"We? Ha!" the man called Williams laughed.

The Professor ignored the remark. "I trust we'll have no more trouble making our way to Washington City."

"That's where you're heading?" Jack asked.

"As quickly as we can get there," Beeler responded. "We are

engaged to perform at Maguire's Theater. I would be honored to have you accompany us to Washington and to be our guests on opening night."

It was just the break Jack had been hoping for. Traveling with a minstrel troupe, he could slip right past the Federal sentries and into Washington City.

Sam wasn't so certain. "You sure you want to go into the enemy camp?" he said quietly.

Jack nodded and turned to Beeler. "As it happens, I have business in Washington City."

"Just what are you doin' with all that gear?" Bingham demanded.

Tarleton unhitched the saddle from his horse and placed it alongside his bedroll and saddlebags. "Preparing to cross the river, Brother Bingham."

"Not with all that, you ain't." Bingham spat. "It'll swamp my boat."

"I can't very well leave it all on the horse, now, can I?"

"Why not?"

Tarleton straightened up and patted the horse on its flank. "It will be difficult enough for him to swim without being weighted down."

A sharp laugh cut through the dusk. "Preacher, the Good Lord may have walked on water but I ain't never seen a horse that could. And I know I ain't never seen a horse that could swim that river."

"He'll manage."

"The horse stays here, Preacher."

Tarleton whirled on Bingham and pinned him with an icy glare. "If you want your money, you will do as I say. And I say the horse comes with me."

Bingham glared at the tall man in black. "You sure ain't like no preacher I ever seen before," he grumbled as he tromped toward the edge of the bluff. He peered out across the river. "Sun's about gone. We might as well get started."

Tarleton hoisted his gear and gathered up the reins. "Lead the way."

Professor Beeler lit a lantern and hung it from a peg on the front of the wagon. "I hope you don't mind traveling in the dark," he called.

Riding alongside the wagon, Jack replied, "Not at all."

The older man nodded. In the wagon behind him, one of the minstrels strummed a banjo while another wailed mournfully on a harmonica.

"They make pretty music," Sam observed. He drew his horse up alongside Jack. "What sort of business do you have in Washington City?"

"My brother's missing," Jack explained, repeating the cover story he had rehearsed on the road from Richmond. "He was captured somewhere down by Petersburg. I'm going to see if the Yankees know where I can find him."

"Good luck," Sam muttered.

"I'll need it."

"Stay close behind," Bingham hissed. "It's tricky finding the way in the dark, and we don't dare make a light." He led Tarleton and his horse down a faint trail stretching from the bluff to the river below. After a few minutes, the path pitched steeply downhill. As they worked their way toward the bottom, the men picked up speed. When they reached the river, they were running at full gallop.

Bingham came to a stop at the water's edge. Tarleton's momentum—added to that of the horse—carried both of them splashing into the river.

"God A'mighty, Preacher!" Bingham hissed. "Quiet down!"

Tarleton pulled himself, then the horse, out of the frigid water. He was soaked from the waist down and the animal was trembling from the cold. Bingham watched from the riverbank, hands on hips. "That's what you get for draggin' that damn horse with you." He picked through the underbrush along the bank, pulled away a clump of dead bushes and revealed a small boat.

"Here she is," he announced proudly. "She ain't fancy, but she knows the way to Maryland by heart." He picked up a pair of rough-hewn oars, dropped them into the boat, and dragged it a few feet to the water. "Come on. Let's get this over with."

Tarleton sprang into the back of the boat, and tied the horse's reins around his right leg. Bingham snarled, "Why in hell are you doing that?"

"You tend to the boat. I'll tend to the horse."

"Say your prayers, Preacher, 'cause here we go." Bingham shoved the skiff away from shore. The horse neighed reluctantly, then followed. Bingham jumped into the front of the boat and began rowing.

They heard nothing but the rush of the river, the oars breaking the surface of the water, and the horse splashing behind them. A thick mist rose around them. Tarleton couldn't see where they were heading. In a matter of minutes, they were sliding through fog so dense they couldn't see one another.

"Where are we going?" Tarleton demanded.

"Nights like these, you don't know till you get there."

"We're drifting south."

"We're fine so long as we don't drift all the way to the Piney Point lighthouse. Now shut up and let me do my job."

The boat glided through the night, shrouded in layers of haze that muffled all sound. As the minutes passed, Bingham's breathing grew more labored. He grunted each time he plunged the oars into the water. Tarleton felt the horse tugging against the reins wrapped around his thigh. He glanced over his shoulder, but the animal was invisible in the murky night.

The rhythmic slap of the oars suddenly stopped. For a moment, the little boat seemed frozen in place. Upstream, a bright flash of orange sparks burst through the fog, followed by a deep boom and the stench of gun smoke. The horse reared back in terror, jerking the boat along with it.

"Patrol!" Bingham shouted, thrusting an oar at Tarleton. "Row like hell!"

A voice called out in a thick Massachusetts accent, "You there, halt!"

"Row, damn you!" Bingham ordered. Tarleton pulled the oar with all his strength.

"They're over there!" the voice shouted. Rifle fire crackled, followed by the splash of minié balls hitting water. Another cannon blast sent a geyser spraying skyward only inches from Tarleton's oar.

"They've got our range!" Tarleton yelled.

"Shut up!" Bingham barked, rowing frantically.

The screaming blast of a steam whistle shrieked through the night.

"She's warning the patrols on shore!" Bingham's voice quivered in fear, his arms moving so quickly that each oar stroke splashed cold water on his passenger. They heard the steamer's captain yell out an order. The vessel groaned as its paddlewheel started churning. The horse reeled back against the reins tethered to Tarleton's leg, pulling him overboard and dragging him underwater.

Tarleton found himself enveloped in icy, inky silence. He fought down panic as he tried to determine whether he was sinking to the bottom of the river or rising toward the surface.

He felt a tug on his leg. That helped him orient himself. He pushed forcefully against the water with his arms and kicked his legs. His lungs were beginning to burn.

His head bobbed out of the water and he gasped desperately. Frigid air slapped him in the face. He reached out and felt something hard and slippery. As his fingers raced across the rough wooden object, Tarleton realized it was the side of the boat. He clutched it tightly, his heart pounding and his lungs furiously pumping.

A wave submerged him for a moment. When he resurfaced, confused voices cut into the fog behind him. Tarleton looked over his shoulder. He saw the glow of sparks in the distance. The shouts were growing fainter as another burst of gunfire thundered into the night. The bullets splashed far downriver. The steamer was heading away.

Tarleton clutched the edge of the boat. The cold water and colder air sapped his strength. As much as he wanted to hoist himself into the craft, he couldn't summon the energy. He held on and allowed himself to drift.

A scraping sound snapped him out of his daze. He realized the boat was no longer moving. He carefully extended a leg. When his foot touched something solid, he felt like letting out a cry of joy. He had made it to Maryland.

Tarleton slogged forward, his feet slipping on the muddy river bottom. At last, he grasped a small tree hanging over the water and pulled himself up on shore. The horse staggered weakly behind him, panting and struggling to maintain its balance. Tarleton untied the reins and let it wander away, then fell back on the ground exhausted.

He might have lain there all night had he not heard a moan. He pulled himself slowly to his feet and stumbled toward the skiff. Inside, Bingham's face was twisted in pain. A steady stream of blood spewed from an open wound on his chest.

Grunting from the exertion, Tarleton hauled his saddle, bags, and blanket roll out of the boat and tossed them to the shore. Then he grabbed the lead rope, wrapped it around Bingham, and lashed it to a fitting on the side of the boat.

Summoning his last reserve of energy, he pulled his long knife from his coat and thrust it repeatedly into the small craft just above the waterline. When he could no longer raise it, he dropped the knife on the bank, put his shoulder against the boat, and shoved it back into the river. Bingham's groans grew faint as the skiff slowly disappeared into the fog, sinking as it went.

The sun was high in the sky when the Professor called for the troupe to stop. Jack and Sam reined in their horses on either side of the wagon.

Walking up the road toward them was a blue-coated sentry. "Halt!" the soldier cried, even though they were standing still.

"Good morning, my dear man!" the Professor replied.

The sentry swept a derisive look over the troupe. "Well, well, what have we here?"

"A traveling band of entertainers," the Professor announced.

"Is that a fact?" He hoisted his rifle. "Let's see a pass or I'll cart the whole lot of you off to the stockade." The Professor calmly handed over a crumpled piece of paper. The soldier examined it, his lips moving silently as he puzzled out the words. Then he looked up, eyes wide. "Beeler's Minstrels?"

"Professor Marcus Beeler, at your service."

"Well, I'll be a son of a gun." The soldier shifted his rifle to his left hand, offering his right to the Professor. "I saw you fellows in Ohio, back before the war. Just wait till the boys back in camp hear about this. They're not gonna believe it."

"If you'll excuse us, sir." The Professor tipped his hat. "We're expected in Washington City."

"By all means, Professor." The soldier stepped aside and let the party pass. "Go straight on through Alexandria and right across the bridge. You can't miss it."

Tarleton pried open his right eye. And instantly regretted it. His head and every muscle in his body hurt. He hoisted himself painfully onto his elbows and scanned his surroundings. He was on the bank of the Potomac, right where he had collapsed the night before. Looking out across the river, he saw no sign of Bingham or his boat. With a satisfied grunt, he clambered stiffly to his feet.

He found his saddle and bags nearby. His horse had wandered up the shore and was grazing contently. The animal showed no ill effects from the night's ordeal. Tarleton loaded the horse and led him up the riverbank.

Thick woods laid bare by the cold weather stretched as far as he could see. He spotted a path leading from the river and followed it onto a farm road. He didn't know where it would take him, but it seemed to be free of Federal soldiers. He mounted his horse and spurred forward.

The animal shot ahead, racing at full gallop along the dirt track. The road veered sharply to the right. Rounding the bend, Tarleton saw a horse and buggy charging directly at him.

The woman driving the buggy jerked sharply at the reins. "Whoa!" she called. "Whoa!"

Tarleton pulled his horse to the right, narrowly avoiding a collision. The buggy rolled to a stop in a small cloud of dust.

Tarleton jumped down. "Are you all right, madam?"

Her eyes were drawn shut, her nostrils flaring as she breathed in quick bursts. "How dare you, sir!"

"Madam," Tarleton repeated, "are you all right?"

"Am I all right?" she snapped, her eyes still closed. "I come across a fool in the middle of the road paying no attention to anything around him. I avoid a crash by the closest of margins. And you ask if I am all right?" Her eyebrows arched high and she turned flashing green eyes toward him. "Sir, I am fine. No thanks to you."

She pinned him with her gaze. He noted the dark red hair trailing down from her pale blue bonnet, falling on a fair face with soft, delicate features. She was beautiful, though Tarleton doubted she would take kindly to such a compliment at the moment.

"And what of you, sir? Are you injured?"

"Not at all, madam. I beg your forgiveness. I should have had my mind on the road, not on the loveliness of the Maryland countryside."

His sincerity seemed to overwhelm her resolve. "I suppose I shall have to forgive you, Mister . . ."

Tarleton swept his hat from his head and bowed deeply. "Reverend Israel T. Harris, madam, the Lord's humble servant."

"Reverend? Now I am embarrassed."

"You needn't be."

"Where is your parish, Reverend?" There was something about her accent Tarleton couldn't quite pinpoint. Not Southern, but not exactly Northern either.

"I am on my way to take the pulpit of a Methodist Episcopal congregation in Washington."

"You'll find plenty of sinners there." She smiled.

"The harvest is great but the laborers are few." Tarleton paused. "You have the advantage of me, sister. You know my name, but I don't know yours."

"Kathleen O'Leary." She extended her hand.

Tarleton bowed over it. "Perhaps you will honor me by attending our services?"

"I'm certain it would be a rewarding experience," she said, adjusting her bonnet, "if I weren't Catholic."

"Our doors are always open to any soul in need."

The woman gave him an appraising glance. "I'm certain they

are, Reverend Harris." She gathered up the reins. "I must be going."

"Would you mind if I rode with you?"

A series of emotions flashed across her face—bemusement, indignation, interest, caution. At last, she tossed her red tresses. "Just the idea!" she said with a warm, throaty laugh.

"Then I bid you farewell." Tarleton bowed again. "Perhaps you would be so kind as to remember the Reverend Harris"— he glanced up under the brim of his hat and captured her eyes—"in your prayers."

"Why, Reverend Harris, what would your parishioners say if they knew you had solicited the prayers of a papist?" She smiled and flicked the reins. "Good day to you, sir."

Tarleton watched her drive away. He made a point to remember the name Kathleen O'Leary. He didn't know how long he would be in Washington, but he knew that before he left, he would see her again. She had rounded the curve and disappeared from sight before he realized he'd forgotten to ask her the way into the city.

Alexandria, Virginia, seemed more armed camp than town. Jack pulled his hat low over his eyes as the minstrel troupe rolled down its streets. There were Federal soldiers everywhere. Guards paced back and forth before mountains of wooden boxes, each filled with cartridges and crackers and bayonets and everything else an army needs. It was a sobering display of military muscle.

Jack had seen the deepening privation in Richmond and, despite the braggadocio of his comrades, he suspected the war was all but lost. Sam's tale of a ragtag army staggering through the woods had strengthened his conviction. But the sight before him drove the point home. It wasn't just the Union army facing the Confederacy, he realized. There was all of this behind it—the entire power of a determined nation channeled toward a single purpose. For the first time Jack understood a truth that had been masked by Southern pride. The Confederacy never had a chance.

They headed onto a long bridge that led into Washington. Crossing the Potomac, the troupe broke into a roaring rendition of "Yankee Doodle," their voices rolling across the broad stretch of water.

The wagon rattled to the end of the bridge and they were in the city. The riverfront, with its narrow streets and seedy buildings, reminded Jack of its counterpart in Richmond—soldiers marching, officers lounging in doorways, teamsters shepherding balky wagons. The Professor blazed a trail through the crowded streets, tipping his hat to people they passed, cheerfully shooing chickens out of their path. They entered broad boulevards lined with stately buildings and bustling storefronts—ladies paying social calls, schoolboys playing hooky, prostitutes and con men mingling among businessmen and shoppers, all on a landscape dominated by a towering white dome.

They finally pulled to a stop in front of a white frame structure festooned in red, white, and blue bunting. An ornate sign hung from the front, proclaiming MAGUIRE'S THEATER AND MUSICAL EMPORIUM.

"Last stop, gentlemen," Beeler called as he dismounted. "Pull the wagon around to the stage door. I'll let our employers know we have arrived."

Jack and Sam followed the wagon to the rear of the building and helped the minstrels carry their instruments, props, and costumes inside. They received a boisterous welcome from the stagehands who greeted the troupe like long-lost relatives.

As the last of the gear was stowed away, the Professor pulled Jack aside. "I was wondering how you and the boy are fixed for lodging."

"Well . . ."

"That's what I thought." Beeler smiled. "I have taken the liberty, if you will pardon the expression, of securing you a room at the Liberty House. We sometimes stay there when we're in Washington."

"That wasn't necessary," Jack protested.

The Professor laid a hand on Jack's shoulder. "Consider it repayment for the help you've given us."

"Really, Professor . . ."

Beeler wagged a finger. "You don't know your way around the city. It can be a treacherous place for strangers." He gave Jack a fatherly smile. "This way, you'll always know where to find a friendly face."

"National capital, indeed," Tarleton muttered as he steered his horse through the muddy streets of Washington City. London, Paris, Rome—those were national capitals, he told himself. This had been a dirty, miserable town the first time he'd visited it a dozen years before. It was a dirty, miserable town now.

A pig scurried noisily out of his way as Tarleton stared up at Washington's new landmark, the just-completed Capitol dome.

He grudgingly admitted it was an improvement over the short, squat ornament it had replaced. On the Capitol steps, laborers were tearing down wooden stands that had been erected for Lincoln's inauguration the previous Saturday.

At the foot of Capitol Hill, a filthy canal stretched toward the Potomac, teeming with the contents of countless chamber pots. Even the brisk winter wind couldn't carry away its overpowering stench. He pressed the back of his hand against his nostrils and spurred the horse forward. He spotted his destination a few blocks ahead—the National Hotel, a dignified brick building standing five stories tall.

As he dismounted, Tarleton decided his first order of business would be a bath and a shave, followed by a new suit of clothes. He carried his bags and blanket roll through the spacious hotel lobby to the front desk.

The clerk glanced at his shabby attire, sniffed, and offered him a bed in the basement. Tarleton produced a sheaf of greenbacks and demanded decent accommodations. Within minutes he was signing the register.

Tarleton climbed three flights of stairs to his room. He dropped his bags and immediately began pulling off his disgraceful black suit. He piled his clothing next to the bags and made a mental note to burn it at the first opportunity. Then he dropped naked onto the bed and fell into a profound slumber.

Breakfast at the Liberty House was late, hearty, and boisterous. The meal was served in a private dining room, where the minstrels could make as much noise as they liked without disturbing the other guests. Jack laughed as hard at their antics around the table as he had watching the troupe's opening-night performance.

The meal included generous portions of eggs, bacon, and ham, sopped up with large yeasty biscuits and washed down with strong coffee. After shoveling food into his mouth for several minutes, Sam leaned back and let loose a resounding belch. The sudden noise brought a stunned silence to the room, followed by an explosion of laughter.

Sam patted his stomach and reached for another biscuit. He winked at Jack. "You reckon they eat like this every morning?"

"They must," Jack replied in a low voice. "Look how fat they all are."

Sam grinned. "Pass the bacon."

After breakfast, the minstrels scattered. Professor Beeler walked with Jack and Sam out of the hotel and paused on the street to pull on his gloves. "Do you gentlemen have any particular plans for the day?"

"I might as well see what I can find out about my brother," Jack replied. "The War Department can't be that hard to find."

The Professor tipped his top hat. "I wish you good luck. I'm off to the theater."

"Again?" Sam asked.

Beeler heaved an exaggerated sigh. "It's a cross I must bear if I am to assure our company's business affairs are in order. Perhaps you'd care to accompany me?"

Sam looked at Jack then back at the Professor. "Why not?"

"Why not, indeed." Beeler linked arms with Sam, gave Jack a wave, and marched off down the street.

Jack took a moment to review his resources. He had a roof over his head, at least as long as the Professor was willing to extend his hospitality. He had enough Yankee dollars to support him for several weeks if he watched his pennies.

What he needed was a plan. He looked up the street at the Capitol dome gleaming in the morning sun. He started toward it, thinking about how he might find Basil Tarleton.

Tarleton consulted his pocket watch. The National Hotel had promised dinner at eight. It was fifteen minutes past the appointed hour and there was no sign of the meal. He decided time must have a more fluid quality in Washington than in any other city he'd visited.

A man beside him offered a knowing smile. "You may be the only person in this hotel who knows how to tell time."

"Or the only one who cares," Tarleton grumbled.

"Punctuality, the mark of a good Yankee."

"The mark of a good businessman," Tarleton politely corrected.

"Is there a difference?"

The men shared a laugh. They shook hands and introduced themselves.

Clarence Logan was a reedy man of about thirty wearing a well-cut dark suit nearly identical to the one Tarleton had purchased a few hours earlier. His pale gray eyes danced in merriment as he handed over his calling card.

The cream of Washington society swirled around them in the salon of the hotel. Gas lamps mounted on paneled walls softly illuminated matrons in stylish gowns who clutched at their men, most of them too old or too fat to serve in the army. The exception was a tall, dashing officer with a strikingly beautiful young woman on his arm.

Logan nodded toward them. "Pretty comfortable way to spend the war."

"A hundred thousand men in the trenches with Grant tonight would agree with you."

Logan arched an eyebrow. "I wonder how many strings he pulled to get this assignment?"

A sly smile played at Tarleton's lips. "I would have pulled twice as many for the chance to stand beside his lady."

"Washington draws women like a magnet."

"Cause and effect. Fill a city with men and it's just a matter of time until you have a city full of women."

"One of them seems to have set her sights on you," Logan stage-whispered behind his hand.

Tarleton followed Logan's gaze to a group of people standing near the dining room doors. A plump young lady turned her head away sharply as his eyes met hers.

"Lucy enjoys being caught staring almost as much as she enjoys staring," Logan whispered.

Tarleton watched the woman chatter to her companion. "I take it you know the lady."

"There's not a soul in this room who doesn't. Lucy Hale is one of the most socially ambitious women in the city. A regular at Mrs. Lincoln's Blue Room receptions, I'm told."

Tarleton added the information to the mental inventory he was taking. The woman wore a gown of rich blue satin. Her drab brown hair was curled and puffed in an apparent attempt to distract from her puffy and plain features. "What can you tell me about her?"

"Her father was a United States Senator." Logan indicated the portly, middle-aged man next to Lucy. "Last November, the good people of New Hampshire decided they'd had quite enough of him, thank you. The Hales live here at the hotel."

"On the outs?"

"Out of Congress, yes. Not out of influence. He seems to be in line for an ambassadorship or some political plum." Logan nudged Tarleton's elbow. "Not bad for a fire-breathing abolitionist, eh? You should have heard the way he railed against Lincoln on the Senate floor. Once, he got so worked up . . ."

Logan continued talking but Tarleton had stopped listening. He cast a thoughtful gaze toward Lucy Hale, the young woman with entrée to the White House. She lifted her head for the inevitable second look and Tarleton's piercing blue eyes caught hers. Crimson rose in her cheeks as she stared for a long moment. Her hand fluttered in front of her face, then she turned away.

Large oak doors behind her swung open. "Dinner is served," a formally dressed black man announced gravely. The buzz of conversation continued while the guests made their way to the dining room. Tarleton fell in beside Logan. He noticed the man was limping and cocked a questioning eyebrow.

"Gettysburg," Logan replied.

Lucy Hale steered her father toward empty seats next to Logan and Tarleton. The former senator nodded to them. Logan handled the introductions. Tarleton bowed formally over Lucy's hand. She responded with another blush and a girlish giggle.

A small army of servants invaded the room carrying trays heaped with beef, mutton, and duck. While it may have lacked the refinement of the more luxurious Willard's Hotel, the National compensated with abundance. Throughout the meal, Lucy darted furtive glances around her father toward Tarleton, who pretended not to notice.

"Did I hear correctly that you're in the mercantile trade?" the former senator asked.

"Yes, sir. In Chicago."

"If you're anything like that one"—Hale shot a glance toward Logan—"I'll spend the rest of the evening hearing how much money you can save the government."

"Now, Senator," Logan protested, "I showed you the figures on those coal contracts. You agreed—"

Hale shushed him with a wave of a biscuit. "I don't discuss business at the dinner table."

"Of course. I apologize." A chastened Logan turned his attention back to his food.

"I'm not here on business," Tarleton assured the former senator. "A maiden aunt of mine recently passed away."

"Sorry to hear it," Hale mumbled around a mouthful of beef.

"Thank you, sir. She was an elderly woman who insisted on managing the family estate in Virginia until the day she died. My father sent me to settle her affairs."

Lucy placed a chubby elbow on the table and propped her chins in her hand. "Will you be in the city long, Mr. Tarleton?" She batted her eyelashes.

"I hope to tidy things up in a couple of days. But there's no rush." Tarleton graced her with his most charming smile.

A bashful smile sent ripples through Lucy's fleshy face. "Don't you think the war must end any day now, Mr. Tarleton? Won't it be wonderful to have all our friends and loved ones home again? How do you think Mr. Lincoln is going to rule the defeated South?"

Tarleton struggled to mask his contempt for women who discussed politics, especially at dinner. Once she started talking, Lucy seemed incapable of stopping. Her prattle continued straight into dessert.

When the table was cleared and the guests began taking their leave, Tarleton rose and extended an arm. "I'd be honored if you would accompany me to the salon, Miss Hale." Her face was aglow as she took his arm.

Lucy paraded Tarleton around the room. He kept careful track of the people she introduced—the wife of a general, an assistant secretary of state, the British chargé d'affaires.

They completed their circuit of the salon and returned to where Logan and the former senator stood by a window framed with dark red draperies. The younger men accepted Hale's offer of cigars to complement their after-dinner sherry. They were raising their glasses in a toast when a flurry of activity across the room drew their attention.

The crowd of people near the salon door parted like curtains at the opening of a play. Between them strode a short, slight man wearing a carefully cut formal suit. His coal-black wavy hair and thick dark moustache contrasted dramatically with his pale, clear skin. He walked into the salon with a swift, sure step, his every move exuding confidence. When he reached the center of the room, he stopped and surveyed his surroundings.

The man's gaze caught Lucy's and she enthusiastically waved to him. His face brightened as he made his way toward her.

"I can't stand to watch this," Hale muttered. He set his sherry glass on a side table and clutched Logan by the elbow. "Let's go get a real drink." They headed out the door as the man reached Lucy and Tarleton.

He paused before them and cast an appraising glance over the couple. "A fine sight, finding my favorite girl with a tall and handsome stranger." His tone was both affectionate and mocking.

"Favorite girl, indeed!" Lucy chided. "As if you don't have the heart of every woman in Washington."

"Every heart except the one that matters."

Tarleton felt he should recognize the man, but couldn't put a name with the face. The newcomer turned toward him. "And just who is this fellow standing in my stead?"

Lucy patted Tarleton's arm. "This is Mr. Basil Tarleton."

The man bowed formally. "John Wilkes Booth, at your service, sir."

Three

THE LEADING MAN

"I saw you on the stage in New York," Tarleton told Booth as they settled in over drinks. When he had accepted the actor's invitation for a nightcap, he expected Booth to take him to some fashionable club. Instead, they ended up in a saloon where most of the patrons wore working clothes and swilled cheap beer. "You were magnificent," he added.

Booth surveyed the men crowded around the bar, nodding to acquaintances. "Which play did you see?" he asked absently.

"*The Merchant of Venice.* It was unforgettable."

"A tolerable production." Booth's eyes settled back on Tarleton. "So what brings you to Washington?"

Tarleton repeated the tale of his fictitious dead aunt and her tangled estate. Booth offered appropriate condolences while his eyes skirted about the room, then returned to the empty snifter in his hand. "I daresay we'll be needing more provisions if we're to make a proper night of it." He pointed toward Tarleton's glass. "Refill?"

"Not just yet."

"You disappoint me, Basil." Booth sighed. "I'll just have to soldier on alone." He threaded his way to the bar and returned with a bottle of brandy and a bottle of whiskey. He made a show of refilling both glasses, even though Tarleton had barely touched his drink. He raised his snifter in salute. "To the Cause."

Tarleton tentatively lifted his glass. "The Cause?"

"The glorious Cause, old boy. The Cause of liberty for my beloved homeland."

Tarleton glanced quickly around the saloon. No one was paying any attention to his famous companion. He realized the actor's pro-Southern sentiment was not out of place here. He sensed an opportunity. "To the Cause," he said at last and clinked his glass against Booth's.

The actor again drained his glass. "Nectar of the gods, my friend." He gave a conspiratorial grin and poured a refill. "So, how are you finding our fair city?"

"It's changed a lot." Tarleton shrugged.

Booth's eyes widened. "You've been here before? I distinctly recall you saying your father's business is in Chicago."

"Most of my father's family was in Virginia."

"Ah, yes. Your dear departed aunt." Booth took a sip of brandy.

Tarleton nodded. "Uncles and cousins, too."

"Forgive me for being indelicate, but if you have uncles and cousins in Virginia, why did it fall on you to settle your aunt's estate?"

"They're all dead." Tarleton shook his head. "This damned bloody war."

Booth raised his drink. "To a swift and just peace."

Tarleton didn't join the toast.

"What is it, Basil? I should think after what your family has endured you would be happy that peace is at hand."

"The war may be ending," Tarleton said in a low voice, "but there will be no 'just peace.'"

"Why not?"

Tarleton hunched forward. His voice took on a low urgency. "It's been eating at me ever since I arrived, Wilkes. My aunt was probably ill equipped to manage the family estate. But I don't think that's what made such a mess of her affairs." He bent over the table and whispered, "Is it safe to talk here?"

"As safe as anywhere."

"I think the Federal army has a hand in this."

Booth rubbed his finger along the edge of the snifter. "And why would the army want to do that?"

"Because," Tarleton hissed, "my uncles and cousins died fighting for the Confederacy." He closed his right hand into a fist. "The courts have been stringing us along for months. The more we try to untangle it, the more complicated it becomes."

Booth nodded slowly. "There are people in this town who might be sympathetic to your plight." He took a long drink of brandy.

"Are they attorneys?"

The actor smiled. "One or two are. Perhaps I can speak to them."

"That would be very kind, Wilkes." Tarleton sipped his whiskey. "I apologize for burdening you with my problems."

"Think nothing of it, old man." Booth regarded Tarleton for a long moment, then rose. "It's been a very pleasant evening, Basil."

Tarleton stood, as well. "I suppose I should be going, too."

"Nonsense." Booth waved him back into his chair. "Stay and enjoy your whiskey. My treat."

"Thanks." Tarleton shook the actor's hand. "I hope we can do this again."

"Oh, we shall." Booth paused at the door and raised his voice to address everyone in the room. " 'To all, to each! A fair good-night, and pleasing dreams and slumber light.' " He bowed to a round of cheers and made his exit.

As Tarleton watched the actor disappear into the night, a thin smile curled the corners of his mouth. He poured a generous whiskey, contemplated the dark liquid for a moment, then gulped it down.

An hour before sunrise, Jack found himself perched on the bench of a delivery wagon operated by the National Lager Company. His attempts to steer the mule team through Washington's alleys was a source of constant amusement to Felix, the large black man assigned to assist with his rounds. As the mules refused to follow Jack's commands, Felix hooted with laughter. He shouted at passersby to step lively and clear the streets. Then he laughed some more.

Delivering beer didn't pay much, but the job offered a more important benefit. It gave Jack a reason to visit dozens of saloons in a relatively short amount of time. He could scout for gathering places of Southern sympathizers who might put him in touch with the operative George Webb.

Jack had talked his way into a job as a teamster by assuring the manager he had experience handling mules. It wasn't completely untrue. He had spent the summers of his youth handling a mule-drawn plow on his father's farm. A single well-broken animal didn't exactly constitute a mule team, but Jack didn't expect two to be much more trouble than one.

He was dreadfully wrong.

"Here we go again," Felix howled as Jack tried to back the team into a cobbled alley behind the tavern where they were to make their first delivery. The big man stood up and pointed behind them. "Watch out for the—"

There was a jolt, followed by a rumbling crash. Jack craned his neck to look back. He had rammed the wagon into the wall of the building across the alley, knocking over the barrels of beer. One lay smashed and leaking on the cobblestones.

Felix propped his hands on his hips and let loose a high-pitched guffaw. "The boss man is surely gonna love that," he howled. "You just cost yourself two days' pay." His body shook with laughter.

Jack could only shake his head as he surveyed the damage. "Welcome to Washington," he muttered.

A pounding thunder roused Tarleton, jolting him upright from a sound sleep. He looked out the window and tried to guess the time. Not long after sunrise, judging from the soft light filling the room.

Another impatient crash, then a third, came from the door. Tarleton bolted across the room and threw it open. A tall, powerfully built young man in work clothes stared at him.

"What do you want?" Tarleton demanded.

"You Tarleton?" the man asked in a thick Southern drawl.

"State your business."

"He wants you to go riding." The man thrust a calling card at him. "Be in the lobby at ten." Without another word, the man turned and lumbered down the hallway.

Tarleton closed the door. J. WILKES BOOTH, the card read. Damned strange way to invite someone for a ride, he thought as he tossed it on the dresser and crawled back into bed.

Three hours later, Tarleton was waiting when the actor strode into the hotel lobby, as dapper and dashing as if he were on the stage. "Good morning, Basil," Booth said cheerfully. He removed a white kid glove from his right hand and shook Tarleton's. "I have to make a brief excursion into Maryland. I'd be delighted to have you accompany me."

"I'm free until this afternoon."

"Then let us take the morning air."

They mounted horses that Booth had waiting at a hitching post and joined the bustling traffic on Pennsylvania Avenue. Along the way, Booth made small talk about the weather, the theater, and Washington society, tipping his hat to admirers whenever they caught his gaze.

Tarleton finally asked, "What sort of lout did you send to drag me out of bed at the crack of dawn?"

Booth laughed. "Lewis Paine. He performs small tasks for me."

"At dawn?"

"Lewis isn't the brightest man in Washington," Booth admitted. "But he has his uses. I apologize for his zealousness."

They reached the Navy Yard Bridge. Booth hailed the sentry, who returned his greeting and waved them past. When they emerged on the other end of the span, the sun was climbing high, promising more warmth than it delivered. They followed a road that led into dense woods. Thick stands of pine stood in ranks on either side of the lane, broken by occasional clumps of oak and birch trees stripped of their leaves by harsh winter winds.

"I've been thinking about your problem," Booth said. "I'm sure you're right. The Federal army is meddling with your aunt's estate. And I know why."

"I told you last night," Tarleton replied. "They want revenge."

Booth raised an index finger. "There's more to it than that. The army is engaged in this bit of chicanery because it has too much time on its hands."

Tarleton peered closely at Booth. "I don't follow."

Booth gestured at the scenery around them. "Do you see any patrols out here?"

"No."

"And you won't. The countryside around Washington is completely pacified."

"What has that to do with my aunt?"

"A lesson from history." Booth tapped the brim of his hat with his forefinger. "What does a military organization do when it has no military duties to perform? Rome under the Caesars, Napoleonic France, Alexandrian Egypt. In each case, once the fighting ended, military commanders turned their energies to civil affairs. All with the same result—tyranny." He looked around at the stark scenery. "It's happening here, too."

"What can anyone do about it?"

Booth laughed heartily. "We can give the army something more important to worry about than your maiden aunt's estate." He flicked the reins and his horse jumped into a gallop. "Come along, Basil," he called over his shoulder.

Tarleton spurred his horse and surged into Booth's wake. They rode hard for more than half an hour before the actor halted at a modest country tavern. Inside, Booth tossed a greeting to a slovenly innkeeper behind a counter, handed him two coins, and snagged a bottle of brandy. He led them into an adjoining dining room. "I took the liberty of arranging a midday repast," he explained as he ushered Tarleton to the table.

Booth grabbed a drumstick from a platter of fried chicken. "We're going to kidnap Lincoln."

He let the words hang in the air as he attacked his meal. Other than the fire crackling in the hearth behind the actor, the room was filled with silence. "You can't be serious," Tarleton said at last.

"I've never been more serious in my life." Booth poured a glass of brandy. "Thousands of Confederate troops are rotting in Yankee prisons. Twelve thousand at Point Lookout alone, not sixty miles from here. If we can get them back, they'll breathe fresh life into the Cause and make the Yankees so sick of the war they'll sue for peace." He leaned toward Tarleton. "And history will richly reward the men who deliver the South its independence."

Tarleton bent forward, his face only inches from Booth's. "You intend to kidnap Lincoln and exchange him for the captured soldiers." Booth nodded. Tarleton leaned back. "How?"

"Lincoln has a fatal flaw. He loves to appear in public." Booth sipped his drink. "The time will come when he makes a misstep. That's when we strike."

Tarleton shifted in his chair and hooked his arm over the back. Despite his air of nonchalance, his mind was working rapidly. He knew Booth was famous, well connected, and could walk through any door in the city. It was certainly possible he could get close enough to abduct Lincoln.

And if Booth could get close enough to abduct Lincoln, Tarleton could get close enough to kill Lincoln.

He wanted to hear more, but he had already made up his mind.

Tarleton planned to stay very close to John Wilkes Booth.

The door burst open. A young man in a mechanic's cap and work clothes stomped into the dining room. He glowered at Booth. "Where the hell have you been?" he snarled.

"Riding," Booth replied with a broad grin. "What are you supposed to be? A boilermaker?"

"Very funny," he said with a sour look. "While you were out touring the countryside, your 'friend' got loose." He stopped, looked directly at Tarleton, then turned back to Booth.

"You can speak freely," the actor assured him. "This is Basil Tarleton of Chicago."

The man's eyebrows twitched suspiciously. "Chicago?"

Booth smiled. "Basil is the scion of an old Virginia family that has suffered mightily at the hands of the Yankee oppressors." He turned to Tarleton. "My dear friend John Surratt has recently returned from Richmond. You might not believe it from his attire, but he helps his mother supervise the family holdings, consisting of this very establishment and a rooming house in the city."

Surratt studied Tarleton with narrow eyes. "Is Wilkes recruiting you?"

Tarleton began to answer, but Booth cut him off. "Early days, John. Suffice it to say I'm satisfied with Basil's commitment to the Cause."

"I hope he's more manageable than Paine." Surratt frowned deeply. "You've got to keep that brute under control."

"What has he done now?"

"I caught him wandering around Massachusetts Avenue. He said you'd sent him on an errand." When Booth didn't respond, Surratt demanded, "Did you?" Booth shrugged. Anger colored Surratt's words. "So you let him roam Washington like some mindless beast."

"He promised he'd go straight back to your mother's house."

"Well, he didn't."

Tarleton interrupted the exchange. "Would someone care to tell me who we're discussing?"

"Lewis Paine." Surratt spat out the name.

"My associate," Booth offered.

"He's thick as a brick," Surratt interjected. "He says the town is laid out crooked. He can't walk to the end of the block without losing his way."

"That will do," Booth said sharply.

"We don't need the risk, Wilkes. Washington is full of spies. There could already be a price on my head. And on yours, too. We don't need that lummox blundering about, getting us all tossed in jail."

"I said that's enough." The color rose in Booth's cheeks. He inhaled deeply and let his breath out slowly. "I told you I would deal with Lewis, and I will. You have my word."

Surratt offered Tarleton a weak smile. "Nice bunch of people you've thrown in with."

"It will all work out for the best." Booth raised his glass. "Our time is almost at hand. I'll take care of some final details, then assemble the players and reveal the plan to everyone."

"It better be soon," Surratt complained. "I'm getting dispatches asking me to come back to Richmond. I can only wait so long."

"Patience, my friend. In a few weeks, you'll take your rightful place in history."

"I don't care about history," Surratt said. "I want those men back in Lee's army. If we wait much longer we might as well give it up."

Booth laid a soothing hand on Surratt's arm. "Soon, John. Very soon."

Surratt nodded toward Tarleton. "A pleasure to meet you, sir. I'm sure this will be an adventure to remember." A sad smile crossed his face. "If we live that long." He turned and strode out of the tavern.

"Is he always that excitable?" Tarleton asked as he watched the man leave.

"Sometimes." Booth drank the last of his brandy and shoved the cork back in the bottle. "The worst part is he's right."

"About what?"

"Everything," Booth muttered. When he spoke again, there was a lighter tone to his voice. "It's not been a lost day. You've agreed to cast your lot with us. Let's meet again tonight. I'll properly introduce you to Lewis Paine."

"I haven't agreed to anything, Wilkes. You'vc drafted me."

"So I did." The actor's charming grin brightened his face. "But what choice do you have? You already know enough to earn a place on the gallows with the rest of us. You may as well come along for the ride."

The sun was setting on Jack's first day as a beer deliveryman, leaving him with strained muscles and a fierce throbbing in his injured leg. He would have liked nothing better than to crawl into bed and sleep until sunrise. But he was sure Tarleton was in Washington. The assassin could strike at any moment. Jack didn't want to waste time.

He plodded toward a saloon he had visited earlier in the day. He paused outside to watch well-dressed customers trickle in and out. A couple approached through the gathering dusk, a lanky towheaded young man escorting a statuesque woman.

"Jack?" Sam Jenkins called. "What are you doing here?" His chest swelled up like a bantam rooster's as he patted the hand of the woman on his arm. She was striking—tall with dark hair, wearing a velvet gown that revealed a great deal of her substantial bosom. As they stepped into the light of a street lamp, Jack could see heavy makeup caked over the crow's-feet around her eyes. She tightened her grip on Sam's arm.

"I could ask you the same thing," Jack replied.

Sam grinned sheepishly. "It was getting toward suppertime, and Olivia—Miss Putnam here—suggested we take a break. She's rehearsing a play." He turned to the woman. "This is the fellow I've been telling you about. We're rooming together."

"So you're the famous Jack Tanner." The actress batted her eyelashes. "Perhaps you would join us for a drink."

"We're meeting some folks from Maguire's Theater," Sam added. "Professor Beeler got me a job there."

Olivia smiled possessively at her escort. "He's going to be the best assistant property manager we've ever had."

Jack looked again at the saloon. If it catered to the theater set, it wasn't the kind of place where he would find information. "I'd better be getting along. Another time, perhaps." He tipped his hat to the actress. "A pleasure to meet you, Miss Putnam."

"Likewise." She tugged at Sam's arm. "Come along. I'm developing a powerful thirst."

"See you back at the hotel tonight?" Sam called over his shoulder.

"Sure," Jack responded. He watched them go with a bemused smile.

Two hours and four taverns later, Jack was ready to call it a night. The weak beers he had nursed along the way did nothing to soothe his aches. And he hadn't made any promising contacts. Limping along yet another unfamiliar street, he felt jolts of pain shooting down his bad leg.

His eyes were drawn to a brightly lit building with a sign reading GRISHAM'S. He peered in the front window. This bar hadn't been on his delivery route. The customers generally were laborers, though a few dandified gents were lounging about as well. A card game occupied a table in the far corner. Just the sort of place he had been looking for.

Jack stepped through the open door and made his way to the bar. He heard a chorus of voices with a wide variety of accents—the clipped tones of New England, the nasal twang of the prairie, the slow drawl of the Deep South.

A voice pierced the din. "What'll it be?"

A stocky bartender stood expectantly before him. "What kind beer do you have?" Jack asked.

"Cold."

"I mean, who's your brewer?"

The bartender gave a vague shrug. "Some place in Baltimore."

"Good enough."

The bartender filled a mug. "Five cents." Jack handed over a nickel and took a deep drink.

A leathery-faced man down the bar gave Jack a cockeyed look. "Kinda particular about your beer, ain't you?"

"I work for National Lager," Jack explained. "I'd hate to pay them more than they pay me."

"Don't seem fair, you payin' for your brew."

"If there's a way to get it for free, I haven't found it."

"You can get most anything for free in Washington." A half-grin creased his face. "You just have to know how."

Jack examined the expensive gray suit and burgundy vest. A gold watch chain and fob stretched across his belly. "I take it you know how."

The man winked. "I do what I can."

Jack decided the man had the look of a gambler and nodded toward the card game in the corner. "Lively place."

"It is at that. Ain't another like it." He slid his empty glass toward the bartender. "I take it you got your fill of the Rebel army."

"I beg your pardon?" Jack gulped at his beer to cover his surprise.

"I reckon Washington City's as good a place to make a new start as anywhere." The man grinned. "It's your shoes." Jack looked down at his worn brogans. "U.S. Army regulation," the stranger continued. "Old soldiers can't wait to get out of them and back into a pair of comfortable boots." He gave Jack an appraising glance. "That makes you an ex-Rebel who ain't got money for proper footwear." He accepted a fresh mug of beer.

Jack knew the man had him pegged. Captured Federal shoes were coveted possessions in Confederate ranks. It had taken some steep haggling to get this pair.

"There's no shame in it." The stranger smiled. "Hell, I was Secesh myself when the war started. That's all behind me now." He sipped his beer, set the mug on the bar and leaned closer. "I know what it's like to be new in this town."

Jack looked squarely into the man's eyes. "Then maybe you can help me. I'm looking for someone named George Webb."

The man straightened up abruptly. He grabbed his beer and took a gulp. He surveyed the bar and lowered his voice. "That's a name you don't say too loud."

"Sorry," Jack whispered back. "You know where I can find him?"

"Maybe." The man shrugged. "Maybe not. Why?"

"I can't say."

The man studied Jack warily. "How do you know this person?"

"I was told to look him up." He added in a whisper, "By a friend in Richmond."

The man nodded. "What's your name?"

"Jack Tanner."

"Where can you be reached?"

"The Liberty House."

The man finished his beer and dropped a coin on the counter. "The person you're looking for can be very difficult to find. I'll ask around. If I hear anything, I'll call for you."

Without another word, the man walked out of the saloon.

As Tarleton approached the tidy three-story white brick house at 541 H Street, he was still debating with himself. He was convinced Booth fervently believed he could abduct Abraham Lincoln. Tarleton was equally convinced it took more than self-confidence to pull off such a spectacular crime.

He spotted the actor pacing impatiently in front of the house. "Opening-night jitters, Wilkes?" he called.

Booth looked up. "You're late."

Tarleton consulted his pocket watch. "I'm four minutes early."

"Never mind." Booth took his elbow and propelled him up the steps to the front door. "Come on in."

A handful of people sat around a blazing fireplace in a cozy parlor. "There you are," John Surratt called as they entered. "I was wondering if you would make it. I think you already know everyone, Wilkes."

"Everyone" turned out to be a pair of young women, who blushed furiously as Booth kissed each of their hands, and a thickset young man, who heaved himself to his feet. Surratt introduced him as Louis Weichmann, a college classmate with whom he currently shared a room.

Weichmann looked Tarleton up and down. "Are you here to discuss business?"

Before Tarleton could answer, Surratt stepped between them. "We're meeting in the back."

"Another of your mysterious deals, John?" Weichmann gave his roommate a sly grin. "Maybe I should join you. I could use a good investment."

Surratt's eyes shifted quickly from Booth to Tarleton. "Perhaps another time, Louis." He motioned toward a staircase. "This way."

A tall, large-framed woman dressed entirely in black approached. She held a tooled-leather prayer book in one hand and a rosewood rosary in the other. Her rich, dark hair, severely parted down the middle, gave a stern cast to her handsome face. "Where are you off to, John?"

"My business meeting, Mother," he explained. "I told you Mr. Booth was bringing a friend by to discuss his oil speculations."

Mary Surratt turned to her visitors. "John tells me your investments are paying off quite nicely, Mr. Booth."

"Indeed they are, madam," the actor responded with a smile. "I think the time is ripe for your son to jump into the market."

The woman held Booth's gaze, then gave him a small nod. "Be sure not to disturb the other boarders," she told her son.

Surratt kissed her cheek. "Certainly, Mother." He led the men up the stairs and through a narrow hallway. He rapped smartly on a bedroom door and pushed it open.

Dirty clothes cluttered the floor. An enormous man cluttered the bed. Tarleton immediately recognized Lewis Paine, the brute who had interrupted his sleep. He sat with his back against the wall, brown hair swept up from his broad forehead, his muscular frame clearly outlined beneath a blue pullover shirt. His gaze locked on Booth.

"Good evening, Parson," the actor said lightly.

"Evening, Cap," Paine replied.

"He is rooming here under the alias of Reverend Lewis Wood," Booth explained.

"A clever pretext," Tarleton replied dryly.

Surratt settled into a chair near the room's only window. "My devoutly Catholic mother is amused that a Baptist clergyman would seek lodging in a papist household." He turned to Booth. "When do we make our move?"

"Before another week is out."

"Finally," Surratt responded. "Let's hear about it."

"In good time." Booth produced a handful of cigars from his coat pocket and passed them around.

"But Wilkes—"

"I want to tell everyone at once," Booth assured him. "I'll notify our associates to join us Wednesday. I've reserved a private room at Gautier's Restaurant for midnight. That's when I'll share the specifics."

Tarleton exhaled a long stream of smoke. "You're still planning to kidnap him?"

"I am."

"Seems like it would be a lot easier to kill him and be done with it."

"Our objective," the actor began slowly, "is freeing our prisoners. A dead body does us no good. Even a president's body."

"There would be a lot fewer headaches."

Booth waved his cigar. "As satisfying as it would be to kill him, and as much as he richly deserves to die, he's worth more to us alive."

Paine carelessly flicked an ash. "Stop that," Surratt demanded. "This is my mother's house."

Paine glared at Surratt as he reached over the side of the bed and picked up an object from the floor. He held it out so Surratt could see. It was a human skull. Paine flicked another ash into it.

Surratt gasped. Booth winced. Tarleton's face remained impassive.

"Some Yankee," Paine explained as he returned the skull to the floor. "Tried to kill me at Second Manassas. I did a better job." Paine puffed on his cigar.

Booth cleared his throat. "Wednesday night, gentlemen, we will set our plan in motion."

"About bloody time," Surratt muttered.

"To avoid suspicion, we should meet that evening. At Ford's Theatre."

"What's the point in that?" Tarleton asked.

"To keep up appearances." Booth smiled. "We'll simply be another theater party treating ourselves to a midnight supper. I've arranged the tickets. John, you bring Paine." He frowned. "Better bring along a couple of women, too. Protective coloration, as it were." He turned to Tarleton. "I'm sure I can manage escorts for us, Basil."

Tarleton nodded. Paine stared mutely at Booth. Only Surratt raised an objection. "You're wasting time, Wilkes. We're all here right now. Just tell us what you're planning."

"We're not all here. Not yet. Patience, John." Booth stepped to the door and placed his hand on the knob. He smiled back at Surratt. "I assure you, in this case patience will be richly rewarded."

Surratt shook his head sullenly. "It had better be."

Tarleton rose and joined Booth. The actor gave a crisp salute to Paine and Surratt and opened the door. Tarleton heard the padding of heavy footsteps in the hall outside. He poked his head through the door and looked to the left, then the right. A chubby silhouette was waddling into the shadows.

Booth followed his gaze. He glanced at Tarleton then turned to Surratt. "You might have a word with your roommate, John. Tell him to stay away from rich foods if he doesn't want to keep trotting off to the privy in the middle of the night."

Four

THE CENTER OF THE WEB

"I was beginning to think you'd forgotten me." Lucy Hale giggled as the buggy bounced along the fashionable part of Pennsylvania Avenue.

Tarleton turned a crestfallen countenance toward her. "How could you say such a thing? One might more easily forget the *Mona Lisa,* or Paris at sunset."

"At least you still remember how to make a girl feel wanted," she said. "Wilkes hasn't a spare moment these days. And I didn't hear from you for the longest time. I thought perhaps I was driving everyone away." She inched closer to him.

Her not inconsiderable weight draped against his shoulder, as if she needed to soak up his body's warmth to ward off the chill. Even though it wasn't that cold, Tarleton did not draw away from her. Lucy might be plain and plump and intolerably self-absorbed, but her knowledge of Washington society was unassailable. She could open doors for him if Booth proved to be nothing but talk. As much as he disliked admitting it, he needed Lucy Hale. "I beg your forgiveness, my dear," Tarleton said with enough feeling to raise the color in her cheeks. "I see you've kept your social calendar full in my absence. The newspaper listed you among the guests at Mrs. Lincoln's salon on Saturday."

"I could hardly miss that. It was the final White House event of the season."

"And how was Mrs. Lincoln?"

"In fine form." Lucy turned to watch the slowly passing scenery. "I wish I could say the same for the president. The poor man looked pale as paste."

"Nothing serious, I hope."

"Serious enough that he took to his bed all day Sunday and Monday. But he must be feeling better."

"Oh?"

"Well enough for a night at Maguire's Theater. With that Clara Harris." Lucy pulled her hand out of her fur muff and waved dismissively as if the name didn't matter to her, which meant it did. "One of Mrs. Lincoln's pets. If there's a function at the White House, you're more likely to find Clara Harris there than Tad."

Lucy lowered her voice. "They say he's addle-minded, you know. He has free run of the White House. Barges in on cabinet meetings just to ask the President of the United States for a nickel. Can you believe it?"

Tarleton shook his head in affected disbelief.

"Papa says Tad is a brat who deserves a daily trip to the woodshed. He'd give it to him, too, if he were Tad's—Oh, goodness!" Lucy clamped her hand over her mouth.

"What's the matter?"

"You won't tell anyone what I've said about the Lincolns, will you?" Lucy turned bovine eyes on Tarleton. "It would ruin my father. The Senate hasn't confirmed his ambassadorship. Promise me you won't say a word."

Tarleton gave her an endearing smile that had melted hearts from Paris to New Orleans. "Of course I won't, Lucy."

She produced a frilly handkerchief and patted her face. "I don't know why I let my tongue run ahead of my brain." She sighed heavily. "You'd think I'd learn, with all the vipers slithering through this city. You never truly know who your friends are."

Tarleton increased the temperature of his smile. "You're sitting beside one now." Lucy giggled and melted against him.

He reined the buggy into the center of the Mall and pulled to a stop at the foot of the unfinished monument to George Washington. As the horse scrounged for bits of grass, Tarleton gestured toward the White House off to their left. "You say he's doing better?"

"Oh, yes. They wouldn't be going to the theater tonight if he weren't."

"Maguire's, you say?"

Lucy nodded. "Why?"

Tarleton offered her another smile. "I was just wondering if perhaps you'd care to take in the play as well."

"It isn't a play." She wrinkled her nose. "It's an opera. I simply couldn't abide it."

"I'm sorry to hear that." Tarleton patted the hand clutching his arm. "Another time, then."

Lucy's face brightened. "Of course."

He consulted his pocket watch. "Oh, my. It's later than I thought." He gathered the reins and flicked them at the horse. "I must apologize. I have an important meeting this afternoon."

"Not another lawyer, I hope."

He turned a weary smile toward her. "I'm afraid so."

Lucy pouted as the buggy rolled past the Treasury Department. "Now, don't look that way," he chided. "Is that how you want me to remember you while I listen to lawyers droning all afternoon?"

The young woman's chubby face brightened. "You think of me when we're apart?"

"The livelong day." Tarleton whipped the horse into a gallop down Pennsylvania Avenue.

An hour after he had deposited Lucy at the National Hotel, Tarleton stood in the Surratt house sitting room watching Booth hold court. The actor was regaling Mrs. Surratt and two young women with tales of his onstage triumphs. Booth glanced up. "Basil!" The actor flashed his famous smile. "What brings you here?"

"I have some news." Tarleton looked quickly at the others. "About those oil speculations."

Booth nodded and rose to his feet. "By all means. Ladies, please excuse us." He retrieved his hat from a table and led Tarleton out of the house.

The actor took a deep breath of chilly air. "A delightful day. Perhaps I shall hire a buggy and take a lady friend for a spin around the Mall." Booth turned to Tarleton. "Unless you think that is too hopelessly romantic, even for me."

Tarleton smiled. "You know best."

"Do I?" Booth's eyes hardened. "Perhaps some other suitor has beaten me to the punch."

The smile faded from Tarleton's lips. "If you have something to say, I suggest you say it."

"Why were you squiring Lucy Hale around the city today?"

"I was returning a kindness," Tarleton replied. "Miss Hale has been gracious enough to welcome me into her social circle. I can hardly turn my back on her." He brushed at the sleeve of his black overcoat. "It wouldn't be gentlemanly, now would it?"

The actor's nostrils flared. "I've invested a great deal of time cultivating Lucy's attentions. I won't have some Johnny-come-lately steal my thunder."

"I assure you I have no romantic interest in her." Tarleton gave Booth a courtly bow. "I could hardly hope to compete with you in that department."

"I should think not," Booth said smugly.

"You seem quite serious about the lady."

"Don't concern yourself with that." Booth sniffed. "I take it we have more important matters to discuss."

"Lincoln will be attending the theater this evening."

Booth nodded. "He'll witness a mediocre production of a second-rate opera."

"You knew?"

"Father Abraham does little that escapes my notice." Booth smiled.

"This could be our opportunity to strike."

The actor shook his head. "We're not ready. Our cast is not yet complete."

"Surratt and that lumbering oaf Paine should be sufficient."

"I assure you, they aren't." Booth rocked back and forth on the balls of his feet. "Not for the plan I have in mind. This is no time to improvise. We must plot our actions carefully and strike only when the moment is right."

Tarleton eyed Booth narrowly. "I'd feel much better if I knew what you were planning."

"You shall, dear fellow." Booth stretched his arms and took another deep breath. "I must say, this weather is invigorating. I really should find a way to take advantage of it." He tucked his hand into his breast pocket. "I hope you don't have plans for this evening."

"Why?"

Booth's hand emerged holding two tickets for that evening's performance at Maguire's Theater.

It hadn't taken Jack long to realize delivering beer was the hardest, least appreciated job in Washington. As he muscled another keg from the back door of the brewery onto his delivery wagon, he vowed never again to lift a glass without offering thanks to the poor soul who had lugged the beverage from brewmaster to barkeep.

Then there was Felix. He towered over Jack each day in a red flannel shirt and pants that had been mended once too often. His harangues were merciless.

"Where'd you learn to drive, in a washtub?" he'd bark.

"How come you roll the barrel that way? You want to wear out your back before dark?" he'd growl.

"Lord," he'd sigh, "do I have to show you everything?"

This day was no different. They rode in stony silence, which was interrupted only by Felix's scolding, jeering, and chiding. They clattered down a brick alley, the mules' clops and the wagon's creaks clamoring around them. At a cross street, they came upon a knot of people gathered round a man standing on a wooden crate. He was decked out in a fancy white frock coat with brown velvet trim that matched his stovepipe hat. One hand clutched a glass bottle as he made sweeping gestures with the other.

"Take it from Dr. Augustus Q. Ezell, late of the University of Medical and Pharmaceutical Disbursement in Cincinnati, Ohio," he proclaimed. "This magic elixir is the wonder of the age."

As the wagon slowly rolled past, Jack noticed Felix taking in the sidewalk show.

The man spoke with the rapid-fire pace of a Gatling gun. "A mere one dollar per bottle is all it costs for a potion of such power, it would have made Samson gape in wonder. I stake my good name on its ability to cure the most reluctant ailments, to restore hope to suffering souls . . ."

The words trailed off as the wagon drew to a stop behind a saloon at the far end of the block. Jack consulted his delivery book, then jumped to the ground. "The fellow who runs this place owes us thirty dollars."

Felix seemed lost in thought. Jack cleared his throat and the big man looked up. "I'll go inside and collect. Okay?"

"Yeah," Felix muttered. "Go on." He turned and looked back down the alley.

Jack followed his gaze, shrugged, and walked through a back door into the saloon. He found the owner, a squat man with a ruddy face and cherubic cheeks who apologized profusely for the delinquent bill.

"I'll have to run across the street to get the money out of the bank." He untied his apron and ordered a burly man with thick side-whiskers to mind the bar. "Give this gentleman a beer while he waits," he called over his shoulder as he scurried out the door. "On the house."

"Much obliged." Jack smiled.

The door rattled open. The man behind the bar scowled at the flamboyant figure entering the saloon. Jack recognized the street-corner barker. "No freeloaders," the barman snarled.

The newcomer tipped his top hat. "You will find, good sir, I have the coin of the realm in hand." He brandished a two-dollar bill. "I have the means at my disposal, and you have the wares at yours."

The barman reluctantly produced a glass and filled it. "How much did you fleece today?" he asked.

The man took a long gulp from his beer, wiped foam from his mouth with his sleeve, placed the half-empty glass on the bar, and beamed at the banknote in his hand. "Two bucks, from the stupidest buck I've ever seen."

Jack eyed the hawker over his beer. "Just what's in the concoction you peddle, mister?"

"A trade secret," the man answered. He downed the last of his beer and waved for a refill.

"Is there any medicine in it?"

"People think it's medicine, and it makes them feel better." A sly grin rippled across the man's narrow face. "It works well for both of us."

Jack shook his head. "Heck of a way to make a living, if you ask me." He took a sip of beer. "Tricking decent, hardworking folks out of their pay."

"Some people want to be tricked, my good man." The peddler took a long draw on his refilled glass. "Take the fellow who just bought two bottles of my elixir. Big black brute in a bright red shirt, didn't have sense enough to pour piss out of a boot. Why, he couldn't give me his money fast enough . . ."

Jack grasped the man's collar and jerked him backward. "Let's just see how that fellow likes being tricked." He gathered up the man's coattail and marched him toward the back door. "Be right back," he told the barman.

The man's arms flailed helplessly as Jack forced him into the alley and thrust him against the wagon. Felix looked down from his seat, eyes wide. "What's going on?"

"Did this man sell you something?"

Felix looked at the hawker. "Yeah." He lifted two bottles from his lap.

"He has something to tell you, Felix." Jack fixed a fierce glare on the peddler. "Go on, tell him. Tell him the stuff in those bottles is nothing but colored sugar water."

The man's face turned bright red. He opened his mouth, perhaps to object, but another look from Jack forced him to close it.

He merely nodded.

"Tell him," Jack demanded, "that you're going to give him his two dollars back and forget the whole transaction."

The man's eyes bulged and he gave his head a vigorous shake. Jack tightened his grip on the velvet trim of his collar. "Now, you wouldn't want word getting around that you were selling this same snake oil down in Richmond last winter, would you?" Jack leaned close and dropped his voice to a hiss. "Trading with the enemy in wartime could earn you a nice long visit to a cold, dark prison."

The man immediately surrendered the two-dollar bill. When it was safely in Felix's hand, Jack loosened his grip. The man bent over, panting and holding his side.

"One last bit of advice." Jack lifted a leg and kicked the man in the seat, sending him sprawling. "Bragging and con games don't mix." The man pushed himself to his feet and brushed the dust from his suit. "Now, get," Jack yelled.

The hawker sprinted down the alley.

When he was out of sight, Jack turned to Felix. "You need medicine?"

"Don't want to talk about it," Felix answered softly.

Jack nodded, wiped his hands on his pants and started back toward the tavern.

"Jack," Felix called, "how did you know that cheat was down in Richmond?"

Jack stopped and put his hands on his hips. He thought for a long moment, then slowly turned around. "Don't want to talk about it."

Each latched a gaze on the other before both erupted in laughter that followed Jack as he returned to the tavern to collect the thirty dollars.

It wasn't the last laugh they shared that day. Whenever Felix started to complain about his driving, Jack would mutter, "Don't want to talk about it." It cracked the big man up every time.

As Jack walked back to his hotel that night, he began to realize just how tired and sore he was. Most evenings, he felt duty-bound to snoop through Washington's watering holes in search of the elusive George Webb. Tonight, all he could think about were the soft warm sheets and feather mattress awaiting him.

A beefy arm reached out and pulled him into a dark alley. A gloved hand clamped his mouth closed. "You want to meet with George Webb, do you, mister beer man?" The voice was low and strident with the accent of the Louisiana bayous. "What makes you think Ol' George wants to see you?"

Jack stood perfectly still. He didn't want to give the man any excuse for violence.

"You better not be working for the Yankees. If you say one word 'bout George Webb to the bluebellies . . . Well, let's just say the Potomac runs mighty cold this time of year. You follow me?"

Jack nodded. In the gloom of the alley, he couldn't make out a single feature on his assailant's face or even guess at the man's height.

"You be at the Crown Oak Tavern tonight at eleven o'clock sharp," the harsh voice continued. "It's just a few blocks down from that hotel where you and that blond-headed boy are staying. Got that?" Jack nodded.

The gloved hand withdrew from Jack's mouth. "Go straight to the last table at the far end. Don't talk to nobody and don't look at nobody. Understand?"

"Yes." Jack's voice was barely a whisper.

"There'll be plenty of eyes on you. No funny stuff." The man shoved Jack out of the alley. When he reached the street, Jack looked behind him. He saw nothing but shadows. He started walking briskly. All thoughts of fatigue and featherbeds had vanished. In a few hours he would finally meet George Webb. He had to convince the Confederate agent to help him.

His thoughts returned to the man in the shadows. There was no mistaking the menace in that voice, the threats implied by his knowledge of Jack, where he worked, even where he and Sam were staying.

After days of uncertainty, Jack knew he was about to take an important step in his mission. And he knew he would have to take that step very carefully.

Tarleton never took his eyes off the box directly across the theater. His gaze remained fixed on the President of the United States.

"What passes for entertainment in this town," Booth mumbled as he watched an overstuffed soprano commanding the stage below them.

Tarleton wasn't listening. He wasn't the only person whose eyes were riveted on Abraham Lincoln. There was a steady rustle and murmur as people throughout Maguire's Theater craned their necks to catch a glimpse of him. Whenever Lincoln leaned forward to look down into the crowd, it was as if an electric spark jumped from seat to seat.

The commotion drew Booth's attention away from the stage. He glared at the president's box. "Know what I see over there?" he whispered. "Not a stupid-looking man and his ugly little wife. I see fifty thousand Southern soldiers back in action."

Tarleton saw something else. He saw how easy it would be to shoot Lincoln. One squeeze of a trigger and he would be twenty thousand dollars richer.

Booth tugged at Tarleton's sleeve. "Come on. Let's get a closer look at our target."

"Do you think that's wise?"

A devilish grin scampered onto the actor's lips. "What's wrong, Basil? Does that bogeyman frighten you?"

They descended to the lobby and strode toward the staircase leading to the presidential box. A soldier blocked their path. "Where do you think you're going?"

Booth flashed a disarming smile. "We just want a glimpse of Mr. Lincoln."

The sentry crossed his arms and shook his head.

"It's all right, Sergeant," a voice called from across the lobby. "Let them pass."

"And who are you?" the soldier demanded.

"Andrew Maguire, owner of this theater." The newcomer drew himself to his full height. "I also happen to be a friend of your commanding officer. I'm certain you wouldn't want him receiving a note describing your insolence toward one of the most prominent figures of the American stage."

"Oh, yeah?" The soldier cast his eyes around the lobby. "Who might that be?"

"That might be me, sir."

The sergeant looked warily at the stylishly dressed man before him.

"John Wilkes Booth." The actor held out his hand.

The sentry's eyes grew wide. "Lord Almighty, I didn't know it was you! I'm really sorry."

"It's quite all right," Booth replied, warmly shaking the man's hand.

"This is an honor, sir," the soldier continued. "I saw you last summer in *Hamlet*. You sure made that play come alive."

Booth stiffened.

A chill stole into his voice.

"That was my brother Edwin."

Embarrassment suffused the soldier's face. He stammered a nearly incoherent apology before snapping to attention and motioning Booth and Tarleton past.

"You'd think I would get used to it," the actor grumbled as they climbed the stairs, "always being mistaken for *him*. I should be known as something more than Edwin Booth's little brother."

Tarleton reached the top of the stairs and said, "You will be, Wilkes."

Booth gave a wry grin. "Indeed I shall. And soon."

The Crown Oak Tavern was tucked into an alley midway between the fine marble halls of government and the squalid riverfront. A few minutes before eleven, Jack stepped through its door and into a thick pall of cigar smoke. In the dim light, he made out a few dissolute characters perched at a bar along one wall. A handful of unoccupied tables was scattered to his left. He took an unsure step forward. No one seemed to be paying him any attention. He had walked a few paces when a voice pierced the gloom.

"George is back yonder." Jack recognized the gravelly baritone of the man who had accosted him earlier in the evening.

In a dark corner beyond the bar, a candle flickered faintly. Walking toward it, Jack made out a dim silhouette at the last table. He stopped and said in a low voice, "I'm here to see George Webb."

There was a scraping noise. Jack felt a chair pushed against his legs. He took that as an invitation and sat down. Across from him, the shadowed figure seemed immune to the feeble illumination of the candle. "George Webb. I'm here to see him."

The figure leaned forward. The shadows parted, revealing the face of the most beautiful woman Jack had ever seen. She smiled. "You've found him."

Jack stared speechlessly at the woman. Her smile brightened. A waiter appeared, placed two glasses on the table and filled them with red wine. He put down the bottle and melted back into the shadows.

The woman lifted her glass. "It's French." She smiled. "Not the sort of thing you'd expect in a place like this. But the proprietor indulges me." She took a dainty sip. "It's quite a respectable vintage. You should try it."

Jack lifted his glass without taking his eyes off her. Her smooth fair skin had the subtle glow of fine porcelain, framed by dark red hair and highlighted by green eyes that sparkled like gemstones. He took a drink of wine and let it linger on his tongue.

She cocked her wineglass toward him. "What can I do for you, Captain Tanner?"

He swallowed his wine. "You know my name."

"I know quite a lot of names."

"How about this one? Matt Johnson." Her face remained poised, offering no reaction. Jack took another drink of wine and put down his glass. "He suggested I find you."

"Go on."

He leaned forward and dropped his voice to a whisper. "Richmond sent me. I'm here on the personal orders of President Davis."

She laughed. "Aren't we all?"

Jack took a deep breath. "I'm here to stop an enemy of the Confederacy from killing Abraham Lincoln."

"Keep talking."

Jack repeated the story—how he had stumbled onto Congressman Standiford's scheme to murder Lincoln, the professional killer who had been hired to carry out the deed, the murder of Harry Kincaid, his meeting with Jefferson Davis. She sat silently through the recital, her gaze never wavering from his face. When he was finished, she took another sip of wine.

Jack felt a stab of exasperation. "Aren't you going to say anything?"

"You tell an interesting tale."

"Don't you believe me?"

"Of course I believe you." She laughed. "If you were going to spin a yarn, I'm certain you wouldn't have concocted one this wild. Just the idea!"

Her laughter jangled Jack's nerves. He didn't know what he had expected, but he certainly hadn't planned on being laughed at. He drained his wineglass and shoved his chair back from the table. "Thank you for the drink, ma'am." He rose. "If you'll excuse me, I have a killer to catch."

"Sit down, Captain," she said firmly. She fixed Jack with a glare that froze him in his tracks. After a moment, he resumed his seat. She picked up the wine bottle and refilled his glass. "Captain John Joseph Tanner, currently assigned to the Richmond Provost Guard. Born and raised on a farm in the Virginia hill country. Parents deceased." She looked into his eyes. "Did your father call you Johnny?"

He fumbled for his wineglass. "Jack." He took a long drink.

"Jack," she repeated. "I like that. It's a good, strong name." She lifted her glass and clinked it against his. "Here's to you, Jack Tanner."

"And here's to you . . ." His voice trailed off in a question.

"Kathleen St. Claire," she answered. "My father called me Kate."

"Here's to you, Kate St. Claire." He lifted his glass in a salute and took a drink. "That's a French name."

"So it is."

"You don't sound like you're from New Orleans."

Kate laughed again. "I'm from Montreal." The woman's laughter, which had been so jarring, now took on a musical quality.

"I'd imagine there are quite a lot of Frenchmen there," Jack observed.

"You're right, much to my Irish father's chagrin." A frown rippled across Kate's brow. "I made the girlish mistake of marrying one of those Frenchmen." The frown melted into a sly grin. "At least he had the decency to die young."

"So how did you end up here? If you don't mind my asking."

"I don't mind." She twirled her wineglass by its stem. "The late, unlamented Monsieur St. Claire met his demise during a business trip to Virginia. He was a tobacco dealer, among other things. That's how I came to be in Richmond when the war began. I offered my services to the Confederacy. I had spent some time in Washington before the war and suggested that might be useful to the Cause. So here I am."

She laughed gaily. "A daughter of clan O'Leary, refugee from the potato famine, immigrant to Canada, saddled with a French last name, and blessed with British citizenship, working for the Confederacy in the capital of the United States." A wicked smile settled on her lips. "Just let the Yanks try to sort all of that out."

Jack smiled back. "Especially if they're looking for a fellow named George Webb."

They shared a laugh and drank more wine. The sparks of confrontation that had flashed between them earlier were now extinguished. As Jack regarded the woman's astonishingly beautiful face, he felt a different kind of spark coming to life. It had been a long time since those feelings had stirred within him. He silently cursed himself and pushed them aside.

"To business, then," Kate said at last. "Tell me about this man who's planning to kill Honest Abe."

Jack leaned forward. "His name is Basil Tarleton. He kills for money, and he seems to make a very good living at it. He has the law looking for him on both sides of the Mason-Dixon Line. No one has ever caught up with him."

Kate nodded. "What else?"

"He apparently left Richmond a few hours before I did. I assume he was heading here."

"What does he look like?"

Jack shrugged. "I've never seen him. I only have Harry Kincaid's description to go on. Tarleton's a sharp dresser, a pretty boy, blond with blue eyes. Harry made a point of that. He said Tarleton's eyes are the brightest, coldest shade of blue he'd ever seen."

Kate drummed her fingers on the table. "Blond hair, blue eyes, nice dresser. There can't be more than five thousand men in Washington who match that description."

"I'm telling you everything I know. I'm sorry he didn't give me a tintype." He looked straight into her shining eyes. "Can you help me?"

A pensive look settled on her face. "I can check my sources around town, see if somebody has heard about this Tarleton fellow."

"That's a good start."

Kate sipped her wine. "Let's meet here again tomorrow night, same time. I'll let you know what I hear."

A wide smile lit up Jack's face. He was gratified to be getting help. He realized he was also gratified by the chance to see this remarkable woman again. "I really appreciate this."

She ran her finger around the top of her wineglass. "Funny, isn't it?"

"What?"

"We've spent four years trying to win independence for the South. Now, this late in the game, we find ourselves trying to keep the Northern president alive."

"War is a strange business." He drank the last of his wine and rose. "Tomorrow evening, then."

"Tomorrow evening," she echoed.

A lanky young man with a sheaf of flaxen hair falling into his eyes stood beside the door to the presidential box. He watched Booth and Tarleton approach. "Can I help you gents?"

"Pay us no mind," Booth said breezily. "We're just going to look in on Old Abe."

The young man furrowed his brow. "I don't think that's allowed, sir."

Booth sized up the teenager. "You're new here."

"How'd you know?"

The actor offered his most sympathetic smile. "It's something of a tradition at Maguire's to have the new lads see after the presidential box. What's your real job?"

"Assistant property master."

"I thought as much. Look, Andrew Maguire gave us permission to pop in on the president."

The young man scratched his head. "I dunno."

"Very well," Booth said. "Maguire is in the lobby. Why don't you trot down there and ask him yourself?"

The young man glanced at the door to Lincoln's box, then at the stairway leading to the lobby. "I don't think that would be such a good idea."

"Then I guess we'll just have to go find him ourselves." Booth heaved an exaggerated sigh. "I'm sure he'll drop everything and come running up here just to satisfy this whim of yours." Booth turned toward the stairs. "Better tell me your name so he'll understand the urgency."

"It's Sam Jenkins," the young man answered reflexively. "But you don't need to bother Mr. Maguire. I reckon it's okay."

Booth gave him a friendly grin. "Stout fellow, Jenkins. We shan't be a moment." He gripped the ivory doorknob and nodded for Tarleton to follow him. Booth slowly pulled the door open. Both men peered inside the box.

Lincoln was sharply silhouetted against the bright lights glowing from the stage. A shorter man was helping him into his overcoat. Mrs. Lincoln was gathering up her belongings.

Booth grasped Tarleton by the collar and tugged him back. "They're leaving," the actor whispered as he pushed the door closed. They backed away, exchanging startled glances. When the door flew open again, Tarleton stepped to one side and Booth scurried to the other. An official-looking man in a dark suit bustled out of the box. Mrs. Lincoln followed, clutching a lace shawl about her shoulders. The president brought up the rear.

He was wiping his nose. Abraham Lincoln glanced at Tarleton and Sam. An embarrassed smile etched deep creases in his cheeks and around his dark, sunken eyes. He stuck his handkerchief in the pocket of his long black coat. He gave the two onlookers a small nod as he shuffled past them and down the stairs.

The door swung closed again. Booth had been standing behind it, his view of the president blocked. "Did you see him?" Tarleton nodded. "Well?" Booth demanded.

Tarleton continued to watch the stairway. "He looked old and frail," he said. He kept his other thought to himself, a thought the assassin savored. Lincoln did look old and frail, he told himself, but mostly he looked vulnerable.

"Major Wingate, sir?"

Drake Wingate looked up from the stack of papers on his

desk. A skinny private in an oversized uniform stood at attention before him. "What is it?"

"Secretary Stanton sends his compliments, sir. He would like a word with you."

Wingate felt the blood drain from his face. In the crowded office around him, the bustle and noise came to an abrupt halt. The other officers stared. He swallowed a lump that had suddenly lodged in his throat. "Very well, Private. Tell him I'm on my way."

"Yes, sir." The soldier turned crisply on his heel and vanished through the door.

"Good Lord, Win," a lieutenant at the next desk sighed. "You've only been here a week, and you're already being summoned before the Throne of Judgment."

The room erupted in howls of laughter and shouts of good-natured insults as Wingate slipped into his blue uniform coat and started for the door. He paused at the door and placed his right hand over his heart. "We who are about to die salute you." He exited to a fresh chorus of cheers and catcalls.

Negotiating the clogged corridors of the War Department, Wingate wondered what he had done during his brief stint in Washington to warrant this kind of attention. Nothing came to mind. At the secretary's office, he passed a hand through his close-cropped black hair and neatly trimmed beard, buttoned his jacket and stiffened his backbone, then knocked on the door.

"Enter," a voice called.

He came face-to-face with a large colonel sporting fierce chin whiskers. "Major Drake Wingate, Intelligence Office, sir. Reporting to the secretary."

They were in a small anteroom devoid of furniture. "It will just be a moment, Major," the officer told him.

Wingate could make out voices from the other room. They

increased in intensity as the conversation grew more animated. Soon, shouts were rattling through the door.

"What kind of a moron orders that kind of troop movement?"

"I can explain, Mr. Secretary."

"I don't want your explanations! I want results! Your orders were explicit!"

"Sir, if you'll let me explain—"

"I've heard all I need to hear. You are relieved of your command, sir!"

"Secretary Stanton, you can't—"

"I can, and I just did! Now get out!"

Wingate felt perspiration sprouting on his forehead. It was clear the stories about the secretary's explosive temper had not been mere barracks gossip. He swallowed hard, wondering if Stanton would leave enough of him to ship home for burial.

The colonel opened a door to the inner office. Out stumbled a brigadier general with an ashen face. The colonel turned to Wingate. "The secretary will see you now."

The Secretary of War was perched imperiously behind a high desk that seemed the size of a railcar. His face was flushed and his towering forehead was creased. He squinted through narrow spectacles as he stroked his flowing gray-streaked beard.

Wingate introduced himself.

Edwin McMasters Stanton fixed him with an intense glare. Wingate felt his salute wilting under the secretary's scrutiny. Then Stanton's features relaxed. He leaned back in his chair and laced his fingers across his ample stomach. "Thank you for coming, Major Wingate. General Sherman speaks highly of you."

"That's quite a compliment, sir."

"I don't think Sherman would commend his own mother unless he felt strongly about it. But I didn't call you here to talk about

Sherman's mother. Sit down." Stanton wagged a finger at a chair in front of his desk.

As Wingate took a seat, the secretary removed a thick stack of documents from a drawer. He laid it on the desk and lowered his glasses to the edge of his nose. He slowly scanned one page after another. "Care to guess what I'm reading?"

"I have no idea, sir."

Stanton placed his palm on the papers. "These are reports of attempts to take President Lincoln's life." He patted the thick stack. "From just the last three months." He settled back into his chair. "Most of them are lunatics, of course. Secesh blowhards, spouting off within earshot of a loyal soldier or citizen. We collect them all, investigate some, and occasionally take action."

Stanton reached back into the drawer and pulled out another, thinner bundle of papers. "These, we take seriously." He dropped the documents on his desk and shoved them toward Wingate. "Go ahead. Take them."

The reports seemed unnaturally heavy to Wingate. He almost felt he was taking the president's life into his hands. He looked up at the secretary. "May I ask why?"

Stanton pointed at the documents. "I'm ordering you to investigate them. I want you to cull out the cranks and the wild talkers. Determine which ones we need to be concerned about. I want you to report to me on anything you feel is necessary to protect the president. Do I make myself clear?"

Wingate nodded. "Very clear, sir."

"The war is winding down, Major." Stanton pulled a handkerchief from the pocket of his black coat and removed his spectacles. "That raises a particular danger. We must be vigilant against any last-gasp efforts from the Rebels."

"I see," Wingate replied.

Stanton began polishing his glasses. "The president is a good man, Major. He thinks that because he means no man harm that no one will harm him." He sighed. "I can't count the number of times I've warned him to stop taking needless risks—flitting around to playhouses and concert halls, riding about in an open carriage. He doesn't listen."

The secretary tucked the handkerchief back into his pocket and settled the spectacles back on his nose. "If he won't look after himself, I will." He pointed a thick finger at Wingate. "No one else is to know about this. And I mean no one, inside or outside of this department. Understand?"

"Yes, sir."

Stanton gathered the thick sheaf of crank reports and dropped them back into his desk drawer. When he looked up, he seemed surprised to find Wingate still sitting before him. "Was there something else, Major?"

"Yes, sir. What shall I tell my commanding officer?"

The secretary snatched up a pen and scratched out an order, signed and blotted it, then handed it to Wingate. "That should satisfy him. If you need anything, come to me. If you find anything, come to me." The secretary gave a dismissive wave toward the door and picked up a document.

Back in the corridor, Wingate folded Stanton's order and tucked it into his pocket. He let out a long breath. Then he looked more closely at the reports the secretary had given him. The one on top concerned a civilian clerk named Louis Weichmann.

Five

THE SUPPORTING CAST

The beer wagon rumbled down a dusty street near the riverfront. The sun was climbing into a cloudless sky. When Jack ran his hand across his brow, it came away damp. The day would be a warm one. And a long one. He sat alone in the wagon. Felix hadn't shown up for work. The foreman at the brewery offered no explanation.

Jack's thoughts began wandering to the Confederate operative he had met the night before. He found it hard to think of "George Webb" without conjuring up an image of the beautiful woman who hid behind the name. The way the candlelight made her smooth skin glow. The way her deep green eyes had flashed in anger then danced in amusement. And her hair, that lustrous, dark red hair.

Jack shook his head vigorously. He couldn't let himself dream. He could not allow himself to think of Kate St. Claire as a desirable woman. He had to focus on her abilities as a Confederate spy and what she could do to help him.

If only he could stop her lilting laughter from ringing in his head.

The mules lumbered through the maze of narrow streets and alleys along the Potomac. Jack made half a dozen stops before noon, wrestling kegs into dim saloons. He struck up conversations with the barkeeps he met, keeping his eyes and ears open for anything that might lead him to Basil Tarleton.

Even without Felix to help him, Jack completed his deliveries by early afternoon. He was in no hurry to return to the brewery. The foreman would probably just give him another load to deliver. So he herded the mules into an alley behind a tavern, parked the wagon, and went inside to grab a bite to eat.

The strain of the day's labors had inflamed his bad leg. He plopped down at a table and propped the aching limb on a chair as he gnawed through a meal of cold roast beef and corn bread.

Another, deeper pain clutched at him. Jack shifted in his seat, trying to ease the discomfort in his groin. It didn't bother him as often as the shrapnel embedded in his thigh. But it returned often enough to remind him why any romantic notions he might have about Kate St. Claire—or any other woman—were empty fantasies.

He remembered what the doctor had told him during his lengthy convalescence at Richmond's Chimborazo Hospital. "The metal cut through you clean as a scalpel," the rumpled and harried surgeon had said. "We stitched you up as best we could, but that's all. The damage is done."

Jack recalled the horror that had mounted within him as the doctor looked into his eyes and delivered the news.

"You'll never have children."

Those four words had crushed Jack's world. Gone were his plans to settle back into the comfortable life he had always known. Gone were his plans to return to his family farm and marry the pretty girl who had grown up not a mile away.

On her next visit to the hospital, she learned the awful truth. The blood had drained from her face as tears drained from her eyes. There was no discussion. She removed the simple gold ring he had given her, placed it in his hand, and went away. He never saw her again, though he later heard she married the son of a dry-goods store owner and was already expecting his second child.

Jack dropped the half-eaten corn bread on his plate and slowly hoisted himself to his feet. These thoughts were getting him nowhere, he told himself. He limped back to the wagon, climbed aboard, and flicked the reins. The mules plodded to the street, then came to a sudden stop.

Traffic was halted all around. In the center of the snarl, a rig lay on its side, crates of live poultry scattered everywhere. An elderly man was on his knees, pushing a chicken back inside its box.

Jack climbed down and walked toward the old man. "Let me give you a hand," he offered.

"Much obliged." The old man straightened up and hefted a crate. He handed it to Jack, then leaned close and whispered, "Change of plans. Be there tonight at eight. Same place."

"What did you say?"

"Be there at eight," the man repeated. "She has something for you." He turned and lifted another crate.

Jack helped gather the scattered load, then scared up some volunteers to right the wagon. The old man clambered aboard, snapped the reins, and drove away.

As he walked back to his own wagon, his step was more brisk

than it had been all day. He finally was on the trail of the assassin.

And he would see Kate St. Claire again.

The plump man stood in the doorway with his mouth gaping. His fleshy cheeks instantly reddened. He raised a chubby finger and wagged it. "See here," he sputtered. "That's my desk."

"That would make you Louis Weichmann?"

The fellow tugged at his vest and brushed his black suit coat. "It would. And I'll thank you to get out of my chair."

"My name is Drake Wingate. I'm with the War Department."

"So am I, Mr. Wingate." Weichmann shoved out his chest. "The Commissary General of Prisoners Office. We may not be in the War Department building, but I assure you our work here is every bit as vital as . . . as . . . wherever it is you are from."

Wingate rose and placed his hands on the desk. "I'm with the Intelligence Office, Mr. Weichmann." He pulled some papers from his jacket pocket. "We need to talk about this."

Weichmann stepped forward and snatched the documents. "I can't imagine what the Intelligence Office would need with me, Mr. Wingate."

"Major Wingate," he said quietly.

Weichmann's eyes snapped up at his visitor. "You're out of uniform."

Wingate looked down at his brown checked suit. "So I am." He leaned forward and whispered, "I'm on a rather delicate assignment. And we need to talk."

Weichmann's gaze dropped to the papers. "What is this?"

"A report about the goings-on at a certain boardinghouse."

The heavyset bureaucrat shot a glance around the office at other men working through piles of paperwork. Weichmann pointed to the door. "Let's take a walk."

"After you."

Weichmann led him out onto Eighteenth Street and began walking south. The squat man set a brisk pace. Wingate noticed he was wearing light blue pants with a dark blue stripe running down each side. "Are you also in the army?"

"I am enlisted in the War Department Rifles," Weichmann answered haughtily. "We are civilian employees ready to assist in any military emergency."

"Like the Rebel army showing up again on the outskirts of the capital. As it did last summer." Wingate stifled a smile. His colleagues always got a laugh recounting stories of such volunteer units melting from view as quickly as the Confederates appeared.

Weichmann appeared not to notice the verbal jab. "If they're foolish enough to try that again." The men crossed New York Avenue and passed an enormous, oddly shaped brick house. Weichmann pointed it out. "That is the Octagon House, where President Madison lived after the British burned the White House fifty years ago. But I suppose you knew that."

"No, I didn't. I've only been in the city a short time."

Ahead of them, the houses thinned out into a stand of trees that cut across their path. Wingate decided they must be making for the Potomac River. "Getting back to the reason I need to talk with you—"

"Shhh!" Weichmann hushed from the side of his mouth, then nodded politely as they passed an elderly woman in a gray print dress sweeping the front porch of her house.

They strode on in silence until they reached a clump of leafless bushes at the street's end. Wingate could hear the river flowing beyond them. Weichmann came to a stop. "We can talk here."

They stood on the marshy edge of the Potomac. A dark Federal ironclad lazily chugged past them with the freshly washed clothes of its crew flapping like pennants as they dried in the wind.

Weichmann thumbed through the papers Wingate had given him. "What do you want to know?"

"You told a coworker that someone where you live is plotting against President Lincoln."

"That's right."

Wingate locked his gaze on Weichmann. "Why didn't you report this directly to the proper authorities?"

Weichmann clenched his jaw and returned Wingate's stare. Then he looked down. "I didn't know who the proper authorities were."

"Tell me about this Reverend Wood."

Weichmann spat on the ground. "He's as big as a tree trunk and every bit as thick."

"That doesn't sound like any preacher I know."

"He's no more a preacher than I am. Sunday mornings, I hear loud snores when I pass his room on the way to church. My guess is, he's never set foot in a pulpit."

Wingate frowned. "How did he come to stay at your boardinghouse?"

"John arranged it."

"John Surratt? The man mentioned in your report?"

Weichmann nodded. "His mother owns the place. She takes in boarders to help make ends meet."

"You've known John Surratt for some time."

"We were at school together. When I came to Washington, he offered to share his room with me."

"Tell me about this meeting three nights ago."

Weichmann shuffled his feet. "John took everyone up to Wood's room. I wasn't invited, but I overheard them."

"Who was there?"

Weichmann wouldn't meet Wingate's eyes. "They said they were discussing investments. Oil. There's supposed to be real money in that."

Wingate fought back a rising tide of impatience. He kept his voice low and steady. "Mr. Weichmann, I'm investigating your statement that someone is planning to harm the President of the United States." He retrieved the report and held it up. "This is not a task I take lightly."

Weichmann reddened. "Nor do I, Major."

"We understand each other, then." Wingate's intense dark eyes pierced the pudgy bureaucrat. "Tell me who was at the meeting."

"Two men," Weichmann muttered.

"Other boarders?"

Weichmann shook his head. "One was visiting from out of town. Chicago, I think."

"And the other?"

Weichmann examined his feet. "A friend of John's."

"Tell me exactly what you heard."

"I'm not sure I got every word."

"Tell me what you heard," Wingate repeated.

"The word 'kidnap' and something about next Wednesday night."

"What else?"

Weichmann jammed his hands in his coat pockets. "They

were discussing Confederate prisoners. I didn't catch much of that."

"Has anything happened since then?"

"John has been gone a lot. I'm not sure where."

Wingate folded the report and tucked it into his jacket. "This boardinghouse sounds very comfortable. Does Mrs. Surratt have any rooms available?"

"Not just now. She turned away a nice couple last week. Good Union people."

Wingate nodded. "The government appreciates your cooperation, Mr. Weichmann."

For the first time, the stubby bureaucrat's face brightened. "It's the least I can do for my country."

The very least, Wingate thought. "I'll be in touch." As Wingate watched him walk away, he concluded Weichmann's officious manner masked a deep-seated insecurity. He was convinced the man was lying, or at least not telling the whole truth. He knew he had to do two things if he was going to make any headway. He had to find out why Weichmann was hiding information.

And he had to get into the Surratt house.

Booth made a hard right turn onto Tenth Street and drew his horse to a halt. He lifted his hat and swept it before him. "My friend," he announced to Tarleton, "I give you the city's newest, and finest, center for the performing arts."

An imposing brick building rose three stories to a sharp gabled peak crowned by a cupola. Five arched doorways stood side by side along the ground level, which was painted a pale gray. A small white sign hanging next to the center door proclaimed FORD'S THEATRE.

"Impressive," Tarleton admitted.

"It's even more impressive inside," Booth assured him. "Almost as grand as the playhouses of New York." He nudged his horse forward. "I expect to give my greatest performance here."

He led Tarleton down an alley and emerged at a small stable behind the building. "Hello, George," Booth called.

A ragged man lounging against a wall looked up at the actor and smiled. "*Ja,* hello," he said with a slight German accent.

"George is a handy man with a hammer and saw," Booth explained to Tarleton. "Aren't you, George?" The man shrugged.

"Remember that proposition we discussed last week?" George bobbed his head excitedly. "Good," Booth continued. "Be at Gautier's Restaurant at midnight Wednesday."

He leaned down from his horse and placed his hand firmly on George's shoulder. "You don't want to miss this meeting."

"*Ja,*" the man replied eagerly.

Booth spurred his horse and rode out of the alley with Tarleton hurrying to catch up.

Once they reached the street, they slowed to a casual pace. "What was that all about?" Tarleton demanded.

"Another piece of the puzzle."

"I don't see what a grubby foreign carpenter can contribute."

"George has spent most of the war secretly ferrying travelers back and forth across the Potomac. He knows that waterway like the back of his hand."

"A fellow like that could certainly come in handy," Tarleton agreed.

"We've found him." Kate allowed herself a satisfied grin.

Jack's eyes widened, reflecting the glow of the candle on the table between them. "That was fast."

A waiter materialized and placed brandy snifters before them, then vanished. Kate raised her glass. "I'll take that as a 'thank you.' "

"Of course." Jack lifted his snifter and tapped it gently against hers. "Thank you." He took a sip of brandy and let it roll across his tongue before swallowing. "That's good."

Kate watched his eyes. They were a deep, warm brown. She could see his gratitude in them. She could see other emotions, too—excitement, wariness, determination. She felt she could look into his eyes all night.

She gave herself an inward shake and sipped her drink. "Tarleton isn't doing much to cover his tracks. He's registered under his own name at the National Hotel."

"He doesn't know anyone is on to him." Jack smiled. "Given enough time, I probably could have found him myself."

"Maybe," Kate said. "But I doubt you would have found out that he's posing as a Chicago merchant in town to settle a dead relative's estate."

"Well—" Jack began.

"Or," Kate interrupted, "that he's moving in the top social circles of the city, squiring around a former senator's daughter."

"Well—" Jack began again.

"Or," Kate continued, "that he's become fast friends with a certain man-about-town named John Wilkes Booth."

Jack threw up his hands. "I give up." A smile creased his

weathered features. He hoisted his brandy. "Here's to you, Kate St. Claire. You're really something."

"I'll take that as a compliment." Her gaze was drawn back to his eyes. She felt herself falling into their brown depths.

"Where is he now?" Jack's words broke the spell his eyes had cast. "How soon can I move on him?"

Kate sat back and swirled her brandy. "Not just yet."

"Why not?"

"We don't know enough."

"We know what he's planning, and we know where he is. We know plenty."

"Do you propose bursting into his hotel room and shooting him full of holes?"

"It's a thought."

"A foolish one." She clenched her hand into a fist. "The Yankee army has this town by the throat. You wouldn't get two steps before they had you."

"Maybe not," Jack retorted, "but at least Lincoln would still be alive."

"And what would you tell the Yankees?" she demanded.

He shrugged. "Nothing."

"Brave talk. You have no idea what they'd do to you."

"You have no idea what the Yankees have already done to me." His eyes bored into hers. "I got through that. I can get through this." She glared back, gritting her teeth and trying to keep her breathing even.

They sat locked in bristling silence. The waiter appeared at the table. "Ready for another brandy?"

Kate turned on the intruder. "When I want another drink I'll ask for it."

The waiter shrank back from the table.

Kate let out a long breath. "I know you're only interested in Tarleton, but there's more going on here. This city is awash in intrigue. Lincoln is surrounded by enemies. We don't know whether Tarleton is in league with them."

Jack absently tapped his finger against the table. "True enough."

"Then there's Booth." A frown furled Kate's delicate brow. "If he's involved, that complicates matters."

"How so?"

"I'd rather not say. At least, not now."

Jack bent forward. "You don't trust me?"

"That's not it." Kate leaned closer until her head was almost grazing his. "The less you know about my operation, the better it will be for you."

"And for you."

"Frankly, yes." Her features softened. "Do you hate me now?"

His eyes again took hold of hers. "I don't think I could ever hate you."

She raised her hand and stroked the coarse stubble of his square chin. "I hope not," she whispered.

The street lamp cast a pale light over the white house on H Street. Wingate had been watching it from the shadows for more than an hour. He hadn't seen anyone enter or leave. He had noticed some movement behind the lace curtains but couldn't identify any of the dim figures. A single flickering light—a candle, he supposed—illuminated a dormer window on the top floor of the house.

In the distance, a church bell tolled ten o'clock. Wingate hunched his shoulders against the chill. He looked around for the hundredth time. Not a soul about. When he turned back, the upper window was dark.

Wingate suspected the boarders were going to bed. Not a bad idea, he admitted. He was about to head home when approaching footsteps caught his ear. He stayed in the shadows and watched.

A portly figure chugged into view. He was walking quickly down Seventh Street, arms swinging heavily. Wingate could hear his breath coming in sharp pants. He turned onto H Street and headed straight for the Surratt house.

As he passed under the pearly halo of the gas street lamp, his face became visible. Wingate rushed across the empty street, grabbed the sleeve of his quarry's coat, and led him into the shadows next to the house.

Louis Weichmann stared, gasping. "My God, Major," he said at last. "You scared the wits out of me."

Wingate shushed him and spoke in a quiet voice. "I need to speak with you, and it didn't seem like a good idea to knock on the door."

"I suppose not." Weichmann took a deep breath and visibly composed himself. "Why do you need to see me?"

"I have a few more questions."

"It's very late. If I don't go inside soon, Mrs. Surratt may lock me out for the night."

"It will just take a moment."

Weichmann craned his neck toward the street and darted a glance up and down the empty pavement. "I don't know."

Wingate took a step back. "You're right. I suppose this can wait." He stuck his hands in his pockets. "I can tell Secretary Stanton you had more important matters than this case."

Weichmann's eyebrows cut an arc high into his forehead. "You know the secretary?"

"Why, yes," Wingate responded casually. "He gave me this assignment personally."

"I see." Weichmann stole another glance down the street. "What do you need to ask me?"

Wingate suppressed a triumphant grin. "John Surratt. You said he's been out of town a lot."

"That's right."

"Do you know where he goes?"

Weichmann's eyes shifted warily. "Not always. He rarely confides in me these days."

Wingate stepped closer. "But he does tell you sometimes, doesn't he?"

"He mentioned a few weeks ago that he had business in Montreal."

"That makes sense." Wingate nodded. "I've done some checking since we spoke this morning. The boys in the Intelligence Office are pretty well convinced John Surratt is a Rebel spy."

Weichmann's gaze dropped to his feet. "I wouldn't know anything about that."

"You wouldn't?" Wingate leaned close to the chubby man. "Are you sure?"

Weichmann pulled back. "What are you saying?"

"An old school chum who works at the War Department would be a very valuable asset for a Rebel agent."

"That's absurd."

Wingate pushed his face close to the shorter man's. "On the contrary, it makes a great deal of sense."

"But—"

"Quiet," Wingate hissed. "Montreal is swarming with Confederate operatives. They've all but beaten a path from there to Richmond." He gathered Weichmann's lapels in both hands. "And your friend, your roommate, goes there at least once a month."

"I didn't know."

Wingate shook him. "I don't believe you, Mr. Weichmann. I think you know exactly what Surratt is up to." He thrust his face forward until his whiskers were scraping against the man's chin. "I think you've been helping him."

Weichmann stared back in horror. His mouth moved, but no words came out. Beads of sweat dotted his forehead. He grabbed Wingate's arm. "No," he gasped. "On my mother's life, I swear it's not true."

"It's not your mother's life I'm interested in," Wingate rasped. "It's yours. And if I find out you've given aid and comfort to the enemy, I won't rest until I see your neck in a noose."

The words staggered Weichmann. He sank toward the ground. Wingate stepped back and let him fall.

Weichmann's shoulders heaved. He held his head in his hands and gave a low groan. "You don't understand," he croaked.

Wingate bent over. "Maybe I do." His voice was gentle. "You were stuck in a mundane, unappreciated job while your friend was off having dashing adventures. You envied him."

"It wasn't adventure I wanted." Weichmann turned his tear-streaked eyes upward. "It was money."

"What money?"

"Oil money." Weichmann wiped at his eyes. "I wanted John to let me join his oil investments. He bragged about how he was cleaning up. He teased me about it, claiming he'd cut me in when the time was right. But he never did."

"That's why you were eavesdropping on him?" Weichmann nodded. Wingate straightened up and helped Weichmann to his feet.

The chubby bureaucrat pulled a handkerchief from his pocket, blew his nose, and dabbed at his swollen eyes. "You must think me a fool."

"What I think doesn't matter. What matters is what you do now."

Weichmann thrust the handkerchief back into his pocket. "What can I do?"

Wingate threw his arm around Weichmann's shoulders. "I'm glad you asked."

Felix was back on the job the next morning. He offered Jack no explanation for his absence nor did he explain his bruised left eye. Jack asked no questions.

At midday, they pulled the beer wagon under a tree within sight of the Capitol Building. Jack had a sandwich he'd bought that morning. Felix munched on a hunk of bread and piece of cheese he had carried from home wrapped in brown paper. They ate in silence for several minutes. Jack stared absently at the sparkling arc of the Capitol dome slicing through the pristine blue sky.

"You probably been wondering about this eye," Felix grumbled at last.

"If you want to talk about it, I'll listen."

"Landlord came around looking for the rent. Didn't have it. He punched me."

Jack nodded sympathetically. He took a bite of his sandwich.

"It's my boy," the black man continued. "The oldest one."

"You have children?"

A broad grin split Felix's face. "Two boys and a girl." The smile evaporated. "The boy took sick about a month back. Doctor said he needed lots of medicine."

Jack remembered how Felix had been taken in by the street hawker's phony elixir. "That's tough."

"Took every penny we had," Felix continued. "Landlord will be coming around again tomorrow. Says he either gets his money or he'll put us on the street." Felix finished his meal and carefully folded the brown paper before returning it to his pocket.

Jack downed the last bite of his sandwich and wiped his hands on his pants. "Maybe I can help."

"Won't take no charity."

"I'm not offering any." Jack took the reins and slapped the mules into action. They pulled the wagon back onto the street. "Maybe you'd like to do a little job for me."

"What sort of job?"

"I'd like you to follow a man this evening. Tell me where he goes and who he sees."

"Why?"

"Do you really care? It pays five dollars."

Felix stroked his jaw. "That's a lot of money."

"And that's just for tonight." Jack pulled the wagon to a halt in front of the next saloon on their delivery route. He lashed the reins to the seat, set the brake, and turned to Felix. "I'll pay you five dollars every time you do this for me."

Felix ran a meaty hand over the top of his head. "You must really want to know what this fellow is up to."

"I do." Jack stuck his hand in his pocket and produced a five-dollar bill. "What do you say?"

Felix fixed his eyes on the money. "Just follow him, right?"

"That's it."

"Tell you where he goes and who he sees, right?"

Jack nodded. "As simple as that."

Felix looked long and hard into Jack's eyes. Then he took the money. "Who is he?"

"His name is Basil Tarleton. He's staying at the National Hotel."

As he made his way home that evening, Jack reminded himself there would be hell to pay if Kate found out what he had done. Walking down the dim corridor of the Liberty House, he found his mind straying to thoughts of her. Her hair, her laugh, her eyes. He willed them away as he opened the door to his room.

The lamp on the table flared into life, momentarily blinding him. He raised a hand to shade his eyes.

"You're doing pretty well for a beer delivery man." The words were followed by the crystalline laugh he had heard in his head just moments earlier.

He squinted against the glare. Kate was perched on the windowsill near his bed. "How did you get in here?"

Her laughter rang merrily through the room. "I wouldn't be much good at my job if I couldn't manage to get into a simple hotel room."

His eyes became accustomed to the light and he could make her out more clearly. Her glorious auburn hair was piled high on her head, exposing her long graceful neck. She wore a simple blue-striped blouse with a ruffle at the collar and a dark blue skirt.

He realized he had never noticed her clothing at their earlier meetings. "I was coming to see you at the Crown Oak after supper."

"I thought this would be a pleasant change." Her green eyes sparkled as they searched his. "You don't mind, do you?"

"Of course not. Make yourself comfortable."

"I already did." She bent down to retrieve a bottle of champagne and two flutes. "May I offer you a drink?"

He accepted it and settled into the chair alongside the bed. They raised their glasses in a silent toast and sipped. The bubbly wine seemed to fill his head with air. He tried not to stare at the beautiful woman before him. He cleared his throat. "I take it you have news about Tarleton."

Kate sipped her wine. "Not really."

"Then what brings you here?"

She placed her flute on the bedside table. "I wanted to find out more about you."

"Not much to tell."

"I disagree." Kate stood up and turned to look out the window. "You said something last night that set me to thinking. You told me I had no idea what the Yankees had done to you." She caught his reflection in the glass. "What did you mean?"

Jack shifted uncomfortably in the chair. "It's not important."

She continued studying his reflection. "I know about Chancellorsville and how you almost lost your leg. I know several pieces of lead are still in it. It's a miracle you can even walk."

Jack offered no response. He took a long sip of champagne.

"There's more," she continued. "I know there's more."

"That's why you came here?"

Her eyes dropped from the window to the glass cradled in her hands. "That's part of it."

He studied her figure, outlined by the dark window. He followed the lines of her back down to the swell of her hip, barely shrouded by the simple skirt. "What's the rest?"

She didn't answer right away. Instead, she finished the champagne in her glass and reached for the bottle. She turned and held it up in offering. He shook his head. She refilled her glass and took a long drink. When she spoke, her voice was barely a whisper. "I wanted to see you again." She peered at him through lowered eyelids. "Is that such a terrible thing?"

Jack felt tension gripping his chest like a vise. He fought to keep his breathing even, his voice level. "I don't think it's a terrible thing. But I don't think it's such a wise thing either."

She walked to him and refilled his glass with champagne. "Just once I'd like to be free to do something foolish." She reached up and pulled a tortoiseshell comb from the back of her hair. The coppery locks were released in a torrent, falling around her shoulders. "It's been a long time."

The glass slipped through Jack's fingers, which were suddenly quite damp. He tightened his grip and took a drink. The champagne fizzed through his brain and electrified his nerves. "Kate," he began.

She placed her finger to her lips and walked toward him. He was mesmerized by the swaying of her hips, the rustle of her skirt, the way her hair bounced lightly with each step she took. When she stood over him, she lowered her finger from her lips to his. "Don't talk."

He gently kissed her finger, then just as gently pushed it away. "There's something you don't know."

"I know everything I need to."

"Not everything."

She bent forward and brushed her lips against the hand that held hers. She raised her liquid green eyes. He felt himself being drawn into the twin pools of warm light. He pulled her hand toward his and kissed it. "You don't know what else the Yankees did to me."

"I don't care." Her arms encircled his neck and she laid her head against his shoulder. "It doesn't matter."

"It does to me." He pulled away. "I may have saved my leg, but that Yankee shell took away something else. Something more personal."

Realization slowly dawned across her face and her gaze dropped involuntarily toward his lap. When she looked up again, his expression was carved from granite. She drew his head to her bosom. "I don't care about that. I just want to feel your arms around me."

He tried to fight down the rising emotion, but it was no use. His longing for her overwhelmed his reason. He pulled her tightly to him. She kissed the top of his head, worked her way down to his ear, then his cheek. He lifted his face. Her lips sought out his. Their kiss began as light as an angel's touch. Then it deepened in strength and intensity until Jack felt as if she were pulling his very soul into her own.

Neither would ever be able to guess how long that first kiss lasted. It might have been a minute, or it might have been a month. When at last they parted, they both knew everything had changed. Each had become a part of the other.

Kate curled up in Jack's lap and let out a contented sigh. "I could stay here forever."

"No argument from me," he replied and kissed her forehead.

"If only there weren't the pesky business of a war to fight and an assassin to stop."

Jack nestled his chin atop her luxuriant curls. "If only," he echoed.

Six

THE CONSPIRATORS

"Just as I thought." Wingate's words echoed against the brick of the chimney. "There's terrible carbon buildup in here." He backed out of the firebox and into the parlor.

"Oh, dear." Mary Surratt placed her hand over her mouth. "I had no idea."

"Good thing I was working in this neighborhood today." Wingate brushed soot from his black coat, earning a stern look from the proprietress of the boardinghouse. "I'd better inspect all the fireplaces."

"Of course. Give me a moment to notify my boarders." She bustled from the room.

When he was certain Mrs. Surratt was out of earshot, Wingate headed for the stairway and crept up the steps. He allowed himself a small smile of satisfaction for coming up with the idea of posing as a chimney sweep to gain entry to the house. At the second-floor landing, he moved toward the room Weichmann had said was occupied by Reverend Lewis Wood.

Wingate placed his ear against the door. When he didn't hear anything, he tapped lightly. There was no response. He twisted the knob and eased the door open.

Curtains were drawn over the lone window. Wingate squinted as his eyes adjusted to the darkness. The room was a mess. He picked his way between a chair draped with soiled clothing and a rumpled bed. He spotted an upended human skull on the bedside table, clogged with cigar butts.

He crossed to a small desk and sifted through papers scattered about it. He found a small rectangle of pasteboard and examined it in the light trickling through the door.

It was a ticket for a box seat at Ford's Theatre that evening. Wingate wondered how an itinerant preacher could afford such an indulgence.

The door slammed, plunging the room into gloom. As Wingate dropped the ticket, a massive body bowled into him. He sprawled across the floor, groaning in pain. A hand as big as a side of beef clamped over his mouth. Another gripped his neck and slammed him against the floor.

"Get out!" The words rumbled through the room. Wingate felt the grip tighten around his neck. His head pounded against the floor again. "Get out!"

Wingate couldn't see his attacker's face, but could tell from the weight pressing against him the man was enormous.

"Get out!" Wingate's head banged the floorboards a third time. Then he felt himself being lifted into the air like a rag doll. The huge man carried him across the room, opened the door, and flung him toward the stairs.

He bounced down the treads, glanced off the wall, and landed on his head before tumbling to a stop. He lay still, gasping for breath. He wiggled his fingers and toes. No broken bones.

Footsteps hurried through the back of the house. He groaned again, rising to his hands and knees and crawling back into the parlor. He lunged toward the fireplace just as Mrs. Surratt reached the doorway behind him.

"My word!" she gasped. "Are you all right?"

Wingate tried to speak but only managed a jumble of slurred words. He propped himself up on his elbows. Mrs. Surratt pressed a finger against his forehead, sending a jolt of pain stabbing through him. "You have a nasty bump. What happened?"

"I fell."

"Don't move. I'll get a cold cloth." She scurried away.

Wingate leaned against the fireplace, fighting to regain his senses. He felt something cold against his bruised forehead and opened his heavy eyelids. Mrs. Surratt stood over him again, dabbing the swelling with a damp towel.

"You're very kind, ma'am. I should have known better than to try to climb up that flue." He nodded toward the fireplace. "I spotted a big chunk of soot. I thought I could knock it loose." He shook his head, then winced. "It's my own fault. I apologize."

"Don't be silly," she replied. "I just thank the Lord you aren't hurt even worse."

With an effort, Wingate rose and steadied himself against the mantel. "I think I'll finish this tomorrow." He managed a thin smile. "I'm sorry to trouble you."

"It's no trouble." Mrs. Surratt held his arm as she escorted him to the door. "Just take care of yourself. You can clean my chimneys when you're feeling better."

"Yes, ma'am." He stepped out onto the porch and walked slowly down the stairs, leaning heavily against the railing. When he reached the street he took a few unsteady steps, then lurched toward the lamppost on the corner. He sagged against it and mopped perspiration from his brow with his coat sleeve, leaving a long, sooty streak above his eyes.

Gathering his strength, Wingate was certain of three things. First and foremost, "Reverend Wood" was extremely dangerous. Second, he needed to apprise Secretary Stanton of the situation inside the Surratt house.

Finally, he needed to be at Ford's Theatre that night.

"It has been too long," Booth said, almost to himself, as he stood at the center of the Ford's Theatre stage. He raised his arms, threw back his shoulders, and projected his voice. "Far too long." The words echoed through the empty house and bounced back from the decorative dome above the rows of wooden chairs.

Tarleton lounged at the edge of the stage, his shoulder propped against the front of the box he and Booth would be occupying that evening. Next to the actor, Harry Ford, the younger brother of the theater's proprietor, thumbed through a notebook. "The set for *The Apostate* will go up Friday afternoon."

Booth stared out into the auditorium. Tarleton watched the actor's gaze drift along the lower balcony, known as the dress circle, until it came to rest on the upper box to their left. A small smile settled on his lips.

"Ticket sales are brisk," Ford continued. "Many of our patrons are quite excited about your return."

"What about him?" Booth jerked his thumb toward the second-story box.

"Oh, we won't know if the president plans to attend until the day of the performance." Ford consulted his notes again. "We can have the stage ready for a dress rehearsal by four o'clock on Friday, if that's acceptable."

"He was here during my latest engagement," Booth muttered, then tossed a glance at Tarleton. "For *The Marble Heart* a year ago last November."

Tarleton tilted his head back and examined the chandelier hanging above him. "Perhaps he'll take in your performance on Saturday."

Booth's gaze returned to the box. "Yes. Perhaps he will." The small smile again flickered across his face. He nodded, then turned back to Ford. "I may be otherwise engaged on Friday afternoon. Let's schedule rehearsal for Saturday morning, say, ten o'clock."

"Very well, Mr. Booth." Ford jotted in his notebook. "I'll post a notice for the cast and crew."

"You're a good man, Harry." Booth gave him a warm smile. "You always take care of me, whether I'm performing at your fine establishment or merely taking in the show."

"It's our pleasure," the young man replied. "We'll see you this evening."

"I'm looking forward to it," Booth called as Ford scurried into the wings. "So what do you think, Basil?"

Tarleton's eyes swept across the theater. Its white walls trimmed in gold shone faintly in the reflected light from the stage. "An impressive venue," he admitted.

"That it is." Booth smirked. "Just the place for a grand drama."

Tarleton frowned. "Is that what you call *The Apostate*?"

"Why not?" Booth laughed. "It will serve until something grander comes along."

A swath of light cut through the center of the darkened orchestra seats. Booth peered out into the theater. A woman strode down the aisle, followed by a tall young man with a box perched on his shoulder. "Olivia!" A cheery smile wreathed the actor's features. "What a delightful surprise!" He sprang from the stage and landed lightly in the orchestra pit. "Basil, come meet an old friend."

Tarleton followed Booth's lead and jumped down from the stage. His landing was not nearly so athletic as the actor's, but his face betrayed no hint of the strain. He bowed over the hand of Olivia Putnam, an actress Booth had known for years.

Her dark eyes flashed as they swept over Tarleton, who responded with a courtly nod. Her gaze stayed on him a moment longer than it had to. Then she turned back to Booth. "My friend Sam here brought some props over from Maguire's."

The towheaded young man hoisted the box from his shoulder and presented it for Booth's inspection. He reached in and withdrew an ornate chalice. "Excellent! Your timing is impeccable as always, Olivia." He held it up for Tarleton to see. "It's for our production on Saturday." He dropped the chalice back into the box and clapped Sam on the arm. "Come along. I'll show you where to put them." He led the young man through a door at the base of the stage.

When they were gone, the woman turned her intense dark eyes back to Tarleton. "I believe we've met before."

"Have we, Miss Putnam?"

She gave him a long hard stare. "The name threw me off. What did Wilkes call you? Tarleton?"

"At your service."

She tapped a buffed fingernail against her brightly painted lips. "That wasn't what you called yourself. Was it Wellington? No, that's not right." A frown furrowed between her severely plucked eyebrows. "Worthington. That's it. Earl Worthington."

"I'm afraid you—"

"Six years ago in New York. You told me you were a theatrical producer from Pittsburgh. You said you were staging *Oedipus Rex*. You thought I would be your perfect Jocasta." She sniffed diffidently. "And I would have been."

"Miss Putnam—"

"'Miss Putnam,' is it? You called me 'Olivia' then. You made yourself very familiar. Very familiar, indeed."

"There's been some mistake—"

"Oh, there's no mistake." Her cheeks flushed red under layers of face powder. "I remember the gifts, the flowers, the expensive dinners. You wheedled your way into my good graces." Her eyes dropped. "And my bed."

"Please—"

"Don't 'please' me." She crossed her arms over the scooped neckline of her dress. "After all that, you simply disappeared. No 'good-bye,' no 'sorry.' Nothing. I was devastated."

Tarleton laid his hand on her arm. "I'm sorry I never had a chance to explain."

She regarded him coldly. "I *knew* it was you."

Hearing Booth and Sam chatting behind the door under the stage, Tarleton lowered his voice. "Can we discuss this? Let me come see you."

"I'm not sure."

The voices grew louder. "Why don't we meet this afternoon? At the very least, you can hear me out."

Olivia's eyes darted to the door. "I'm renting a place not far from Maguire's." She gave him directions and said she would be home at three o'clock. Each took a step backward just as Booth and Sam burst into the orchestra pit.

"Thanks again, Mr. Booth," the young man said. "Your play sounds like a real humdinger. Maybe I'll come see it."

"Do that, my young friend." Booth clapped him on the shoulder. "Here he is, Olivia, safe and sound."

She smiled at them, but her eyes strayed toward Tarleton. She snaked her hand through Sam's arm. "Let's run along, dear. We don't want to be late for rehearsal."

As she shepherded him up the aisle, Sam turned back to Booth. "It was sure nice seeing you again." He looked toward Tarleton. "And you, too."

When they had disappeared through the auditorium door, Booth chuckled. "You and Olivia seem to have gotten chummy in a hurry."

Tarleton spread his hands in a helpless gesture. "What can I do, Wilkes? It's a gift."

Booth guffawed as he strode through the theater. Tarleton matched him step for step. "What did that young fellow mean when he said it was nice seeing us again?"

Booth halted at the door leading to the lobby, hooked his thumbs in his vest, and struck a thoughtful pose. "He meant he has seen us before, you and I. He was at Maguire's the night we looked in on Father Abraham."

"I see."

"No you don't." Booth clenched his teeth. "He saw us there, Basil, and he saw us here. He's seen us together twice now, once in the presence of Lincoln. That young fellow could be a big problem."

"Don't worry, Wilkes," Tarleton said slowly. "I'll take care of it."

"That's all?" Jack snapped the reins and the mules pulled the wagon away from the brewery. "He met two men at a boardinghouse and they all went out to supper?"

Felix nodded. "I followed him from the minute he left his hotel until he went back again."

"You're sure it was Tarleton?"

"Tall, fancy white man with blond hair and cold blue eyes."

"That's him."

Felix grunted. "You give me five dollars to do a job, I get it done." He crossed his arms defiantly.

Jack chewed his lower lip. "Tell me about the other men."

Felix offered a brief description: two white men, below average height, slender, dark hair and moustaches. "I probably couldn't have told them apart," he admitted, "except one is that famous fellow."

"What famous fellow?"

"Booth." Felix searched Jack's face. "You don't know who he is?"

Jack shook his head. Felix roared with laughter. "What's so funny?" Jack demanded.

"Pull over," Felix ordered, still chuckling. Jack steered the wagon to the side of the street and reined the mules to a halt. Felix jumped down and trotted to a brick wall plastered with handbills. He tore one down, then returned and thrust it up to his partner. "That's him."

Jack examined the poster. *"Ford's Theatre presents* The Apostate, *March 18."* In slightly smaller letters was the name *"J. Wilkes Booth."*

"He's an actor," Jack mumbled.

"These things are plastered all over town." Felix climbed back onto the wagon and resumed his seat. "You should pay more attention, Jack. It might save you a heap of trouble one day."

"I need proof, Major." Secretary Stanton squinted at Wingate through small gold-framed glasses perched on his nose. "Evidence that will hold up in court."

"Sir, we already have enough evidence for a military court." Wingate gestured at the report he had placed on Stanton's massive desk. "It's all there. The meetings between Surratt, Wood, and the others. The attack on me. What more do we need to arrest them?"

Stanton removed his spectacles and jabbed them in the air. "We're entering very dangerous territory."

"These are dangerous men."

"It's not just these men that are dangerous. It's the times." Stanton held up his glasses and inspected the lenses before settling them back on his nose. "Every day, the war comes closer to its conclusion. Once it ends, the military's authority will be dramatically curtailed."

"Yes, sir." Wingate clenched his hands. "All the more reason to move quickly."

An expression spread across Stanton's face that Wingate had never seen before. The secretary smiled. "That's our dilemma, Major. We must move quickly, but we must move carefully."

Stanton shook his head. "I'd like nothing better than to have you clap these scoundrels in irons. But before I can order that, I need incontrovertible proof that they are conspiring against the president. Proof that will satisfy a civilian court." He leaned forward and lowered his voice. "Grant is preparing to break into Petersburg. In a matter of days, he could be in Richmond. Once he is, the president will insist on restoring the civilian rule of law."

His chair creaked as Stanton shifted. "So on the one hand, you must collect sufficient evidence to convict these men. On the other, you must move quickly enough to prevent them from carrying out their plans."

"Yes, sir."

"There's one other thing." Stanton looked over the top of his spectacles at the young officer. "Listen very carefully to what I'm about to say." He paused to lick his lips.

Wingate leaned forward.

"If you believe these traitors are prepared to move against the president, I expect you to take whatever steps you deem necessary to stop them." Stanton narrowed his eyes. "Do you understand?"

"I do, sir." Wingate felt the words scratching against his throat, which had gone dry.

"If it comes to that," Stanton continued, "I expect you to act with the utmost discretion. Anything you do must not be seen as an official action of this office."

Stanton's statement pounded in Wingate's ears. The secretary was telling him to kill the conspirators if he had to. He also knew that if something went wrong, he was completely on his own.

Wingate rose. "I'll do my best, sir."

"I know you will, Major." Stanton pushed back his chair and stood up. He looked down at Wingate. "Your country is counting on you."

The back door of the Crown Oak Tavern stood open as Kate passed it on the way upstairs. She heard a mule bray and glanced out. Her breath caught in her throat.

There was Jack, unloading a wagon in the alley. She melted into the shadows behind the staircase as he wrestled a keg into the tavern's storeroom. She felt a tingle of excitement watching him work. His white cotton shirt, slightly damp with sweat, clung to his broad shoulders. Muscles rippled along his arms when he hoisted the keg upright and shoved it against the storeroom wall.

He ran his hand across his forehead. She stepped forward. His eyes widened. A grin stretched across his face. "It's good to see you."

The distance between them vanished and she was in his arms. She nuzzled his neck, breathing in his warm, masculine scent. She gave him a quick peck on the cheek, then disentangled herself. "We have things to discuss."

His face lost a bit of its glow. "I'd like to, but I'm working."

"Can't you take a break?"

"Let me talk to my partner."

Kate followed him to the door and watched as he talked to a large black man lounging against the wagon. Jack nodded at the doorway. His partner's eyes darted toward her. She felt suddenly embarrassed and stepped back into the shadows.

A moment later, Jack was throwing his arms around her again. "He'll pick me up on his way back to the brewery."

She led him to a room she kept upstairs. Kate's agents had collected some information she knew Jack would want. When they reached the room, it suddenly seemed unimportant.

He looked at her, head slightly atilt, like an inquisitive puppy. His brown eyes latched onto her and pulled her to him.

They kissed. Any thought of discussing his mission evaporated. She felt that tingle again. Her hand ran down his shirt, feeling the taut skin beneath the damp fabric. Her hand strayed lower. She glanced up at him, her eyes asking an unspoken question.

His eyes gave her an unspoken answer.

Later, as she lay against his chest, watching the rhythm of his breathing return to normal, deep contentment settled over her. When Jack had described his injuries, she had assumed they had left him incapable of physical love.

She was wrong. And she was delighted. She rolled away from him and jumped up from the bed.

"Where are you going?"

"We don't have much time." She stepped to the wardrobe on the other side of the bedroom. Kate could feel his eyes on her, taking in the lean lines of her back, as she walked. She slipped on a chenille robe and turned to face him as she knotted the cloth belt at her waist. "We've been watching Tarleton pretty much around the clock." Her voice took on a businesslike edge. "It's just as I feared. He's getting help."

Jack hoisted himself onto his elbows. "From the actor?"

Kate lifted an eyebrow. "You mean Booth?"

"His name's plastered all over town."

Kate withdrew a white blouse and russet-colored skirt from the wardrobe. "It's more complicated than that." She pulled off the robe and slipped into the blouse.

"Aren't you going to put something on under that?"

"No time." She stepped into the skirt and pulled it up around her hips. "Don't worry. I won't present myself in public until I'm decently dressed."

Jack rolled out of the bed and picked up his own clothes. "If Booth isn't the problem, it must be the other fellow. What's his name . . ." He held his shirt in his hand as he stared at the ceiling. "The fellow from the boardinghouse."

"John Surratt."

Jack snapped his fingers. "That's the one."

Kate nimbly buttoned her short boots and straightened up. "How do you know about him?"

Jack shrugged. "I have a lot of practice digging up information."

"What do you have on Surratt?" she demanded sharply.

"Enough to know he's mixed up in Tarleton's plans." He turned toward her. "That's more than you ever told me."

Her cheeks turned fiery red. "I've told you everything you need to know."

"Have you?" He stood with one leg in his pants. "I need to know everything about Tarleton, but you won't even tell me who he has supper with."

Kate reached blindly into the wardrobe and yanked out a black riding jacket. She threw it on and buttoned it with flashing fingers. She retrieved a flowered bonnet from the wardrobe and jammed it over her unruly auburn curls. "I've told you everything I can. If you can't understand that . . ." She gave her head an angry shake and stomped out of the room.

"Wait a minute. Come back," she heard Jack calling after her. As she fled down the stairs, he shouted her name. She ran into the alley and didn't slow down until she no longer heard his voice.

Olivia ran her fingers through the thatch of blond hair on Tarleton's chest. Their coupling had completely disarranged her bed. Even the canopy of silk scarves draped across the high bedposts had been dislodged and they hung limply, like flags on a windless day.

Her thick black hair, as tangled as the bedclothes, swished across his chest as she turned her head. "Oh, dear. The time." She pushed herself up and looked into his eyes. "I have to go soon. I'm meeting Sam."

Tarleton ran his hand over the swollen mound of her breast. "That's too bad. I was just getting started."

"You're incorrigible." She straddled his hips. "If it were up to you, we'd never get out of this bed."

"There's a delicious thought." He grabbed one of the scarves loosely hanging from the bedpost.

"What're you going to do with that?" Olivia grinned.

He wrapped it around her wrists. "I'm making certain you don't escape."

"Oh, no," she cried in mock dismay. "Please, mister, I'll do anything you want." She raised her wrists, now bound snugly together. "I'm helpless." He wrestled her off him and onto her back, then snatched another scarf.

"Wait until you see what I do with this." He held it before her face and folded it lengthwise. Her eyebrows inched high as he placed it across her eyes.

"Ooooh," she cooed. "Someone is being a very naughty boy."

He wrapped the scarf around her head and tied it. "Hold still," he whispered. He brought the trailing ends together at her throat, then looped one through the other in a knot and jerked it tight against her skin.

"Wait," she gasped in surprise. "That hurts."

"Does it, Olivia?" he breathed into her ear. He yanked the knot tighter. The silk cut deeply into her throat. Her mouth worked furiously, gasping for air. Her bound hands flailed powerlessly against his chest. She bucked her hips, trying to push him away. He pulled harder.

Her struggles continued for several minutes as the life drained from her body. When at last she lay still, Tarleton gave the scarf another sharp yank, then climbed down from the bed and put on his clothes.

He removed the glass chimney from a lamp and doused oil over her body. He sprinkled it around the bed and, for good measure, splashed the last drops on the curtains. He withdrew a cheroot from his jacket and struck a match. Tarleton walked to the bedroom door as he puffed the small cigar to life, then tossed the match onto the bed.

He heard the satisfying "whoosh" of oil igniting as he left through the back door.

Jack clumped glumly down the stairs. He could never catch up with Kate. With Felix due to pick him up any minute, he couldn't hang around the tavern waiting to see if she would return. At the bottom of the stairs, a short, barrel-chested man with a few wisps of gray hair plastered against his bald head blocked his path.

"A word with you, Captain?"

Jack froze. The man's low, gravelly voice sounded familiar, but he couldn't place it. "I just need a moment of your time." He gave Jack a smile that didn't quite reach his slate-gray eyes and led him into the deserted saloon. He pulled a chair from a table and gestured for Jack to sit down.

Recognition dawned as Jack slid into the chair. "You're the waiter."

"Among other things." The man sat in the opposite chair and propped his elbows on the table.

Jack looked closely at the broad, grizzled face. "I met you in another saloon, didn't I? You steered me to Kate."

The man nodded. "More than once. I prodded you along in a dark alley one night, and delivered a message in an overturned chicken wagon."

Jack's mouth fell open. "That old man was you?"

The man nodded again. "Call me Rufus. I work for Kate."

"Are you the one following Tarleton?"

Rufus shook his head. "She has other agents on that detail."

"What do you want with me?"

"A word of caution." Rufus knitted his shaggy brows. "About the lady. She has a great deal of responsibility. She can't afford any distractions. And you, Captain, are becoming a distraction."

Jack felt his ire rising. He pushed himself away from the table and rose. "I don't see how that's any business of yours. Now, if you'll excuse me—"

With surprising quickness, Rufus shot his hand out and grabbed Jack's wrist. He tightened his grip until Jack was gritting his teeth in pain. "Everything that woman does is my business," the older man growled. "She has to concentrate all her energy on her mission. If she loses focus, everything could come crashing down like a house of cards. People could die." He squinted his steely eyes. "She could die. Is that what you want?"

A long, loud whistle came from the alley. Felix called, "Let's go, Jack."

Jack looked down at the beefy fist wrapped around his wrist. "I have to leave."

Slowly, the grip eased. Rufus stared into Jack's eyes. "Remember what I said."

Jack didn't reply. Once outside, he rubbed his throbbing wrist. Felix, sitting on the wagon, laughed heartily. "If that woman made you hurt there, you surely were doing something wrong!"

The fire brigade could do little more than watch the small house burn to the ground. A crowd gathered as firemen in long leather coats pumped a stream of water from their steam-powered engine onto the fringes of the blaze. At most, Tarleton decided, they were trying to keep it from spreading to surrounding houses.

He watched the flurry of activity from the back of the crowd. A fireman talked to an old woman next door. She was shaking her head and gesturing with her hands. He was nodding and scribbling on a pad. He finally put it away, tipped his long-brimmed helmet, and walked across the street. He unbuttoned his coat and dug a tobacco pouch and pipe out of an inner pocket.

He was exhaling a stream of smoke by the time Tarleton approached him. "Could you tell me if that's Olivia Putnam's house on fire?"

The fireman puffed his pipe. "That's what the neighbors say."

"Oh, dear." Tarleton sighed. "She will be devastated."

"Friend of yours?"

"I attended one of her plays at Maguire's. She's an actress, you know."

"So I hear," the fireman mumbled around the stem of his pipe.

Tarleton shook his head. "Such a lovely little house. She had decorated it beautifully. She was so proud of the way Sam helped her with the painting."

"Who's Sam?"

"Her gentleman friend. A tall, strapping fellow with blond hair. He works at Maguire's, too." Tarleton raised an index finger. "Now that you mention it, I just passed him a moment ago. He was heading that way." Tarleton pointed away from the burning house. "He must have been late."

"Why do you say that?"

"He was practically sprinting. I called to him, but apparently he didn't hear me." Tarleton looked over his shoulder at the flames. "Does Olivia know yet?"

The fireman shrugged. "A policeman went over to the theater to see if she's there."

"If you should speak with her, please say that I asked after her." Tarleton produced a calling card from his pocket and handed it over.

The fireman glanced at the name: CLARENCE LOGAN, ALLEGHENY COAL COMPANY, ALLEGHENY, PENNSYLVANIA. He shoved it in his coat pocket. "If I see her, Mr. Logan."

"Thank you." Tarleton tipped his hat. "Good luck with the fire."

The creaks and groans of the wagon were amplified by the silence of the men riding it. Felix had tried to cajole his partner into talking about what happened at the Crown Oak. Jack didn't rise to the bait. The warning from the man called Rufus gnawed at his mind. Was he really putting Kate's life in danger? The thought horrified him.

He was equally horrified at what would surely happen if he abandoned his mission. He was certain Tarleton was already stalking Abraham Lincoln. It was only a matter of time—days, perhaps—before he would make his move.

If he tried to stop Tarleton and failed, he would have to live with the consequences. If he didn't try to stop Tarleton, he would never be able to live with himself.

Jack realized with chilling clarity that his only option was to do everything he could to prevent Tarleton from killing Lincoln.

Even if it meant sacrificing the woman he loved.

Jack jerked the mules to an abrupt halt. Felix rocked back on the seat. "What are you doing?"

Jack handed over the reins. "Take the wagon back to the brewery." He jumped to the street.

"What'll I tell the boss?"

Jack jammed his hand in his pocket. "Say I got sick. Or quit. Tell him anything you want." He pulled out a wad of currency, counted out five ones, and pressed them into Felix's hand. "After you drop off the wagon, follow Tarleton."

Felix stuck the money in his pocket. "Whatever you say, Jack."

"See you in the morning." He didn't look back as the wagon rattled away.

He walked aimlessly, his mind a whirling muddle. The sun was hanging low. Ahead, a lamplighter on his evening rounds sent a sudden burst of illumination onto a two-story white frame building. Jack stared at the sign hanging out front. Maybe here, he could take his mind off his worries for a while. He walked up to the door of Maguire's Theater and Musical Emporium.

Kate counted on Lucy Hale to provide her with nuggets of intelligence. Not that the younger woman realized it. She was just doing what came naturally, prattling on about "Mrs. So-and-so this" and "Colonel So-and-so that" from the time they settled into their chairs in the lobby of the National Hotel. Tonight, however, Kate had little energy for sorting through the gossip. She smiled politely, nodding now and then.

Why, she asked herself, did I ever let Lucy rope me into this outing? She fretted with the fringe of an embroidered shawl that matched her rich green gown. She had spent the afternoon at her brick town house in Georgetown reliving her confrontation with Jack.

As she had gone through the motions of preparing for the evening—piling her curls high atop her head, selecting a gown and shoes—she kept coming to the same conclusion. Jack didn't trust her.

"Here they are," Lucy proclaimed breathlessly.

Kate looked toward the door. John Wilkes Booth doffed his hat, bowed, and scraped his way around the room, kissing a lady's hand, slapping a man on the back, throwing his head back in laughter as he drew all attention to himself.

When he reached them, Booth dropped to one knee and folded his hands over his heart. "Dearest Lucy. My life, my breath, my very soul." As he kissed her hand, a flush spread across the young woman's fleshy cheeks.

Kate couldn't decide which of them was guiltier of overacting. A man in a long dark coat holding a flat-brimmed hat stood behind the actor. He was tall with a sharply handsome face. A faint smile played across his thin lips as he watched Booth fawn over Lucy.

When he glanced her way, Kate felt a stab of recognition. There was something about his eyes. They were a frigid blue that should have seemed almost transparent, but there was a hidden depth in them. She felt she had seen those eyes before.

"And the glorious Mrs. St. Claire." Booth bowed over her. "Radiant as always."

Kate tore her gaze away from the stranger. "You appear to be in fine fettle this evening, Mr. Booth."

"And what man wouldn't be, sharing such splendid company!"

Lucy joined Booth and slung her arm possessively through his. "I so enjoy a theater party, don't you, Kate?"

"Of course." She rose. "Are we ready to go, then?" She cast another glance at the strangely familiar man.

"Where are my manners?" Booth slapped his forehead. "Introductions are in order." He turned to the man. "Allow me to present the fairest flower of the northern provinces, Madame Kathleen St. Claire. Kate, this is Basil Tarleton."

An icy hand clutched at Kate's heart. The assassin was accompanying them to the theater? She pasted an insincere smile to her face as she gave him a small curtsy. He dipped his head in response.

"Oh, dear!" Lucy was digging through her handbag. "I've forgotten my opera glasses. Excuse me, Wilkes. I must fetch them."

"Certainly, my dear. That will give me a chance to see if the rest of our party has arrived. Basil, you wouldn't mind entertaining Kate, would you?"

"Of course not."

"Good man." Booth scurried toward the door as Lucy waddled up the main staircase.

Tarleton waited until both were out of earshot before turning to Kate. "I must say you don't look much like a St. Claire." A sly grin wormed its way onto his face. "With your coloring and complexion, I expected to be introduced to a Mrs. Riley or a Mrs. McConaughey." He leaned close to her. "Or perhaps a Mrs. O'Leary."

She eyed him coolly for a moment. Then she remembered—the early-morning encounter on a Maryland road the week before. "And might I say, Mr. Tarleton, that you cut a very dashing figure for a man of the cloth." She whispered, "How is Brother Israel Harris faring with his new congregation?"

Tarleton lifted his eyes to hers. She felt their cold intensity seeping into her. They held each other's gaze, then he looked away, slowly surveying the people scattered about the lobby. "It would seem that you and I have something in common."

"And what would that be?"

"Secrets."

A hand-scrawled sign hung crookedly on the front of the Maguire's Theater box office: ALL PERFORMANCES CANCELED UNTIL FURTHER NOTICE.

Jack's shoulders sagged. He had hoped a happy crowd would

pick up his spirits. There were voices in the auditorium. Perhaps Sam was there. He had barely seen the young fellow, even though they shared a hotel room. Maybe they could get a beer.

The auditorium was ablaze with light. People milled around on the stage while two uniformed police officers spoke with Professor Beeler. Jack stayed in shadows cast by the balcony. He certainly didn't need the law taking an interest in him.

He moved around the theater, hugging the darkened outer wall. Professor Beeler swept his hands wide and turned his head from side to side. In midgesture, his eyes met Jack's. Without missing a beat, he waved over one of the minstrels and engaged him in the conversation. Then he motioned for Jack to join him backstage.

When they were safely out of sight, the Professor slumped into a chair, fanning himself with his hand. "What's going on?" Jack asked.

"Horror capped by tragedy, my friend." Beeler heaved a deep sigh. "Olivia Putnam is dead."

"What?"

The Professor quickly shushed Jack. "There was a fire at her home."

"That's terrible."

"It gets worse," Beeler whispered. "They think Sam had something to do with it."

Jack blinked as he tried to comprehend the words. "Sam?" The Professor nodded sadly. "Where is he?" Jack asked.

The Professor led Jack to a door behind the stage. "He's down there. Please be quiet."

Jack picked his way down a darkened staircase. The musty smell of damp earth rose to greet him. "Sam?"

"Over here." The voice came from his right. Jack carefully descended the last few steps and was inching his way through the gloom when a match blazed to life. By its light, he saw Sam huddled under the staircase.

"Are you all right?"

Sam nodded glumly. "For now. Reckon that'll change if the bluebellies find me."

"What happened?"

"I don't know." Sam shook out the match. "I was working here all afternoon, painting sets and fixing up props."

Jack squatted on his haunches. "Did you see Miss Putnam today?"

"We went over to Ford's this morning. Then we came back here for rehearsal. She left about half past two and I didn't see her after that."

"And you were here all afternoon?"

Sam struck another match. "I swear, Jack, I never left this theater." He set his lips in a thin, determined line.

Jack patted his shoulder. "I believe you. We just have to figure out how to make the police believe you." He saw gratitude reflected in the young man's eyes. "Who else was here?"

Sam shrugged and dropped the match on the dirt floor. He watched it burn out before responding. "Couple of stagehands. Someone up in the box office."

"Professor Beeler?"

"Sure. And most of the minstrels."

Jack straightened up, flinching as pain shot through his bad leg. "Stay here." He felt his way along the basement until he reached the staircase. As he began climbing, he heard snuffling under the stairs. He called quietly, "Don't worry. I'll take care of it."

From the front window of the Star Saloon, Wingate watched people arriving at Ford's Theatre next door. He nursed a beer as his eyes continuously swept the steady stream of foot traffic and carriages on Tenth Street.

Somewhere out there, he knew, Reverend Lewis Wood was on his way to the theater. After their violent encounter, Wingate had as much difficulty imagining the lout was a patron of the arts as he did believing Wood was a man of God. He seemed like the type who would feel more comfortable at a cockfight than a stage play.

Wingate sipped his beer as he scanned the crowd. Most of the men wore working clothes and the women were dressed simply. Many clutched the hands of young children. They were waiting to climb three flights of stairs to the cheap seats in the theater's family circle. It occurred to him that he hadn't even checked to see what was playing.

The line of carriages moved sluggishly along the street. Each stopped in front of the theater and discharged its fashionably dressed passengers. The ladies wore fancy shawls or embroidered coats over brightly colored gowns. The gentlemen were dressed in dark suits with tall silk hats.

A coach carrying two men and two women pulled to a stop directly in front of him. One of the men was Lewis Wood. Based on Weichmann's description, the other man had to be John Surratt. Wingate dropped his glass on a table and rushed to the door.

He hurried onto the sidewalk. Turning toward the theater, he ran headlong into the largest, blackest man he had ever seen. Wingate tumbled to his backside.

The huge man towered over him. He shot a glance at the stream of carriages, then looked down at Wingate. "Beg pardon, sir." His voice was a low rumble.

Wingate stood up. "My fault," he mumbled.

The man hitched up his homespun trousers and tucked in the tail of his bright red shirt. With a final look at the street, he walked briskly away.

Wingate shouldered his way through the line of people. Lewis Wood stood with Surratt and the two young women, obviously waiting for someone. Wingate studied the carriages. Two couples occupied the next one that stopped. He didn't recognize the blond-haired man or the redheaded woman with him.

The other couple, however, was different. A heavyset young woman stepped to the ground with some struggle. Her handsome companion riveted Wingate's attention.

Everyone knew that face. Wingate was shocked to see John Wilkes Booth join the party of the barbarian Lewis Wood.

The four men and four women stood on the sidewalk until the theater doors flew open and the crowd headed inside. People pushing their way toward the upper balcony jostled him. Wingate held his ground long enough to see Booth, Surratt, Wood, and the others sweep through the entrance.

He felt a tug on his sleeve. A mop-haired girl looked up with bright eyes. "Excuse me, mister," she said politely. "Are you going inside?"

Wingate smiled. "Why do you ask?"

"Because, sir, you're holding up the line."

Wingate looked around. He was, indeed, blocking the entrance to the family circle. "I apologize, young lady." He swept his hat off his head. "Please forgive my lack of manners."

A man placed his hand protectively on the child's shoulder. "What'll it be, mister?" he asked. "Are you going to see the play?"

"Yes, sir." Wingate plopped his hat back on. "I do believe I'll see the play."

Jack watched from the wings as the two policemen continued interviewing Professor Beeler. The taller one was doing all the talking. His short, ferret-faced partner was taking notes.

"Everyone here will tell you the same thing," Beeler explained. "Sam was in the theater all afternoon."

"I'll be more than happy to talk to everyone in this theater, and everyone in the city of Washington if I have to." The tall officer smiled down at the Professor. "After I talk to the lad. And not a moment before."

"I think we can arrange that." Jack walked across the stage.

"Can we, then?" The policeman gave Jack a once-over. "And who might you be?"

"A friend of the boy's. I think I can get him to talk to you."

"I'd gratefully appreciate that."

"On one condition," Jack added.

"I'm investigating a murder." The policeman squinted up at him. "I'll have no conditions holding me back."

"This one won't hamper you," Jack assured him. "Why do you think Sam was involved in Miss Putnam's death?"

The officer's features relaxed. "A witness saw him leaving her house at the time of the fire."

"What witness?"

The policeman studied Jack's face. "I believe I've said enough. Produce the boy."

Jack stepped to the edge of the stage. "I've heard a thing or two about firebugs. After they set a fire, they like to hang around and watch people try to put it out. They even offer tidbits of information to the police." He looked down at the officer. "Of course, the information is false."

"You've heard quite a lot."

"Is it possible that your 'witness' is really the person who set the fire?"

The policeman shook his head. "He's a respectable businessman from out of town."

"So you've talked with him?"

"Not yet." The officer looked away.

Jack pressed on. "I'll get Sam. But, just out of curiosity, what does this 'respectable businessman' look like?"

The policeman's eye hardened. "The fireman who talked to him said he was a gentleman, well dressed."

Jack nodded. "Any physical description?"

"Tall. Slim build. Blond hair. Blue eyes."

Jack's pulse quickened. "Did he say anything else about the eyes?"

The policeman frowned. "As a matter of fact he called them 'the palest, coldest blue anybody ever saw.'"

Wingate hated admitting defeat, but he had no choice. He had prowled around the family circle, trying in vain to get a glimpse into the lower box on the left side of the stage where Wood and his party were seated. He had even drifted down to the dress circle on the floor below. From there, he could see into the upper boxes—including the one the president often used—but the lower boxes remained out of sight.

By the time the play was building to its climax, he gave in and retreated from the theater. Across the street, a row of brick town houses provided him an unobtrusive vantage point.

Within minutes, the theater doors opened and people began pouring out. He caught sight of Wood, with Surratt and the rest of the party. Booth chatted with the women and the tall blond man. Wood stood dumbly under the street lamp and Surratt kept sweeping his gaze up and down the street, as if he were standing lookout for a gang of thieves.

A carriage drew up in front of them. The women climbed aboard. Wingate expected the men to follow. Instead, Booth made a grand farewell gesture and sent them on their way. Then he led the other men off on foot.

His curiosity piqued, Wingate followed, keeping pace from across the street. Booth kept up a stream of chatter, occasionally eliciting laughter from his companions. They turned a corner and Wingate lost sight of them for a moment. When he reached the intersection, he spotted them again. He was about to cross the street when a flicker of color caught his eye. A figure lurked in the shadows. All he could make out was the bright red of the man's shirt.

Wingate melted into the darkness of a storefront and watched closely. The man was keeping abreast of Booth's party. They reached a restaurant called Gautier's and went inside. The man finally emerged from the shadows, looked at the entrance to the restaurant, then turned and hurried off down the street.

As he disappeared into the night, Wingate whispered to himself, "That truly is the biggest, blackest man I have ever seen."

Sam hadn't said a word as they walked back to the Liberty House. He was still obviously shaken from his brush with the law. Jack let him be, and concentrated on what he had learned from the policeman. They were in their room when Sam finally broke the silence.

"I don't know why that stupid Yankee wouldn't just take the Professor's word and leave me alone."

Jack kicked off his shoes and unbuttoned his shirt. "He was just doing his job. And doing it pretty well."

Sam sprawled across the bed. "How do you figure?"

"You're not in jail." Jack poured water into the washbasin and started scrubbing his hands and face.

Sam raised his voice to be heard over the splashing. "I didn't do nothing."

"He didn't have to let you go." Jack reached for a towel. "He could've locked you up on suspicion while he sorted things out." He dried his hands. "You should be thankful to him."

"Pardon me if I don't throw him a parade." Sam kicked off his boots, letting them fall with a thud to the floor.

Jack felt a pang of sympathy for the young man who had saved his life. Sam was coping with the death of someone close to him. But that didn't change the fact that he had become the target of a deadly predator. "You'll need to watch your step for a couple of days," Jack cautioned.

"I don't give a damn if the Yankees—"

"It's not the Yankees." Jack crossed the room and sat on the bed. "You have a bigger problem than that." He lowered his voice. "I have to tell you something very important. And I have to ask you to keep it to yourself."

"What're you talking about?"

"I didn't come to Washington looking for my brother. Truth is, I don't have a brother." Jack took a deep breath. "I'm a captain in the Confederate Provost Guard. I'm on a personal mission for President Davis."

"You're joking."

"I've never been more serious in my life." Jack clasped his hands between his knees. "I'm after an assassin named Basil Tarleton. He's planning to kill someone in Washington."

"Who?"

"That doesn't matter. The point is—from what the police told me, I'm convinced Tarleton killed Olivia Putnam."

Sam's face turned ashen. "Damn."

"And he tried to pin the blame on you."

Sam stared at Jack, emotions playing across his face—anger, fear, confusion. Finally, he asked, "What are you going to do to stop this Tarleton?"

"Anything I have to," Jack replied flatly.

Sam looked him squarely in the eye. "Tell me what I can do to help."

Booth's little company was finally assembled. Tarleton had rarely seen grown men tear into food so ravenously. They made short work of platters filled with meat, cheese, and bread, washing it all down with bottles of champagne. Tarleton had joined John Surratt and Lewis Paine as Booth introduced the others.

Michael O'Laughlin, a boyhood friend of the actor's, wore a loud striped suit. He'd arrived from Baltimore with Samuel Arnold, another Booth crony, who seemed quite eager to enjoy his host's hospitality. George Atzerodt, the immigrant carpenter, stank of sweat and sawdust. A thin teenager Booth called Davey Herold, a druggist's clerk, sat nearby.

They had the restaurant to themselves. When Booth had arrived, the manager asked him to lock up when he was finished, since the staff was going home. Booth cheerfully agreed.

Surratt raised the business at hand. "Enough food and drink, Wilkes. It's time to hear your plan."

"Very well." Booth strode to the center of the room. "It's as simple as it is elegant. We will seize Lincoln during a performance at Ford's Theatre and carry him to Richmond, where we will offer to exchange him for all Confederate prisoners of war."

Booth began pacing. "When the time comes, I'll give a signal." He paused to place a hand on O'Laughlin's shoulder. "Michael will turn off the houselights." He nodded toward Arnold. "Sam will take the stage, armed and ready to stop any interference." He moved on to Paine and laid both hands on the man's broad shoulders. "Lewis and I will be outside the State Box. When the lights go out we will seize Lincoln, tie him up, and lower him to O'Laughlin and Arnold on the stage. Lewis and I jump down from the box and we'll exit through the stage door."

Booth turned toward Tarleton. "Basil, you'll have a carriage behind the theater, plus horses saddled and waiting. Lincoln goes in the carriage and we speed away before an alarm can be sounded."

Booth strode to the buffet table and poured a glass of champagne. "We'll cross the Navy Yard Bridge and meet John in Maryland. He'll take us to his family's tavern." He tipped his glass toward the youngest conspirator. "Davey, you'll be there with additional arms and gear. We'll take the back roads to Port Tobacco." He turned to Atzerodt. "George will ferry us to Virginia." He sipped at his drink. "Then it's on to Richmond." A broad grin creased his cheeks. "And into history."

Booth surveyed his audience as if he were expecting applause. Instead, he got a lengthening silence.

Surratt stared into his champagne glass. O'Laughlin stroked his moustache. Arnold's face was twisted into a frown. Atzerodt's eyes nervously skipped from Booth to the floor and back again. Paine stared impassively at the actor, while Herold smiled trustingly.

Tarleton lit a cigar.

Arnold finally spoke up. "That's the most preposterous idea I've ever heard."

Booth's eyes flashed angrily. "You have misgivings about our prospects?"

Arnold spat out a derisive laugh. "That's not the half of it. Don't you think someone will be keeping an eye on Lincoln? Do you really think we can just waltz out with him?"

"We'll have the element of surprise," Booth countered.

"Maybe," Surratt pointed out. "But the army would be on our heels within the hour."

"We'll be deep in Maryland within the hour." Booth leveled his eyes at Surratt. "Unless someone betrays us."

"Another thing," Arnold interjected. "There's the eight of us, plus Lincoln. We'd need a steamboat to hold us all."

Booth whirled on his old chum. "This is how you repay my friendship?" he snapped. "After all I've done to keep you out of Baltimore's gutters—"

"Friendship's got nothing to do with it." Arnold stood up. "I'll be damned if I throw my life away on some half-baked scheme."

The actor took a step forward and raised his voice. "You'd abandon us?"

"If it comes to that."

The two men glared at each other as if they were about to come to blows. Tarleton took his cigar from his mouth and examined the glowing tip. "Does it have to be at Ford's Theatre, Wilkes?"

Booth spun toward him. "That's where I've laid it out."

Tarleton flipped an ash on the floor. "Perhaps your plan could be put into play somewhere less crowded."

"Lincoln likes to ride in the country," Surratt noted.

Tarleton nodded. "A secluded road might offer a ripe opportunity." The suggestion was greeted with grunts of approval.

Booth studied the faces around him. "I see." His gaze settled on Tarleton. Their eyes remained fixed on each other. The actor raised his glass. "We're in agreement, then. We shall take Lincoln on an isolated road."

There was a murmur of assent as the men raised their glasses. "I salute you," Booth proclaimed, "the liberators of our Southern people."

"To seize the King!" Arnold cried.

"To seize the King!" The words echoed around the room.

Tarleton offered a silent toast of his own:

"To kill the King!"

Seven

THE TRAP

As he watched Felix contentedly munch his noon meal of hard bread and cheese, Jack fought back the urge to demand a report on Tarleton's movements. He nibbled at a boiled egg, though the emotions churning in his stomach robbed him of any appetite. A steady stream of foot traffic passed the beer wagon, parked under a tree on the Mall.

"They went to the theater," Felix finally mumbled through a mouthful of food.

Jack wiped his lips with the back of his hand. "Tell me what happened."

Felix recounted his observations of Tarleton the night before. He described each member of the assassin's theater party—the actor Booth and his companion, who Jack now knew was Surratt. The third man was a stranger. Felix painted a vivid portrait of a muscular hulk in an ill-fitting suit.

"They had women with them," Felix continued. "One was plump and plain and hanging on to Booth for dear life."

"Who was with Tarleton?"

Felix took a big bite of cheese and chewed deliberately. When he looked at Jack, his eyes were hooded. "You're not gonna like this." The big man's face was creased with concern.

"Just tell me."

"She was batting her eyelashes at him the whole time, touching his arm, sashaying around. It was all I could do to keep from walking over and giving her a good slap in the face." Felix shook his head. "It was that redheaded gal. Your lady friend."

Jack cocked his head. "Who did you say?"

"You know who." The words were spoken with mixed disdain and sympathy. "The one you saw at the saloon. Your woman, Jack."

Invisible hands shoved Jack's chest. He reeled back. "You're sure?"

"Sure as I'm sitting here." Felix spoke so softly he could barely be heard.

Jack's head was spinning wildly. He felt as if a hundred cold shards were piercing him, slicing a hundred cuts into his soul. "Kate?"

Felix nodded slowly, sadly, acknowledging the pain his confirmation was causing.

Jack swung his head away. What was Kate doing with Tarleton? Realization hit him in the gut. She was helping the assassin. Everything she had said the day before suddenly made sense. Now he knew why she was so reluctant to move against Tarleton. Now he knew why she was unwilling to share all that she knew.

Now he knew. The woman he had entrusted with his mission,

the woman he had entrusted with his heart, was playing him for a fool.

"Damnation."

"You say something?" Felix's words brought him back to the moment.

Jack hadn't realized he had spoken aloud. "No, I didn't." His voice was thin and shaking.

The tromping of horses passing nearby beat relentlessly against Jack's eardrums. On the Mall, children played noisily in the thin sunshine.

"What're you gonna do?" Felix asked at last.

Jack straightened his shoulders. "I'll do what has to be done." He picked up the reins and whipped the mules into action. It was clear now. The time he had wasted waiting as Kate had spun her web and snared him in it was over. He knew what he would do, and he would do it fast.

"Don't expect me to show up at work tomorrow," Jack said as the wagon clanked onto the street.

Felix nodded. "She done you wrong. A man's gotta set things right." He turned to face his partner. "Let me help you."

Kate held a dispatch before her, but her eyes refused to focus on it. She chided herself for neglecting her duties. Richmond wouldn't have sent the message if it weren't important. But try as she might, she couldn't concentrate on it.

Her mind was on Basil Tarleton. She had seen how he had

infiltrated Washington society in mere days. From what she had heard him tell Booth, she concluded he already had contacts with important people such as Lucy Hale's father. Tarleton was smooth, she had to give him that.

And, she reluctantly admitted, strikingly handsome. Kate understood why men were drawn to him and why women fawned over him. Especially the mindless young belles who swirled in Lucy's orbit. If he put his mind to it, Tarleton could probably wheedle an invitation to the White House. He might be brazen enough to slit Lincoln's throat under his own roof.

She watched the afternoon sunlight falling on the opposite wall. It shimmered on a massive engraved print of Benjamin Franklin at the French Court that dominated the cozy dining room of Kate's brick Georgetown town house. The polished mahogany table and matching buffet she had brought from Montreal reminded her of her homeland. She felt safe and secure in this room and did much of her thinking here. Now, she churned over the problem posed by the beguiling Tarleton.

Wily as he was, she had no doubt her operatives could eliminate him. But he seemed chummy with Booth and Surratt. And that was the problem.

Her eyes finally focused on the dispatch. Richmond wanted still more quinine and other medical supplies. She would alert her operatives at Washington's hospitals and supply depots to collect what they could and turn it over to smuggling teams for the trip south.

One team included John Surratt. And, when the occasion required, John Wilkes Booth.

She needed to deal with Tarleton without drawing notice to them. Maybe she could have the killer abducted. People disappeared all the time.

After all, there was a war going on.

Kate folded the paper and locked it in a long, narrow metal box. She slid aside a concealed panel under the table and slipped the box into a hidden compartment. She was putting the panel back in place when the doorbell rang.

Footsteps sounded in the entry hall. Kate heard her maid open the front door and exchange words with the caller. She made out a man's voice.

Her heart beat faster. Had Jack found her home? Had he come to apologize for the way he treated her yesterday? Kate forced herself to relax. She picked up a book of poems and was thumbing through it when the young black woman entered the dining room.

"A gentleman to see you, ma'am."

Kate didn't look up. "Who is it?"

"He says his name is Wingate."

She frowned. "I don't know anyone named Wingate."

"He says he has information about a certain Mr. Surratt."

Kate felt a twinge of doubt. There shouldn't be anyone in Washington who could connect her to Surratt. Perhaps Richmond had ordered someone to follow up on the dispatch. She closed the book. "Very well. Show him in."

"Yes, ma'am." The maid disappeared into the hallway.

Kate quickly patted her hair, then folded her hands on the table.

She gave her visitor an appraising glance as the servant showed him in. He was of middle height with slender shoulders. His full beard was clipped short and was as fiercely black as his hair. And his eyes. He wore a brown checked suit and held a brown beehive hat in his hand. "Please take a seat, Mr. Wingate."

He settled into a chair and waited until the maid withdrew before speaking. "Despite appearances," he said with a gesture toward his clothing, "I'm actually a major in the United States Army attached to the War Department."

Kate's breath caught in her throat. This was the moment she had dreaded since she began playing her dangerous game. Here was a Federal officer, right in her own home. But if he had come to arrest her, why was he sitting calmly at her dining table? She pasted a thin smile to her lips. "What can I do for you, Major?"

Wingate placed his hat on the table. "Last night, you were seen in the company of a known Rebel sympathizer."

"I was in the company of a great many people last night." Kate kept her tone light. "Several hundred, in fact, at Ford's Theatre."

"Not all of them were in the lower box on the left side of the stage."

"Just the idea!" Kate forced herself to smile brightly. "Can you imagine how crowded that would have been?"

Wingate's face remained impassive. "We have reason to believe a member of your party poses a grave threat to the United States government."

"It wasn't my party, Major. I was invited by Miss Lucy Hale." Kate tilted her chin up and looked down her nose. "Do you know *Senator* Hale's daughter?"

"No, ma'am."

"Perhaps I should introduce you. I'm sure she'd be more than happy to answer your questions."

Wingate idly skimmed the hat brim with his finger. "I don't think that will be necessary."

"I see." Kate scooted her chair back from the table and rose. "If there's nothing further—"

"You're on very shaky ground." His voice took on a sharp edge. "You're consorting with the enemy. The army doesn't take that lightly." He rose and fixed a heated stare on her. "You're in league with a man who's conspiring against your government."

"My government?" Kate crossed her arms. "*My* government? I am a proud subject of Her Majesty Queen Victoria. If you have any complaints about my behavior, direct them to the British Embassy."

The color drained from Wingate's face. "You're British?"

Kate impatiently tapped her foot. "I believe I've said quite enough, Major. You know the way out."

"I—"

"Good day, Major."

Wingate scooped his hat from the table and hurried from the room. Kate stood perfectly still until she heard the front door close behind him. Then she marched into the parlor. She pulled a small sheet of paper from her desk and called for her maid as she began writing.

"Find out all you can about a major named Wingate at the War Department. Urgent."

The servant appeared at the doorway. "Take this to Rufus," she said as she folded the message and handed it over. Then she added, "And tell him I need to see John Surratt first thing tomorrow morning."

"She's not here." Rufus glared at Jack through the smoky dimness of the Crown Oak Tavern.

"I didn't come to see Kate."

"Good," Rufus grunted. "She doesn't want to see you."

The words tightened the knot in Jack's stomach. As much as he wanted to set things right with Kate, the time had come to complete his mission. "I was looking for you."

"What do you want from me?"

"I need a gun."

Rufus passed a hand through his fringe of white hair. "Why?"

"I'm going after Tarleton."

"Are you mad?"

"Maybe." Jack set his jaw. "But it's what I came here to do and I'm going to do it."

The grizzled operative scowled. "How do you intend to pull that off?"

"I have a plan. And the men to carry it out."

Rufus thrust his face up at Jack. "If you've compromised Kate—"

Jack waved off his protest. "You don't have to worry about that. They don't know anything about her." He leaned down until his nose was almost touching the older man's. "And she doesn't need to know anything about this. Understood?"

"Why not?"

"For her own protection." Jack cast a quick glance around the murky saloon, then lowered his voice. "If the Yankees catch wind of what I'm doing, they may try to stop me. Things could turn sour. There's no need to put her at risk."

Rufus regarded him skeptically. "Besides," Jack added quickly, "it will all be over in twenty-four hours. After that, no matter what happens, you'll never see me again."

Jack felt the older man's gaze boring through his skull. It was as if Rufus were trying to see right into his thoughts. At last, he looked away. "All right."

Jack let out a long breath. "Thanks."

"Don't thank me." Rufus stabbed his forefinger into Jack's chest. "I won't tell Kate anything before tomorrow night. And I'll get you a pistol. But get this straight. If your plan fails and the Yankees are breathing down your neck, you'll use that pistol on yourself."

Jack looked Rufus squarely in the eye. "Count on it."

"And if you don't," Rufus concluded, "I will."

John Surratt was waiting on the street in front of his mother's boardinghouse the next morning when Kate pulled her buggy to a stop. "Get in," she said brusquely. Once he was seated beside her, she flicked the reins and the buggy lurched toward Pennsylvania Avenue. "I have a message," she said quietly. "From George Webb."

Surratt's eyebrows lifted. "I'm not part of his operation."

"He has a message for you all the same." She looked up at the cloudless morning sky and breathed deeply. "You can smell spring in the air."

Surratt huddled inside his coat. "It's cold out here."

"What would you say to a spin around Lafayette Park?"

Before Surratt could answer, the buggy was passing the White House. He shot a nervous glance toward the mansion. "Why here?"

Kate leaned close. "Someone is asking questions about you. A Federal major named Wingate."

Surratt shook his head. "Never heard of him."

"He's heard of you." Kate nodded toward the buildings next to the White House. "George Webb says he works over there, in the War Department. He's an intelligence officer."

Surratt rubbed his chin. "That's not good."

"Indeed. Perhaps you should think about going away for a while."

The buggy turned onto Jackson Place and inched along the west side of the park. "An excellent idea," Surratt agreed. "The timing couldn't be better. I just received word. I'm leaving town today."

"I can drop you at the train depot," Kate offered.

"Thanks, but I have an errand to run first." Surratt offered an enigmatic smile. "I'll make a quick stop on the Seventh Street Road, then Washington City will see nothing more of me."

Harsh sunlight stabbed Tarleton's eyes as he rolled over in bed. He pulled the blanket to his chin.

"Don't hog the covers." The woman beside him tugged the blanket.

He had met her while slumming in Murder Bay, a disreputable and dangerous neighborhood along the canal where he had spent the night blowing off steam. He tried to pry her name from his memory.

Hilda. A big-boned redhead who served watered-down whiskey at a back-alley card game. Last night she reminded him of Kate St. Claire. In the light of day, there was no resemblance.

As he was deciding how to rid himself of her, there was a sharp rap at the door. A voice called, "Message for Mr. Tarleton."

"Slide it under the door." A slip of paper skidded across the wood floor. He flipped aside the blanket and sat up. The motion made his head spin and churned the bile in his belly. He closed his eyes until the dizziness passed, then let loose a powerful belch.

"You need the hair of the dog, sweetie," Hilda cooed. "Why don't you get us both a drink?"

Tarleton climbed out of bed and retrieved the message. *"The curtain is going up. Be at the ready. J.W.B."* So the actor's time has come, he thought as he lit a cigar. He touched the match to the paper and dropped them both in a large brass spittoon. The message flamed brightly, sizzled, and disappeared. His own moment was also at hand.

"How about that drink, then?"

He turned to the woman. Tangled hair obscured most of her face. All he could see clearly was her slack mouth. A tooth was missing. "I think not." He picked up his pocket watch and saw the day was heading toward noon. "Time for you to go."

Hilda groaned and rolled over. "I was just getting comfortable."

The last traces of the hangover faded as Tarleton began mentally listing all he must do to be ready to strike. He scooped a frayed plaid dress from the floor and flung it on the bed. "I have business to tend to. Now, get dressed and get out of here."

She turned bleary eyes toward him. "No need to get snippy. I can take a hint."

"Good." Tarleton filled the washbasin with water and scrubbed his face. This was the day, he realized. Abraham Lincoln's last day alive. The day Basil Tarleton entered the ranks of the greatest men in his select profession. As he vigorously toweled himself, he caught sight of the woman in the mirror. "You'd best go down the back stairs. We don't want the desk clerk seeing you."

She gave a crooked smile. "You sound like we have something to be ashamed of."

He crossed to the bureau and fished around in the breast pocket of the jacket he had worn the night before. His fingers slid along the smooth handle of his narrow knife. Then he recalled Booth's message. "A certain degree of discretion is in order."

"Oh, I can be very discreet," she chuckled. "Especially with a man who shows me proper appreciation."

Tarleton ran his finger down the knife handle before moving it aside. He withdrew his wallet. "Just how much appreciation do I need to show you?"

Her crooked, gap-toothed smile grew wider.

Felix waved Jack and Sam aboard as the beer wagon pulled up in front of the Liberty House. A canvas tarp obscured the words NATIONAL LAGER painted on either side.

"What did the boss say when I didn't show up this morning?" Jack asked as he settled onto the seat beside Felix.

"He said he's looking forward to seeing you on Monday." A wide grin split the broad black face. "So he can fire your ass."

"I hate to disappoint him."

Felix slapped the reins and the mules reluctantly pulled the wagon down the street. As they picked their way through the morning traffic, Jack introduced Felix to Sam.

"It's pretty straightforward," Jack said from his position in the middle of the wagon bench. "Sam and I will go inside the hotel. I'll send a note to lure Tarleton into our trap."

"You sure he'll fall for it?" Sam asked with a trace of uncertainty.

Jack shrugged. "It's the best card we have. You just stay and delay Tarleton in case he gets any ideas about leaving early. He has to be there when Felix gets back."

"Oh, you can count on that. He won't leave until I say he can."

There was a steeliness in the words that worried Jack. "No scenes, Sam. There's too much at stake to risk losing him now."

Sam stared at the whirling wagon wheel below his feet.

"Promise me," Jack insisted.

"I promise," he said without looking up.

"And me?" Felix asked, a little too eagerly.

"You'll take me out to Maryland and drop me off in the woods," Jack said reassuringly. "Then come back, pick up Tarleton, and bring him to me."

"Devil take him," Sam said as he spat at the wheel.

"With any luck, he will," Jack said flatly.

Felix steered the mules onto Pennsylvania Avenue. The National Hotel loomed a few blocks away. Jack pulled a handful of greenbacks from his pants pocket. "Once Felix has Tarleton, hurry over to the stable and get our horses." He passed the money to Sam. "That should cover it."

When Felix pulled the wagon to a halt in front of the hotel, Jack and Sam climbed down. "You sure you can find the Rockville Road?" Jack asked as they made their way onto a sidewalk crowded with shoppers, soldiers, and former slaves.

"I'll find it," Sam assured him. "You've only repeated the directions about thirty times."

"Once we have Tarleton, we'll hitch the horses to the wagon." Jack glanced at the wagon. "They can pull it a bit faster than the mules. We'll need to make tracks back to Richmond."

A formally dressed black man opened the door for them.

"I'll bring the horses." Sam's voice was husky as they stepped inside the busy lobby, but his gaze was fixed on the floor. "But I'm not going to Richmond."

Jack's head snapped around. "Why not?"

"Hell, Jack. There ain't nothing for me back there."

"Where will you go?"

Sam scratched his head. "I reckon I'll just stay here." He eased down on a red velvet settee and added, "It's not such a bad place. Once you get used to it."

"It won't be the same without you."

"Don't you have a message to send?"

Jack looked at him, this boy who had seen so much more than one his age should have seen, had felt so much more than he should have felt, and let a wave of admiration sweep over him.

"The front desk is over there." Sam pointed.

"So it is," Jack said at last. He strode across the lobby and waited behind a fussy western congressman who was disputing his large bill.

"May I help you?" a sad-eyed clerk with a sagging moustache asked as Jack stepped forward.

"I need to send a message to one of your guests."

The clerk picked up a pen and wearily dipped it into a gilded inkwell. "Go ahead."

"Say, 'I must see you. We have urgent business to discuss. Will send a ride for you promptly at two P.M. Don't be late.' "

"And how do I sign it?" the clerk asked as he scribbled.

"John Wilkes Booth."

The clerk folded the sheet in half. "Mr. Tarleton seems to be a popular man today. I will see he gets this message, too." He was writing Tarleton's name and room number on the paper as Jack walked away.

"Much obliged," he called and shot one last glance across the lobby. He spied Sam already flirting with a blond girl. Jack was reminded again how young his comrade really was and wondered if he could be trusted with his assigned task.

He had to come through, Jack thought as he returned to the bright sunshine of the street. The threat to Lincoln had to end once and for all. Tarleton had to be stopped, and he had to be stopped today.

Wingate waited until Kate's buggy was lashed to a hitching post before he stepped out from behind a sturdy elm tree in front of her brick town house. A few blocks away, a church bell began tolling the noon hour. "Mrs. St. Claire," he called.

Kate paused on the steps and gave him a hard look. "What is it now, Major?"

"I don't like it when people lie to me." He hurried over to her. "I think you'd better come along."

"I'd rather not."

Wingate placed his hand gently on her elbow. "Don't make me drag you away in irons." He steered her to the sidewalk. "You're not British," he said. "You're Canadian."

"Canada is part of the British Empire, Major, and I am a subject of the crown, no matter which side of the Atlantic I call home." She held her head high, refusing to meet his eyes. "Where are we going?"

"Keep walking." Wingate's voice was conversational. Anyone who passed would assume they were out for a midday stroll. "Tell me what you said to Surratt."

"At the theater?"

Wingate tightened his grip on her elbow. "This morning during your little buggy ride around Lafayette Square. I saw you."

She gazed coldly at him. "I wanted you to see us."

"Why?"

"To prove I have nothing to hide."

Wingate jerked Kate to a halt. "You haven't answered my question. What did you say to Surratt?"

"I should think you'd be more interested in what he said to me."

"I'm asking the questions here."

She sniffed derisively. "And you're not doing a terribly good job of it. I will give you the information you're looking for, Major. Then I shall return to my home, and you will never darken my door again."

"And if I say no?"

Kate smoothed the fabric of her burgundy jacket. "Then you won't have the information you want."

"And you'll be trading your comfortable brick home for the cold stone of Old Capitol Prison."

"I think not." Her eyes flashed angrily. "Lay a hand on me again, Major, and the British ambassador will make certain you are cashiered from the army before nightfall." She turned and began walking again. "Perhaps it will be you, not I, sampling the accommodations of Old Capitol Prison."

"Wait," Wingate called. Kate stopped but didn't look back.

"We'll do this your way," he said as he reached her. "But one false move and I'll bury you so deep Queen Victoria herself won't be able to dig you out."

"Very sensible, Major. Now, pay attention. I'll only say this once. You can stop troubling yourself over John Surratt. He's leaving Washington City."

"When?"

"Today." A triumphant look settled on Kate's face.

"Where's he going?"

"He didn't say. But he made it clear he won't be coming back."

Wingate scratched his beard. He couldn't imagine why Surratt would turn tail and run, unless this woman had warned him the authorities were closing in. Whatever the reason, the threat to Lincoln seemed to be disappearing.

"Thank you, Mrs. St. Claire. You've been most helpful."

"Good day, Major."

As he watched her go, Wingate felt a growing sense of satisfaction, knowing the president's safety was no longer in doubt. But an unanswered question wriggled in the back of his brain. He sprinted after her. "Just a moment," he called.

She looked over her shoulder. "What is it now?"

"Did Surratt say how he would be traveling?"

Kate didn't slow her step and Wingate had to hurry to keep up. "No," she replied. "I even offered to take him to the train depot, but he declined."

"Did he say why?"

Kate let out an exasperated breath. "If you must know, he said he was running an errand out on the Seventh Street Road before he left town."

"I see." Wingate slowed to a stop. "Thanks again."

She gave him a dismissive wave as she strode briskly down the street. He called after her, "One last thing. Where's the Seventh Street Road?"

"My Lord, Major, don't you know anything? Go north on Seventh Street out into the country. You can't miss it."

Jack chewed on his fingernail as he reviewed his plan with Felix one last time. "What kind of place did you say this was?" he asked.

"Used to come out here and buy corn liquor." Felix held the reins loosely in his hands as the mules plowed up a cloud of dust in the road ahead of them. "Army shut it down a few months back. I've been out here about every other weekend, hoping they were back in business. Nobody there."

"Good." Jack fell silent as the rolling countryside of Maryland slid steadily past them. He mopped his damp forehead with the back of his hand. "Now, Tarleton is probably going to ask you some questions. You can't say anything that might make him suspicious."

"Won't tell him nothing," Felix promised.

Jack nodded and sank back into thought. After several minutes, he asked, "Did you bring a rope?"

Felix grunted. He steered the mules into a wooded lane and stopped. "Here we are." A run-down shack stood at the end of the short lane. Trees shrouded them on all sides, providing an oasis from the blinding midday sun.

"This will do just fine," Jack said.

"Can I ask you a question?" The big man lashed the reins to the seat and turned to face his partner. "You gonna string that Tarleton fellow up or just shoot him in the head?"

Jack recoiled at the question. "Neither."

Felix shook his head. "This man messed with your woman. You got the right to do with him what you want." He nodded toward the wagon bed. "You got enough rope to hang him from the highest tree. And don't think I didn't notice that pistol tucked in your belt."

Jack patted the back of his jacket where it covered the revolver Rufus had given him. "I don't plan on killing him in cold blood."

Felix's eyes bored into his partner's. "I heard you talking to the boy about Richmond. That where you're going?"

Jack nodded. "Tarleton, too. Tied up, in the back of the wagon."

"You taking the wagon?"

"Yeah." Jack let his gaze drop away. "I'm going to steal the wagon."

"And I get to explain it back at the brewery."

Jack peered around the brim of his hat. "Well, I'm leaving the mules."

Slowly, a grin spread across Felix's face. "Some friend you are." He threw his head back and let out a long howl of laughter.

Jack jumped to the ground. "You'd better get back to town and pick up Tarleton."

"When this is over, will you tell me what it's really all about?"

"I'll tell you what I can."

Felix nodded. "Good enough."

Jack extended his hand. "Thanks for doing this, Felix. I'm proud you call me your friend."

Felix gave his partner a firm handshake. Then he whipped the reins and the mules began the long trudge back to Washington.

Wingate drew a nod of recognition from the sentry at the south gate of the White House. He gave the man a cheerful greeting, as he always did when he cut through the grounds on his way to the War Department. He had made it a point to get to know the soldiers who stood guard over the mansion.

Not because he was concerned about the president's safety. At least, not at first. He had been more interested in becoming a fixture around the grounds so he could occasionally nick a meal from the White House mess. The faint aroma of roasting meat tickled his nostrils. Perhaps he could sneak over for a bite of lunch before heading back to the office.

Wingate's access let him keep close tabs on the president's movements. Crossing the south lawn, he spotted a squat man in sweat-stained clothes sweeping out a black carriage that gleamed in the early afternoon sunshine. "Howdy, Bert," he called.

The man smiled. "Catch any Rebels today, Win?"

"A whole regiment since breakfast." Wingate walked across the graveled driveway and pointed to the carriage. "Is the old man going for a ride?"

"Not anymore. He was supposed to visit the boys at Campbell Hospital, but there's been a change in plan." Bert pulled a red bandana from his hip pocket and mopped his face. "Some folks came over and picked him up for a meeting at the National

Hotel." He shook his head. "The fellows at the hospital will sure be disappointed."

"That's a shame." Wingate stuck his hands in his pockets. "Maybe he can still squeeze in the trip after his meeting."

"Won't have time." Bert grunted as he tugged at the rigging. "Campbell Hospital is all the way out on the Seventh Street Road."

Wingate's face went cold. "My God," he whispered. Kate St. Claire's words rang in his mind. John Surratt was "running an errand" on the Seventh Street Road. Then he would leave Washington forever. It was all clear now.

The conspirators were planning to attack the president on his way to Campbell Hospital.

But Wingate knew something they did not—their target wouldn't be on the Seventh Street Road. And if he acted quickly, he could round up the whole gang and quash the threat.

He shot a glance at the carriage. "Bert, I need a favor."

"Excuse me, sir." A toady little desk clerk hovered at the foot of the stairs as Tarleton descended to the lobby of the hotel. He was just the sort of self-inflated functionary the assassin despised—greasy moustache, greasy hair, greasy smile, palm ever poised to be greased. "I was just about to send this up to your room." The clerk extended a folded piece of paper.

Tarleton snatched it from him and scanned the florid handwriting. He checked his pocket watch. It was nearly two o'clock. He grunted as he hurried into the lobby.

"Will there be anything else, sir?" the clerk called after him.

He didn't respond. His mind was leaping ahead. Booth would pick him up in a matter of moments and he would be on his way.

And he would not look back. He carried everything he needed in the pockets of his black overcoat. Anything still in his room could be left behind without a second thought. By nightfall, Lincoln would be at his mercy, and Washington City would be a receding memory.

"Mr. Tarleton?" A tall, blond young man stood just inside the front door twisting a hat in his hands.

"Yes?"

"I was hoping to have a word with you."

Tarleton took a closer look. "I know you."

"Yes, sir. Sam Jenkins. From Maguire's Theater."

An alarm sounded in Tarleton's head. The police should have hauled in this whelp for Olivia Putnam's murder. Yet here he was, walking about free. "I'm late for an appointment." As he brushed past Sam, he felt a tug on his arm. He glared at the young man.

"This will just take a moment."

Tarleton shook the hand off his sleeve. "Speak up, then."

Sam shuffled his feet. "I wanted to know if you had spoken to Miss Putnam. You know, on the day she . . . she . . ." He cast his eyes down as his words sputtered to a stop.

"I saw her that morning at Ford's. Other than that, no. Now, step aside."

"One more thing."

Tarleton grabbed Sam by his shirt collar and pulled him forward. "I said step aside."

"And I said, 'One more thing.'" Sam's eyes flashed angrily. He grasped Tarleton's wrist and pushed it away. "I know what you did to her." The young man's voice was a menacing whisper.

"You know nothing." Tarleton's hand shot forward and wrapped around Sam's throat. "Now listen very carefully." He tightened his grip. "If I ever lay eyes on you again, my face will be the last thing you ever see."

Tarleton shoved Sam and sent him reeling into a large mirror on the wall. It shattered, sending a shower of glass down onto his head. The ornate golden frame splintered, spraying pieces in every direction as Sam fell under the debris.

Tarleton spun around and marched to the door. Footsteps scurried across the marble floor. The desk clerk was rushing toward him. He produced a twenty-dollar bill from his pocket and dropped it behind him. "For the damages," he growled as he stepped out onto the street.

He squinted in the brilliant sunshine and swept his eyes along Pennsylvania Avenue. He saw no sign of Booth, only a mule-drawn wagon parked at the curb.

"You Mr. Tarleton?" a large black man called from the seat of the wagon. "Mr. Booth sent me."

"It's about bloody time," Tarleton grumbled and climbed aboard. "Let's go."

The matched pair of carriage horses trotted northward on the Seventh Street Road. Wingate clutched tightly at the reins, his eyes shifting from side to side. The lane led into a thick patch of woods that seemed a million miles from the bustle of Washington City. Laurel and poplar crowded the road. He drove deeper into the trees as the sun disappeared behind a thick cloudbank.

For the first time since he had talked his way into taking the president's carriage, Wingate's mind was shrouded by doubt. It had seemed such a brilliant idea—using the rig to draw Surratt and his gang into a trap. Now he realized he had no way of knowing how they would react when they saw they had been tricked. Just how desperate were they?

He gathered the reins in one hand. The other settled on the thick bulge in his coat pocket. If he'd had a little more time, he could have rounded up an armed squad to accompany him. He had settled for borrowing a revolver from a White House sentry.

A rustling noise made his head snap to the left. Wingate peered intently at the underbrush. He heard it again—something moving in the thicket. His eyes strained to find the source.

A grayish blur darted across the road. The revolver was halfway out of his pocket before Wingate recognized it. A rabbit dashed between the horses, making them start in fright. They reared up and bellowed, shaking the carriage violently.

Wingate had a sudden vision of the president's carriage twisting and flipping along the road. He pulled forcefully on the reins and shouted at the horses.

The battle of wills raged for several minutes until Wingate regained control. The carriage came to a stop, the horses panting in the middle of the road, their big eyes rolling from side to side.

Hoofbeats rumbled from behind. A single rider galloped toward him. Wingate couldn't make out his features. He reached for the pistol.

The rider spurred his horse into a full gallop. Its hooves resounded on the hard dirt road like cannon fire. Wingate kept his eye on the emerging figure.

He felt a sharp jerk on the reins. The jittery horses had bolted at the sudden noise. The carriage shot forward, nearly throwing

Wingate from the seat. He struggled to regain his balance as he fought to rein in the team. He cast a quick look over his shoulder.

The rider was only a few yards away and closing fast. In the fleeting glimpse, Wingate recognized the horseman's face—the pale skin, the deep-set dark eyes, the flowing black moustache.

It was not John Surratt.

The mules plodded through the Maryland countryside, hauling the wagon over a rough track. Tarleton wondered again why Booth had sent such a sluggish conveyance to carry him to their rendezvous. He had tried engaging the driver in conversation. The massive black man had grunted a few replies, then sat as silent and stolid as a slab of granite.

Tarleton scanned the rolling terrain. He tried to visualize how Booth would strike at Lincoln. There wasn't a lot of cover—some scrubby bushes and a few trees—but there were hollows and gullies on either side of the road, perfect spots to lay an ambush.

Tarleton raised his eyes to the western horizon. Thick clouds obscured the sun. He considered what effect rain might have on Booth's plan. A good shower could help him elude pursuit after the deed was done.

The driver steered the wagon into a narrow path and stopped. "Here we are, sir," he grumbled.

Tarleton looked around. "Here?" He saw no sign of Booth or the other conspirators, just a tumbledown shack. His hand stole into his coat pocket and rested lightly on his long, narrow-bladed knife. "Booth told you to bring me here?"

"*I* told him to bring you here," a voice called.

Tarleton's head jerked toward a man approaching from the shack. "Who the hell are you?"

The man cocked a revolver and pointed it at Tarleton's head. "Captain Jack Tanner of the Confederate States Army. You're under arrest for the murder of Harry Kincaid."

It took all Wingate's strength to keep the horses from racing out of control as the carriage flew down the road. He shot another look over his shoulder. The rider was almost abreast of him. "Booth," he muttered under his breath.

Ahead, Wingate saw a man walk out of a small building and into the middle of the road. It was a toll taker, signaling the carriage to stop.

"Out of the way," Wingate called. He checked over his shoulder. Booth had pulled alongside the carriage and was looking inside. The actor's eyebrows rose in surprise.

Wingate turned his attention back to the man who stood in the road waving his hands above his head. "Out of the way," Wingate shouted again.

The man froze. The horses were barreling straight toward him. Wingate stood up and pulled back on the reins with all his might. The horses refused to break stride. Wingate wrapped the reins around his left wrist. His right hand dove into his pocket and pulled out the pistol. "Clear the way," he shouted. Then he fired a shot into the air.

The toll taker dove aside as the carriage roared past. Wingate gave the reins another fierce yank. At last, the horses slowed their pace. He looked behind him. Booth had stopped. Five more riders were galloping toward him.

The actor wheeled his horse about, took off his hat, and waved it at the others. They pulled up short as Booth spurred toward them, shouting as he rode. Wingate raised the gun and aimed at the receding figures. The carriage bounced beneath his feet. He took a last look at the six figures shrinking in the distance, then put the pistol back in his pocket and took up the reins in both hands.

"Step down from the wagon," Jack ordered. He looked closely at the man he had been tracking for weeks. The assassin's arctic blue eyes returned his gaze. He sat perfectly still, one hand in his pocket. "Let me see your hands."

Something like a smile flickered across Tarleton's face. The hand flew from his pocket. Jack caught a glint of steel. "Look out, Felix," he called.

The tip of a knife materialized at Felix's throat. "Drop your gun," Tarleton barked, "or I'll take his head off."

Jack's aim remained steady. Felix fixed his eyes on his partner as he dropped the reins and balled his hands into fists.

"Give it up, Tarleton," Jack demanded. "You can't get away."

Tarleton pressed the knife against Felix's skin. "Have you ever seen a man with a severed carotid artery? The blood comes gushing out like a geyser. I've seen it spray more than five feet in the air." He applied more pressure to the blade. A thin stream of blood trickled down Felix's throat.

Jack took a step toward the wagon. "It won't do you any good. You won't get away alive."

"Maybe not." Tarleton dragged the knife lightly along Felix's throat, leaving a thin trail of blood. "But this man will be dead before you can pull the trigger."

Felix sat motionless. "Do what you have to do, Jack."

"That's right, Jack." Tarleton spat out the name like a bad piece of meat. "Do what you have to do." He jabbed the point of his knife into the wound on Felix's neck. "And sign your friend's death warrant."

Jack looked from Tarleton to Felix and back again. "I know why you're here. I know why Harry Kincaid gave you all that money. I guarantee you'll never live to collect the rest of your fee."

"You've already seen to that." Bitterness cut through Tarleton's words. "If I surrender, what do you plan to do? Take me back to Richmond?"

"That's right."

"And the gallows."

Jack nodded.

"If I don't surrender, you'll kill me."

"Count on it."

Tarleton shook his head. "I don't like those options." He fastened his eyes on Jack's. "Here's another. Let me go."

"Why would I do that?"

Tarleton nodded toward Felix. "To save his life."

"I'm not a fool. You'd head straight back to Washington City."

A small smile creased Tarleton's face. "I'll leave town."

"And walk away from all that money?"

Tarleton shrugged. "I have plenty. I don't care much for Washington anyway. Not civilized enough." He lifted an eyebrow.

"What do you say? You go your way, I'll go mine, and this man stays alive."

Jack searched his friend's large brown eyes but found no answers there. He looked back at Tarleton. "Release him."

Tarleton tightened his grip on the knife. "He's my insurance that you'll live up to your part of the bargain. Give me enough time to get back to town and I'll let him go."

Jack lowered his pistol. "He has nothing to do with this. He doesn't know anything."

"Good." Tarleton nudged Felix in the shoulder. "Get us out of here."

Felix eyed his friend. "Jack?"

Jack jammed the revolver into the waist of his trousers. "Go on, Felix. I'll see you back in town."

Tarleton kept the knife close as Felix whipped the mules into motion. Jack watched the wagon disappear into the fading afternoon light. When the clop of their hooves and the rattling of the rigging had faded, he set off on foot.

At the Rockville Road rendezvous, Sam gave him a questioning look. Jack silently mounted his horse and spurred the animal toward Washington, leaving Sam scrambling to catch up. They rode hard in the failing light. As they raced past the shack where Jack had faced Tarleton, large drops of rain began to splatter in the dirt road. Within minutes, a heavy downpour drenched them.

Jack rounded a bend and pulled his horse to a sudden stop. Ahead, he saw the beer wagon slewed in a ditch. The mules were gone. A figure was slumped on the seat. He bounded off his horse and ran toward it.

Felix was sprawled on his back, his eyes staring sightlessly into the falling rain. A deep gash across his throat leaked a trickle of blood. Jack grasped his wrist and felt for a pulse. He couldn't find it. He tossed his hat aside and thrust his ear against the big man's chest. Silence.

Sam came sloshing up beside him. "Oh, Lord. What happened?"

Jack pushed himself away from the body. He reached up and pressed Felix's eyelids shut. He closed his own eyes and lowered his head.

"God bless you, Felix," he whispered. "And damn you, Tarleton."

Eight

THE INTERMISSION

Sunday, April 2, 1865

"They've disappeared. Just vanished." Kate's lips barely moved through a brilliant smile. She put her arm through Jack's and pulled close to his side. Their feet crunched the gravel path in Lafayette Park. "It's as if they were whisked away in the middle of the night."

"You've still got men on it, don't you?" Jack asked.

"Everyone I can spare. But my resources are melting away. With Grant almost in Richmond, they want to go home. That doesn't leave many agents to troll saloons and whorehouses for Tarleton and his friends."

They had met almost daily over the past two weeks, sharing what little information came their way, talking over hunches and hashing out their worries. Often they posed as lovers out for a stroll, as they did this Sunday afternoon. It felt natural, her arm in his, her gait matching his longer strides. But it tore at Jack's heart that he had to pretend to be what he most dearly wanted to be—the man in Kate's life.

He pulled the brim of his hat lower, shading his eyes from the dazzling sunshine. Around them, a swarm of people drank in the break from wintry weather—soldiers promenading with women decked out in church finery, children scampering on still-brown grass, old men sitting on benches happily swapping lies.

"That big brute who hangs around Booth is still in town." Kate clutched Jack's arm more firmly. "Maybe he'll lead us to the others."

Jack nodded at a passing army officer. The man tipped his hat to Kate, a boyish smile stretching his side whiskers. Once he was beyond them, Jack whispered, "How hard can it be to find a man as famous as Booth?"

The smile froze on Kate's face. "Are you suggesting I'm holding something back?"

"Of course not."

They stopped in front of the park's centerpiece. A uniformed Andrew Jackson towered over them astride a tarnished green steed rearing on its hind legs. Old Hickory held his hat aloft in salute to the Executive Mansion across the street.

"I didn't mean anything like that." Jack's words were clipped and his voice a husky whisper. He let out a long breath. "I'm sorry. All this waiting around is hard to take. From what you've told me, Booth is no shrinking violet. I don't understand why he isn't cutting his usual swath through Washington society."

"Neither do I," Kate admitted. "He took the stage at Ford's for one night last month, then melted away." She gazed up at the heroic statue. "As for Tarleton, it's as if he never existed."

Jack jerked his head toward the White House. "What about *him?*"

"He's visiting Grant's army in Virginia."

"What about that fellow from the boardinghouse, Surratt?"

"He said he was leaving town." Kate's eyes shifted from side to side, making sure no one was within earshot. "I don't know if I believe him, but he has the connections to make himself scarce. It wouldn't surprise me if he skedaddled it to Montreal. From there, he could go anywhere."

"Tarleton's gone, Booth's out of sight, and Surratt is off to parts unknown." Jack pushed his hat back and stared across the street at the White House. "Meantime, Lincoln is surrounded by Grant's army. That's the safest place he could be right now."

Jack patted her hand. "Maybe we've turned the corner. Maybe we can finally dare to hope for the best."

Monday, April 3, 1865

As he opened the War Department's polished wooden door, Wingate was met by frenzied excitement. Boots trod heavily, hurriedly down plank floorboards. Sabers jangled against running thighs. Shouts and countershouts mingled with the nonstop staccato click of telegraph keys. This was no typical Monday morning, he thought as he turned into the corridor leading to his office.

"Make way!" A young captain ran toward him so fast Wingate barely had time to draw back against a wall.

Ahead, two civilian clerks exchanged animated gestures. "What's the big fuss?" Wingate asked as he walked up to them. "You'd think there's a war on."

"It's been like this all morning," a tall, gangly man answered. "We've been here since midnight."

"We'll likely work straight through till midnight tonight, too," his gray-haired companion sighed. "Our boys are marching into Richmond at this very moment."

Wingate's spine tingled at the news he and everyone else in the North had waited four blood-soaked years to hear. Richmond had fallen! "Thank God," he murmured.

"Amen," the gray-haired man seconded.

"Not that's there's much of Richmond left," the other clerk went on. "It's been burning all night."

"Why did we torch the town?" Wingate asked.

The thin man shook his head. "We didn't. The Rebs did, right after Jeff Davis and his bunch ran away."

"They burned their own capital?" Wingate tried imagining the desperation that would compel people to set their own city afire.

"The game's up now." Smug satisfaction settled on the older clerk's face. "Grant is already chasing old Lee just as fast as he can skeedaddle."

"That's great!" Wingate clapped each man on the shoulder.

There was a fresh bounce in his step as he reached his office in the back of the building. The room was buzzing with the morning's developments. He had no sooner settled at his desk than the same captain who had flown past him in the hall blew into the room, summoning him to see Stanton.

Wingate felt a new tingle. He jumped from his chair and raced out of the room. The corridors were filled with men, officers of ever-higher rank the closer he got to the secretary's domain. The small reception room was packed with colonels and brigadier generals.

Stanton's aide asked Wingate to wait. The room was thick with cigar smoke from the throng of officers who filled it. He stood against the wall. And he listened.

"They didn't fire a shot!"

"I'd give anything to see Old Glory floating atop the Rebel capitol. That must be a sight."

"Too bad they weren't able to catch Davis."

The door to Stanton's office swung open. Wingate heard the most amazing thing yet that incredible morning. Stanton was laughing.

Two major generals walked out of the office, stopping to light cigars and trade congratulations.

"Major Wingate," the aide called over the noise. "The secretary will see you now."

He smoothed his suit, took a deep breath, and walked inside.

"There you are." Stanton's voice was now cold and businesslike. "Close the door. You've heard the news?"

"Yes, sir. It's wonderful."

Stanton looked anything but happy as he stroked his long beard. "Wonderful news for the army, for the country, yes." He paused. "But you and I know differently."

Wingate blinked in confusion. "Sir?"

"The Rebels are desperate, Major. They've lost their capital. Their pride has taken a beating." His eyes narrowed to steely slits. "The threat to the president has never been greater than it is right now."

"Don't you think surrender is imminent, sir?"

"You think the Confederacy will disappear into history without one last strike?" Stanton opened a desk drawer. "Early this morning, a sentry spotted someone in the bushes near the White House. A rough-looking character in beat-up clothes. He had this." He reached into the drawer, withdrew a revolver, and handed it across the desk. "Look at the marking."

C. S./RICHMOND VA. was stamped in small letters by the hammer. Wingate recognized the mark of the Richmond Arsenal.

"He was an amateur," Stanton continued, "and not a very smart one. Probably acting alone. The Rebels aren't dumb enough to equip their spies with telltale evidence."

"Well done, sir." Wingate heard a nervous quiver in his voice.

Stanton stared at the revolver. "The danger is more acute than ever before." He looked up. "Tell me about this Rebel you've been following around. What's he up to?"

"Sir?"

"Surratt!" Stanton snapped. "Good God, man, don't you even know the name of the man you're supposed to be watching?"

"Of course, Mr. Secretary. I'm on top of his every move."

"You know where he is, what he's doing?"

"Absolutely. He can't scratch his neck without me knowing about it."

"Very good." Stanton relaxed into his chair. "Major, let me make this abundantly clear. With peace at hand, you must be especially vigilant. Should you slip up and some evil befalls the president . . ." Stanton left the threat dangling overhead like a hatchet blade.

Wingate swallowed hard. "Yes, sir."

Stanton held out his hand and Wingate returned the revolver. "This will never happen again, will it, Major?"

"No, sir."

Stanton placed the gun on the desk, then looked up with a

smile so warm and sincere it startled Wingate. "I'm glad we've had this chat. Now go off and celebrate the day's glorious news."

"Thank you, sir." Wingate headed toward the door.

"One more thing, Major."

Wingate paused with his hand on the doorknob. "Sir?"

Stanton's voice cut through the office like a scythe. "Don't let that traitor out of your sight."

"I won't, sir." Wingate let himself out, passed through the smoky reception room and into the corridor.

Picking his way back to his office, his mind kept repeating the question he had been asking himself for the past two weeks.

Where was John Surratt?

Wingate decided it was time he learned the answer.

New York City
Monday, April 3, 1865

Sounds from the street told Tarleton there was news. He peered through a film-coated window still sealed against winter. Shopkeepers left stores, mingling with passersby. People shifted from group to group, stopping to whisper and listen, then moving to the next for more details. As the afternoon wore on, the buzz from a hundred excited conversations rose to the third-floor room.

When night fell, the door flew open and a full-bosomed woman ran inside. "Richmond has fallen!" She launched herself into his arms. "The war is ending!"

Tarleton said nothing as he leaned into her mouth and kissed deeply, running his hands down her blouse. Her clothing fell to the floor, accompanied by the muffled percussion of distant explosions. As they tumbled naked into bed, the bright reds, blues, and whites of fireworks painted a kaleidoscope on the dirty window.

He thrust into her with a brutality that seemed to terrify and thrill her. It was more a coarse, savage assault than coupling. Their bodies collided and exploded in a frenzy that left him exhilarated and left her exhausted and asleep.

He rolled from the bed and went to the window, watching as bright, dancing sparks fell on the rows of rooming houses, old sheds, and shops that surrounded the woman's rented room, an anonymous cranny that had provided a safe haven since he had fled Washington.

Memory stabbed at his pride. He had turned tail. Ran. And why? Because some bristle-chinned Southern soldier got the drop on him. He shook his head in disgust.

That's what I get for letting someone else do my planning for me, he told himself. Never again.

The thought of Booth left a bad taste in his mouth. He had let the actor charm him into joining his half-baked scheme. In the days since he had taken flight, Tarleton had devoured the newspapers but found no mention of any attempt to abduct Lincoln. It was small consolation that Booth's failure was as grand as his own.

Bed linen rustled. Tarleton glanced toward the part-time singer, part-time prostitute who sheltered him. She was one of his female devotees, spread through cities across two continents, kept on a string for just such a purpose.

He watched her until he was convinced she was sleeping soundly. Then he dressed and left with the same suddenness that had marked his arrival two weeks earlier. No note, no farewell kiss, no token of appreciation or affection. Just a door slowly closing.

Minutes later, Tarleton was in Chatham Street, nudging through throngs of elated New Yorkers—young and old, working men and businessmen, ladies of society and ladies of the street—all smiling, cheering, singing patriotic songs. He pushed and shoved, and was pushed and shoved in return. It was too much, too big. He slipped onto a side street where the crowd thinned into smaller groups, equally jolly but not so suffocating.

A tall, trim army officer in full dress uniform walked toward him with champagne bottle in hand. "Raise a glass, good fellow!" his voice boomed in slurred words. "Tonight all of New York must drink. Drink, I say!" He held out the bottle and poured into a glass that didn't exist. Neither, for that matter, did the champagne.

"Thanks." Tarleton nodded as he took the make-believe flute.

"Don't mention it, General." The officer stopped, leaned forward, and peered closely. "Why, you're not General Dilworth."

As the officer wobbled before him, Tarleton studied his build and frame. Their height was almost identical. Their spare bodies seemed crafted by the same sculptor.

"No," Tarleton said, "I'm not the general. But I saw him down the street." He slipped an arm around the drunken man's shoulder. "Let me take you to him."

"Obliged. Much obliged, sir."

Tarleton hauled his new companion down the street. He noticed the insignia on the uniform—a colonel's eagle. "Right this way," he said soothingly. "The general will be glad you're here."

Inebriated emotions sent a quiver through the officer's voice. "That noble soul is celebrating more than any man in this town tonight."

"I'm sure he is," Tarleton said, turning toward an alley.

"And no one deserves it more than he does." The colonel pressed his nose against Tarleton's cheek. "After what this war did to that fine man, I say let him drink all night!"

"Hear, hear." Tarleton guided the man into the alley, darkened by brick buildings on each side.

"What those Rebels did at Antietam, why, it was—" The words were lost as the men were swallowed by shadows.

There was no sound of struggle, no anguished cry. Only a thin dark red stream flowing from the alley into a ditch.

In time, Tarleton stepped back into the street, dressed as comfortably in the colonel's uniform as if it had been tailored for him. Epaulettes sat squarely on his shoulders, the double row of gilded buttons elegantly tapered down to the large gilt belt buckle with a Union eagle spread across it, a sword swaying lazily from his black leather belt.

He put the colonel's kepi on his head and walked back into crowded Chatham Street. Two laughing soldiers lounged against the front door of a bakery. "You there!"

The privates snapped to attention. "Yes, sir!" they replied in unison.

"What's your unit?" Tarleton called as he approached them.

"Sixteenth Massachusetts Infantry, sir," one answered in a Boston accent.

"Fine regiment." Tarleton smiled. "Tell me, men. Where is the nearest train station?"

Washington City
Wednesday, April 5, 1865

Jack peered through a window into a dimly lit saloon. "How long has he been there?"

"I dunno." Sam hunkered down beside him. "I spotted him when I walked in with the stagehands from Maguire's. I slipped out the door and made myself scarce."

On the other side of the window, John Wilkes Booth tossed back a glass of dark liquor. "Good idea," Jack muttered. "He might remember you."

Sam nodded. "That's what I thought. And that's why I came for you."

Jack stood up. "I'm going in to have a beer." He looked at Sam. "Why don't you get one, too—somewhere else—while I take a look inside."

"See you later." Sam buried his hands in his pockets and walked off as Jack took another look through the window.

Booth was gulping down another drink. Jack scanned the small crowd of men gathered around the actor. Tarleton wasn't among them, nor was he anywhere else in sight. Jack entered the saloon and went straight to the bar.

He ordered a beer, positioning himself where he could keep an eye on Booth's table and an ear on his conversation. It wasn't difficult with the actor's voice booming through the room.

In a few minutes of eavesdropping, Jack learned Booth had recently spent time in Boston and Baltimore, had returned to Washington the night before, and was flat broke. He also learned

Booth had an astonishing capacity for drink. He was sucking down brandy as quickly as he could cajole his companions to buy it for him. Yet he remained poised, articulate, seemingly clear-headed.

Booth raised his empty glass. "We must send for reinforcements," he proclaimed. "Who's buying?"

There was an awkward, shuffling silence. "Come, come," he demanded. "Surely one of you gentlemen will assist a comrade in need." He looked from face to face of the men seated around him. "Graham? Simon? Ed?"

"What do you expect?" The one called Graham shrugged. "We're just bit players. Not leading men like you."

"Don't sell yourself short, my man." Booth leaned across the table. "I saw your Puck in Providence. You're a thespian of the first order."

"Save your flattery, Wilkes. It won't earn you a drink." The small crowd joined Graham's laughter.

"Earn it, you say?" Booth's eyes lit up. "If that's what it takes, then I shall earn it."

"How?"

"A friendly wager."

Graham's eyebrows drew together. "What sort of wager?"

"I can recite any work of the Bard that you choose. If I win, you supply me with a libation."

"And if you lose?"

Booth let out a derisive laugh. "I'll not only buy you all a drink, I'll go hang myself in the Capitol dome!"

Graham held a whispered consultation with the other two men at the table. Then he held out his hand. "It's a bet."

They shook on it. "Pick a title. Simon, call out the act, and Ed, you shall select the scene. Agreed?" Three heads nodded in unison.

"How about something from *King John*?" Graham offered.

"Act three," the small man named Simon added.

They turned to their companion. Ed stared ahead in drunken silence. Simon nudged him. "Scene four," he murmured at last.

Booth rose, grasped his lapel with one hand, and raised the other. "Gentlemen, I give you *King John*, act three, scene four."

Jack watched with growing wonder as a transformation came over Booth. His eyes focused on something far, far away. His jaw jutted out defiantly. His voice, already strong, became fuller and richer, resounding through the room.

"A sceptre snatch'd with an unruly hand
Must be as boisterously maintain'd as gain'd;
And he that stands upon a slippery place
Makes nice of no vile hold to stay him up."

Booth finished his recitation with a deep bow. Applause erupted from the men clustered around the table. A triumphant smile spread across his face. "Satisfied, Graham?"

"Damn you, Wilkes." He jammed his hand in his pocket and pulled out a handful of coins, dropping them on the table. "That's all I've got. You've cleaned me out."

Booth scooped up the money. The men cheered and whistled as the bartender brought the actor another drink. Booth hoisted it above his head, bowed to the crowd, and downed the brandy in a single swallow.

"Forgive me, friends, but I must take my leave." He put the glass on the table and picked up a pair of gray gloves. "I thank you for your hospitality."

He pulled on his gloves, lifted a hat from the back of a chair, and placed it on his head. With a jaunty wave, he started toward the door. Then he paused and turned back to the crowd. "Let me leave you with this, from *Henry the Sixth, Part Two,* act two." His gaze fell upon Ed. "Scene four.

> "*'Tis not my speeches that you do dislike,*
> *But 'tis my presence that doth trouble ye.*
> *Rancor will out.*"

Booth bowed grandly, then made his exit. Jack took a last swig of his beer, dropped a nickel on the bar, and followed the actor into the night.

Thursday, April 6, 1865

It had been weeks since Kate called on Lucy Hale. With her force of operatives dwindling rapidly, she decided to see if the former senator's daughter might offer some helpful gossip. Crinoline rustled against the polished marble floor as she walked across the lobby of the National Hotel.

When she reached the main stairway, a strong hand grabbed her wrist. "Good afternoon, Mrs. St. Claire." The Union major who had been such a bother the previous month spoke in low tones. "Will you kindly step this way?" He gestured to the far end of the lobby where a squad of armed soldiers waited.

"Really, Major Wingate." Kate sniffed. "Intruding on a widow's home—twice—was bad enough."

Wingate tugged at her wrist. "This way, please."

"Where are you taking me?"

"Someplace where we can speak in private."

Kate looked around the lobby. People were stopping and staring. "What is it you wish to discuss?"

Wingate tightened his grip. "We can have the discussion here." His voice dropped to a whisper. "Or someplace much less comfortable. You decide."

Kate's eyes strayed to the seven soldiers arrayed in the lobby. She shook free from Wingate's grasp. "Very well, sir. I am at your disposal."

Wingate directed her to a small business office. The soldiers took up station as he closed the door. He pulled a chair away from the wall and held it out for her.

"I prefer to stand," she said curtly.

"I don't." Wingate settled into an identical chair across a plain wooden table. "Sit."

Kate sat. She fixed him with a hard stare.

"A lot has changed since our last conversation."

She didn't reply.

"Your capital has gone up in smoke," Wingate continued.

"I read the papers, Major," she said evenly. "I believe London is safely out of harm's way."

Wingate's black eyes flashed angrily. "You can drop the pretense, Mrs. St. Claire. We both know where your loyalties lie. Queen Victoria is eager to patch things up with her American cousins. I'm not sure you'd find yourself welcome back in Canada." Wingate pulled a cigar from his pocket and stuck it in his mouth. "Of course, you could stay here." He lit the cigar and blew a thick cloud of smoke. "If you tell me where I can find John Surratt."

Kate sighed wearily. "We have been down this road before."

"Then here's a new avenue." Wingate jabbed the air with his cigar. "Why did Surratt try to kill Secretary of State Seward last weekend?"

Kate's jaw dropped in astonishment. All of Washington was talking about the terrible injuries Seward had suffered when his carriage overturned on a country road. Doctors initially thought they would be fatal. But he had survived and was convalescing in his town house across from the White House.

"Carriage horses can be such skittish animals." Wingate rolled the cigar between his fingers. "They jump at the slightest thing—a rabbit darting across their path, an unexpected gust of wind." He puffed a cloud of smoke into the small room. "Or a gunshot."

Kate waved her hand in front of her face. "Must you smoke that infernal thing in my presence?"

Wingate went to the window and raised it a crack. "Horses are very queer animals," he continued. "One minute they're trotting happily down a peaceful lane. Then . . ." He snapped his fingers. "They bolt like the hounds of hell. Puts a damper on a Sunday ride in the country."

Kate smirked. "If you are suggesting that I was skulking around a country road on Sunday . . ."

"Oh, it wasn't you." Wingate leaned back against the windowsill. "It was John Surratt."

"Then you should be talking to him."

"I've had it with you, lady!" Wingate's face flushed. "If you don't tell me what you know, I'll toss you in prison and keep you there till the year 1900."

"I'm telling you the simple truth," Kate replied evenly. "I knew nothing of Secretary Seward's mishap until I read the newspapers." She lifted her chin defiantly. "And I have no idea where John Surratt is."

Wingate drew furiously on his cigar, his eyes welded to hers. "I know."

Kate cocked her head to one side. "Then why are you harangu-ing me?"

"Because you know Surratt." He held up a hand to cut off her protest. "And I know Surratt is plotting an attack on the presi-dent. He has already tried once."

Kate sat in stunned silence as the news sank in. The Federal army had apparently picked up the same scent she and Jack had been following for weeks. What else did this major know? "Are you certain?"

"There was an attempt to intercept the president's carriage on a deserted road last month." Wingate examined the glowing tip of his cigar. "So when a member of the cabinet is nearly killed be-cause his carriage overturns on another deserted road, I see a pat-tern."

"You have proof Surratt was involved in the attempt on the president?"

"Let's just say," he said with a hint of a smile, "I know enough to put John Surratt's neck in a noose." His expression sobered. "If I can't produce Surratt, I'll have to settle for one of his asso-ciates."

Kate felt as though the jaws of a giant steel trap were closing on her. If she didn't turn in Surratt, she would end up in prison for a crime that neither of them had committed.

But she couldn't turn in Surratt.

She didn't have him.

She groped for something she could give Wingate to get him off her back. "There are two men who might have something to do with this business. I would be willing to give you their names, if you do something for me."

"You're in no position to bargain, Mrs. St. Claire."

"I'm not seeking a bargain. Believe it or not, in this matter we share a common interest."

"What might that be?"

"Protecting Abraham Lincoln's life."

Silence hung between them as thick as the cigar smoke that cloaked them. Wingate's face remained impassive, but Kate could see he was weighing her words carefully. At last, he said, "Tell me about these men."

"If I do, I want you to keep me posted on what you learn about them."

Wingate clenched his jaw. "I'll offer you a better deal, Mrs. St. Claire. Tell me what you know and you won't spend tonight in prison."

Kate settled back in the hard wooden chair and clasped her hands in her lap. "They've been cooking up something with Surratt for weeks. They claim they're involved in oil speculations, but that's just—" She waved her hand daintily in front of her face. "A smoke screen."

"Who are they?" Wingate demanded.

"One is a well-known actor by the name of—"

"John Wilkes Booth."

"That's right. He's known Surratt for some time. He has even visited him at—"

"The Surratt boardinghouse." Wingate gestured impatiently. "Go on."

Kate grudgingly admitted the major was quite good at his job. "Whatever Booth and Surratt have been up to, they aren't the real threat."

"Then who is?"

"A man who joined their circle about a month ago. He claims

to be a mercantile trader from Chicago. In truth, he's a hired killer. His name is Basil Tarleton."

Wingate shook his head. "Never heard of him."

Kate straightened her back and fixed him with a determined glare. "The first time you and I met, you claimed to know about a theater outing I attended with Surratt."

"So?"

"One of the other men in the party was tall and slender, with blond hair and blue eyes."

"He was your escort that night."

Kate leaned forward. "That was Basil Tarleton."

Wingate shifted the cigar from one side of his mouth to the other. "If he's a hired killer, who hired him? And what's he doing in Washington?"

"Sit down and I'll tell you everything I know." She motioned Wingate toward his chair. "And put out that foul cigar."

He pulled the cigar from his mouth and regarded it intently. Then he tossed it out the window.

Saturday, April 8, 1865

Tarleton paused before a shop window and studied his reflection. He had to admit he cut a fine figure. The dark blue uniform complemented his fair complexion.

Why, he asked himself, have I never thought of disguising myself as a military officer before? He took one last look and resolved to bury the Reverend Israel Harris forever.

Tarleton meandered through midday crowds, picking his way around people bustling in and out of stores, lounging outside saloons, or gathering to chat under the sunny sky. Since his return to Washington, he had stalked these streets, watching, listening, poised to pick up the trail he had abandoned weeks before.

The lethargy that had held him captive in New York melted like the last of the winter snow. There was firmness in his step and a sense of purpose in his bearing.

A stray line of overheard conversation sent him hurrying toward the massive Navy Yard that sprawled along the Anacostia River. He passed bored-looking sentries who didn't bother acknowledging his uniform. A shrieking whistle drew him to a wharf. A steamboat with the name *River Queen* painted across its paddlewheel was inching to a halt. Soldiers held back the crowd gathering at the landing.

Tarleton approached a private leaning against his musket. "What's going on?"

The young man snapped to attention. "The Old Man's coming home, sir."

"Which old man?"

"President Lincoln, sir."

Tarleton's heart beat faster. He felt in his breast pocket for his small pistol and gave it a reassuring pat.

Sailors on the deck of the riverboat lashed ropes to thick wooden posts as the steamer creaked to a stop. Tarleton studied the blue coats all around him. Could he chance shooting Lincoln here? He might succeed in killing his target, but he would never get away.

The presidential party emerged onto the deck and the crowd sent up a rousing cheer. The president gave a tired smile as he made his way down the gangplank. The crowd ignored the man in a green vest following Lincoln. Tarleton did not.

It was Robert Standiford, the Confederate congressman who had set the assassin on his task.

Standiford was speaking with Lincoln. The president took the Rebel legislator's hand in his giant paw and gave it a weary shake. Then an army officer led Lincoln to a waiting carriage. People cheered one last time as the president rode away.

Tarleton strode through the thinning crowd and tapped Standiford's shoulder.

The congressman glanced his way. "Something I can do for you, Colonel?"

Tarleton said nothing. Standiford peered into the assassin's face. His features went pale. His mouth opened, closed, then opened again. "I suppose I shouldn't be surprised to find you here."

"Well, I'm certainly surprised to find you here." Tarleton nodded toward the riverboat. "How did you—"

"We served together in Congress twenty years ago. He sent for me while he was in Richmond. He wants me to use my influence to help him 'heal the wounds of war.'" Standiford spat on the ground.

"I have plans of my own. I'm leaving this godforsaken country. I asked Lincoln for permission to travel to Washington. So he offered me a ride." A smile creased the congressman's cheeks. "Little does he know he's abetting my escape."

Standiford paused to let a squad of sailors push wheelbarrows filled with coal past them. "I expected to hear from you long before now," he said in a low voice.

"There have been . . . complications," Tarleton responded.

"Spare me your excuses." Standiford pointed at the road the president's carriage had just traveled. "You see how easy it is to reach the man. I could have strangled him myself if I'd—"

"But you didn't." Tarleton's tone was frosty. "Because you couldn't. You don't have it in you. That's why you need me."

The two stared at each other. "I don't know what more we have to talk about," Standiford grumbled. "It's finished."

"No it isn't. You hired me to do a job. I intend to do it."

"The war is over."

"That changes nothing."

"It does for me," Standiford insisted.

Tarleton's blue eyes grew colder. "We have a deal."

"We *had* a deal," Standiford corrected.

Tarleton's nostrils flared. "Twenty thousand dollars. That's what you promised me. That's what I expect to collect. By week's end. Payment in full."

Standiford swallowed hard. "I haven't got it."

"Then get it. I'll live up to my part of our bargain. You'd better live up to yours."

Standiford's chin dropped. "I can't pay you."

"You'll pay," Tarleton said. "One way or another, you'll pay."

Sunday, April 9, 1865

"Met a man last night." Rufus swallowed a mouthful of cold fried chicken. "Wants to meet you real bad."

"Who is he?" Kate handed Rufus a linen napkin from the picnic hamper she had carried to the little room where he boarded.

He wiped his mouth and fingers. "I don't rightly know."

She opened the hamper and began repacking it. "You must have some inkling."

He shook his head. "He came right out and asked if I was Rufus Youngblood."

Kate froze. "He knew your name?"

"Gets better. He says he wants me to find a woman. I tell him Washington is full of whores. He tells me that isn't the kind of woman he's looking for. Says he's after one who goes by the name George Webb."

Kate steadied herself against the bed.

"Then," Rufus continued, "he says, 'That's a mighty strange name for a pretty redheaded woman.' " He shook his head. "I tell you, Kate, it made the hair stand up on the back of my neck."

"Who is he?" Kate asked again.

"Wouldn't give a name, not even a phony one. Says he just came up from Richmond. Says he heard you could help him. Wants to talk with you as soon as possible."

"What did you tell him?"

Rufus shrugged. "I said you'd meet him at the Crown Oak Tavern at three o'clock."

Kate pressed her lips together. How could a stranger know so much about her? "I'd better be there, hadn't I?" She looked at Rufus, but he refused to meet her eyes.

"There's something else." He licked his lips and spoke in a low, even tone. "This is the last straw, Kate. I been with you nigh onto four years now. But this cuts it. Some stranger blows into town tossing around my name and yours . . ." He raised his eyes and trained them on her. "Time to get out while the getting's good."

The words hit Kate like a mule's kick. She fought to keep her breathing steady as she sat down heavily on the bed. "You're leaving?"

His eyes dropped again. "I reckon I am."

"Where will you go?"

Rufus squirmed. "West. Always wanted to see Texas. There hasn't been much war out there. No one will know me."

Kate tried to swallow. The lump in her throat wouldn't budge. Her voice came out thin and cracked. "When?"

"Tonight."

She sniffed back a tear. "And you're just telling me now?"

"Just made up my mind." He laid his hand on hers. "You could come with me."

She shook her head. "I have a job to do."

"War's over, Kate."

"General Lee is still in the field." Kate rubbed her eyes. "So long as there's a fight, I'll be in it." She rose. "Will you be at the Crown Oak this afternoon?"

" 'Course I will." Rufus stood up.

"Jack should be there, too."

"I'll round him up." His warm gray eyes peered deeply into hers. He opened his brawny arms and she flung herself into them. She left tearstains all over his massive shoulder. He didn't seem to mind.

Three hours later, the door of the Crown Oak Tavern opened, admitting a spear of daylight. It disappeared abruptly when the door closed. Kate sat at her usual table in the back corner watching a figure move through the shadows.

She forced a smile, knowing it was neither sincere nor effective. "Sit down, Jack." He took a seat beside her. Kate fought the urge to inch away. "Nice of you to come on such short notice."

"Didn't have anything better to do. Except look for a missing killer." He offered his own feeble smile.

He looks like a little boy, she thought as she studied his disordered dark hair, the simple honesty in his brown eyes, the strong jaw of a good man. "Did Rufus tell you what this is all about?"

"As much as he ever explains anything."

"Then you know as much as we do." Kate looked down at the wooden table, studying the rings left by countless damp glasses. The silence between them was uneasy.

She was about to speak, was forming the words to say she was sorry, when daylight again stabbed through the room. She sat up in her chair. "Our guest is here."

An elegant middle-aged man emerged from the smoky haze. He nodded to Kate. "George Webb, I presume?"

"And whom do I have the pleasure of addressing?" She extended her hand, which he took with polished refinement.

"A friend." He took a chair and raised an inquisitive eyebrow at Jack. "And this would be . . ."

"Another friend," Kate replied.

"Very well, Mrs. St. Claire. Or would you rather I call you Mr. Webb?"

Kate swallowed a mouthful of air, trying to keep her rattled nerves under control. "You may call me whatever you wish. How is it you came to ask for me?"

Rufus appeared and placed three glasses of cherry cordial on the table, then was gone.

"I just came from Richmond," the man explained.

"A difficult journey at the moment," she countered.

"Not if you know the right people. Which reminds me." He fixed a broad smile to his face. "Matt Johnson sends his kind regards." He picked up a cordial. "That should settle my bona fides." He took a sip that seemed almost delicate.

Kate felt her patience leaking away. "Who are you?"

"Who I am is unimportant. What I am—that's another matter. I'm a loyal citizen of the Confederacy and a fugitive. I'm seeking assistance."

Kate fired a glance at Jack. He sat expressionless, eyes fixed on the stranger. "What sort of assistance?" she asked.

"I must travel to Montreal immediately." His smile curled into a smirk. "I believe you have some acquaintance with that city."

Kate absently ran a finger up and down her cordial glass. "Getting our people into Canada is not my expertise. It can be done, but it will take time."

"That's a commodity I do not have, I'm afraid. I must leave today, if possible."

Kate shook her head. "It isn't. It will take a few days, at the very least, to make the arrangements."

The man tapped his forefinger against the table. "I suppose I can find a way to pass a few days." He rose to his feet. "A grateful heart thanks you."

"Where can we find you?" Kate asked.

He winked. "I'll find you." He disappeared into the tavern, the only evidence of his passing a lance of daylight as he exited.

Rufus slid into the seat he had vacated. "What the hell was that all about?"

"I wish I knew." Kate's shoulders sagged. "What do you think, Jack?" He stared into empty space. "Jack?"

"The man has gall." He blinked his eyes rapidly. "Do you know who that was?"

She took a big sip of cordial. "Whoever he is, he thoroughly scares me."

"That was Congressman Robert Standiford," Jack said gravely.

Kate's eyes grew wide. "The man who hired Tarleton?"

"The same. I recognized him the moment he sat down. We were wrong about Tarleton," he said through clenched teeth. "He hasn't gone away. Lincoln is in more danger than ever."

Nine

THE CURTAIN RISES

Monday, April 10, 1865

Tarleton pounded on a weather-beaten door. He had invested two days in finding this run-down one-room house a few blocks from Ford's Theatre. He banged again.

"Go away," a woman called groggily.

Tarleton reared back and kicked. The door crashed open in a hail of splinters.

The woman sat up in a large bed that occupied most of the room, clutching a dingy white sheet against her chest. Her brown hair stood at all angles. "Who are you?" She cowered against the headboard as Tarleton marched toward her. "What do you want?"

"Shut up and get dressed."

"I'm calling the police."

Tarleton fixed his fiercest gaze on her. "Get dressed."

She scrambled from the bed and retrieved her clothing.

Tarleton nodded at the inert figure still lying under the sheet. "Is he drunk or dead?"

"Dr-drunk," she stuttered. "He's done nothing but drink for three days straight." The woman pulled on a skirt and blouse, fingers flying so quickly she missed every third button. When she was fully, if wildly, clothed she headed to the door.

Tarleton grabbed her arm. "Not a word to anyone. Not to the police, not to the people at Ford's, not to your best friend."

Her head gave the slightest bob.

"Go. Now."

Her tiny feet dashed out the shattered doorway.

Tarleton grabbed a porcelain pitcher from a washbasin and emptied it onto the patch of thick black hair poking out of a ragged quilt.

"Damnation!" John Wilkes Booth roared. "Why the hell did you do that?"

"Wake up."

First one eyelid peeled open, then the other. Booth blinked twice. "Basil?"

Water trickled down Booth's neck, branching across his muscled shoulders. The actor looked around. "Where's—"

"Your whore?"

"Now see here," Booth sputtered, pushing himself upright. "What gives you the right to barge in this way?"

"This does." Tarleton produced a newspaper from under his arm and threw it in Booth's face. The actor scowled at it.

GREAT DAY OF REJOICING!

WAR FINALLY OVER!

LEE SURRENDERS!

VICTORY FOR OUR GLORIOUS UNION!

The paper slid from Booth's fingers to the floor. "So it's over."

"The war, yes." Tarleton leaned over the bed. "But not our mission."

Booth's face lit up. "You're right! Now is the perfect time to strike. We can snatch the Ape and—"

"Not snatch," Tarleton corrected. "Slay."

Booth took a moment to digest the word. "Slay," he repeated. "I'll reassemble my men and—"

Tarleton cut him off. "*My* men."

Booth's ebony eyes shone like angry coals, met by the icy blue of Tarleton's stare. They locked in a silent battle of wills, each determined to break down the other.

Booth finally looked away. "*Your* men."

Tarleton smiled, not in victory, but in reconciliation. "As far as the men know, it's still your operation, Wilkes," he said in a softer voice. "Only my role has changed, to that of a strategist."

The light returned to Booth's eyes. "Yes. Strategist. That's a splendid idea."

"Put on your trousers," Tarleton said. "There's work to do."

"I'm getting mighty sick of lugging props and scenery around," Sam sighed.

Jack grunted in sympathy as they trudged to their shared room at the Liberty House. The sun was dipping low. With news of Lee's surrender spreading through the city, they knew a celebration was coming in which neither could share.

"Why don't you turn in early tonight?" Jack suggested. "The rest would do you good."

Sam shook his head. "I can't get any rest, Jack. I lie awake thinking about what happened to Olivia. Then I think about Felix. Then I think about Tarleton out there someplace, running free with blood on his hands. How can a fellow rest with all that going through his head?"

"Would you like to tend to an errand for me? It'll take your mind off your troubles."

Sam shrugged. "Why not? I've got nothing else to do."

"It's a little dangerous."

Sam's face brightened. "Now you're talking!"

"You mentioned Felix." Jack dropped his voice to a whisper. "I feel bad for what happened to him."

Sam's face tightened. "I do, too."

"He said he had a wife and family. I'd like you to take this to them." Jack handed him twenty dollars. "That should see them for a while."

Sam looked up. "That's the last of your beer-delivery money, ain't it?"

"Never mind where it came from. Will you take it?

"Sure. What was Felix's last name?"

Jack's face went blank. "You know, I don't recall him ever mentioning one."

"Where did he live?"

"Over in Murder Bay."

Sam's mouth fell open. "You want me to go there? With night coming on?"

"I told you it was dangerous," Jack said blandly.

Sam looked at the wad of currency in his fist. "I'll do it . . . for Felix."

Jack patted him on the back. "Good man. Just ask if anyone knows a Felix who worked for National Lager. Sooner or later someone will point you in the right direction."

Sam bent down and put the money in his shoe. He adjusted his foot to accommodate the bills, then grinned. "This is gonna be fun."

Jack tried to suppress a smile. "Not too much fun, you hear? Be sure to come right back when you're done. I don't want to stay up all night worrying about you."

"I'll be home before your head hits the pillow." Sam started off down the street, whistling "The Rose of Alabama."

"That's a pretty song." A woman's voice came from the shadows of an alley.

Jack spun around. "Kate."

"I suppose I could say something like 'we need to talk,' but that would be very predictable, wouldn't it? Me—predictable? Just the idea!" She laughed as she stepped from the shadows. "Why don't you do the gallant thing and invite me to your room?"

Jack stood for a moment, uncertain. She seemed to be reaching out to him. Or was he only hoping she was? He decided to move cautiously. "Be my guest." He gestured.

They said nothing more until they reached Jack's room. He sat on the foot of the bed. Kate sat beside him.

"I've missed you," she began.

He stared at the floor. "We've met almost every day."

"I've missed *you.*"

Jack looked into her eyes, eyes that showed the openness of her soul. "I've missed you, too."

She touched his forearm. "You really hurt me, you know."

His head snapped back in surprise. "*I* hurt *you?*"

"When you questioned my commitment to your mission. You all but accused me of trying to sabotage it."

Jack's throat tightened. "What was I supposed to think? I was trying to stop Tarleton, and all the while you were gallivanting around town with him."

Kate's eyebrows climbed high on her forehead. "What are you talking about?"

He took a deep breath to regain his composure. Then he told her what Felix had seen—her trip to the theater with Tarleton and Booth, her betrayal of his mission, the pain that cut through his heart as his trust in her was shattered.

Through the long recitation, she stayed silent. Her hand rested lightly on his arm. At last, he covered it with his own. "How do we get over that, Kate?"

She squeezed his hand. "Let's begin with the truth. The only time I ever saw Tarleton was the night we went to Ford's Theatre. Lucy Hale set it up. I had no idea he would be there." She stroked his unruly brown hair. "Can you believe that?"

Relief flooded through Jack's veins. He felt a heavy burden lift from his heart. "I want to."

"Well, that's a start." She placed her hand on the back of his neck and drew his head to hers. "I love you, Jack Tanner."

He took her in his arms and kissed her. Their embrace grew more passionate and within moments their bodies were locked, their flesh guiding them to a place where all was forgiven. They were finally, once again, one.

They lay in each other's arms for a long time afterward. Her cheek rested against his chest. "Have you given any thought to what you'll do when this is over?"

He toyed with a stray curl of auburn hair. "Go home, I reckon."

"Home." She let out a long breath that tickled his ribs. "I'm not sure I know where that is anymore."

"I know a nice little farm in the Piedmont you might like."

Kate rolled her head to look up into his face. "Are you sure it's still there?"

"The land's still there." Jack pecked her forehead. "The Yankees can't take that away."

"Don't be so sure."

He thought that over for a moment. "I reckon I'll just have to find some other field to plow."

"Rufus said he was going west." Her finger traced the outline of his lips. "I like the sound of that."

He kissed her fingertip. "West it is, then."

Kate pushed herself up. "Why don't we go now?"

"What?"

Her eyes lit up. "We can leave tonight. We'll strike out for the frontier, see what kind of life we can make for ourselves." She reached for the undergarment she'd flung aside. "I'll run back to my house and grab a few things. We can meet at the depot. There's a midnight train to St. Louis." She began wriggling into her clothes.

He grasped her arm. "I can't. I have a job to finish."

"But—"

"No 'buts,' Kate. I won't ride off and leave Tarleton on the loose." He pressed his lips together so firmly the blood drained out of them. "Not after what he did to Felix."

Emotions chased each other across Kate's face—exasperation, puzzlement, defiance, and finally determination. "If I can't talk you out of it," she said at last, "then I'd better do everything I can to help you. The sooner we wrap this up, the sooner we can put this city behind us."

He grabbed the silky fabric of her undergarment and pulled her to him. "First thing in the morning, you round up all your agents and put them on Tarleton's trail."

Kate shook her head. "There aren't enough of them left. I've been losing men every day since Lee's surrender."

Jack cradled her in the crook of his elbow. "Then we'll just have to do it ourselves."

"Maybe not." Kate tilted her head, her eyes seeking out his. "There's someone else who might be willing to help us."

"Who?"

"The Yankees." Before he could respond, she continued. "They have resources. We don't. If we tell them about Tarleton, if we let them know Standiford is in town, if we lay it all out for them, they'll surely see the danger."

Jack had been fighting the Yankees for so long, he had trouble imagining them as allies. But he couldn't deny Kate's idea made sense. "Just how would we bring the Yankees in on this?"

She gave a sly smile. "I happen to know a certain Federal officer. He'd be a good place to start."

Monday, April 10, 1865
Dusk

Tarleton walked across Pennsylvania Avenue and headed south. The broad boulevard stretching from Capitol Hill to the White House separated more than branches of government. It was also the line between the socially acceptable and the unacceptable. At that moment Tarleton felt the need to indulge in the diversions the unacceptable had to offer.

The neighborhoods grew poorer and filthier until he stepped into the heart of what proper Washington disdainfully called Murder Bay, seventy acres of vulgarity sprawling almost within view of the White House. An occasional run-down building rose up among a forest of shanties and lean-tos, erected by the newly freed blacks who had flooded the city. Squalid wooden shacks barely big enough for two people housed two families, or three.

Bounding Murder Bay on the south, the long-abandoned Washington Canal served as the dumping place of choice for chamber pots and privies, for garbage and trash, even dead cats, dogs, chickens, and hogs. Its pervasive stench seemed permanently suspended over the slum.

Tarleton tried to ignore the miserable conditions as he passed through. Babies cried, voices hummed in soft chatter, and old black men staggered aimlessly through the dirt streets. Most of the windowless shanties didn't even have fireplaces. Small spaces barely three feet wide created a maze of passageways between the flimsy structures.

A few old buildings housed saloons and brothels and gambling dens. In a specific building at the end of a specific street, there was a specific dark Caribbean woman Tarleton wanted.

People were shadowy forms in the failing light. He moved among them, one of the very few white people on the streets, unbothered because of the army uniform he wore. He kept his head down to avoid attracting attention. Rounding a corner, he walked directly into another person.

"Excuse me." A white teenager drew back from him. "I didn't see you coming."

Tarleton looked at the lean, blond-headed figure. In the fading sunlight, he faintly made out a face. The boy looked at him, too, staring into his eyes, glancing at his uniform.

Tarleton brushed past. He took three steps, then he remembered—the Maguire's Theatre hallway, the orchestra pit at Ford's Theatre, the National Hotel lobby. It was the same lanky teenager he had seen each time.

Tarleton spun around. The boy's eyes widened in recognition. He ran off. Tarleton hurried after him.

The boy was nimble, easily swinging out of the way of dogs, children, an old woman pushing a rag cart through the gathering darkness, who cursed him for almost knocking her down. Tarleton followed and was cursed, as well.

The boy disappeared between two shanties. Tarleton heard a stumble, followed by the pained wail of a cat. The boy emerged onto a street and melted into the shadows of buildings. Tarleton lost sight of him. He stopped and gasped at the foul air. His heart was racing, his side aching. He leaned against a wall and felt curls of chipping paint press into his back. He berated himself for letting the boy get away.

A slight sound, something completely out of place, seized his attention. He held his breath and tried to figure out what it was. He heard it again. A barely audible creak. He tilted an ear. It was directly overhead.

Tarleton looked up. The building, dimly outlined against the rapidly darkening sky, was a decaying church. He heard another creak, this time fainter. Something was moving toward the steeple.

Creeping as lightly as he could, Tarleton felt along the wall to the door, slowly pushed it open, and slipped inside. His hands followed the wall, his feet sliding noiselessly across the floor. He found the stairway and started up with a forceful step, deliberately stomping loudly as he climbed. No need to be secretive now. There was only one way into the steeple, and only one way out. He wanted the boy to know he was coming.

The stairway turned, then turned again. Tarleton's thudding steps carried him higher, closer to his prey. One last turn, then he saw stars shining through the open belfry. As he rose into it, something smashed on top of his head. Tarleton gripped the handrail, steadying himself. The boy was on him, striking him savagely.

Tarleton shoved hard with both hands. The boy went flying back, his head crashing against a thick support beam. Tarleton hurried up the last steps and bent down to examine the motionless boy. It was too dark to see clearly, so he touched the face. There was no blood. He pressed his hand against the boy's chest. There was a heartbeat. The boy was alive, but unconscious.

Tarleton looked around. He made out a huge bell framed against the starlight. He groped around until he located the thick rope he knew had to be there. He tied it around the boy's neck and heaved him upright.

Tarleton pushed. The boy fell, disappearing into the space beneath the bell. The rope jerked taut and the bell lurched, sending a heavy *bong* pealing through the darkness. The bell swung back. The rope slapped wildly. Tarleton peered into the opening. He couldn't see the boy, but heard him flailing, struggling, and gasping for breath. The bell rang again. Tarleton covered his ears and backed away.

He watched the bell swing rhythmically, chiming again and again. The gyrations of the rope slowed until at last it hung straight down. He looked out the belfry to the street below. Dozens of people were converging on the church, eyes raised toward the tolling bell. He raced down the stairs, reaching the front door before anyone came inside.

"What's going on?" a heavyset black man demanded, echoed instantly by others gathering in front of the church.

Tarleton raised both hands. "Good people, the Day of Jubilee has come. The war is over! General Lee has surrendered!"

Wild cheers broke out. People clapped their hands, lifted them to heaven in praise. Some locked arms and danced.

"We're ringing the bell to let you know you are forever free! Now, go celebrate with your families!"

The crowd did as ordered, heading back to their huts and shanties, telling the good news to others who rushed up. Within minutes, singing and banjo music filled the air.

When the street was deserted, he returned to the church. The bell was tolling less frequently, less forcefully, as he climbed the stairs to attend to one last detail.

Tuesday, April 11, 1865
Morning

Peace may have returned to the nation, but it didn't look that way inside the War Department. Blue uniforms hurried up and down its halls as if Rebel forces had just appeared across the Potomac.

Jack led Kate into an office jammed full of desks and workers.

He hung back at the door, but she bustled through the room as if she belonged there. Heads swiveled in her wake. "Major Wingate!" she called.

Wingate looked up. A bemused grin slowly lifted the bristles of his short black beard. They exchanged greetings in voices so low Jack couldn't catch the words. The major accompanied Kate to the door. She introduced him to Jack.

"Mrs. St. Claire says we have something to talk about," Wingate said as he directed them to a small room across the hall. "We won't be disturbed here." Inside, a long wooden table was covered with maps. More were pinned to the walls. "I'll have to ask you not to touch anything." A twinkle lit up his dark eyes. "Unless you want to show me where the last Rebel armies are hiding."

"Just the idea!" Kate laughed brightly. She and Jack sat on one side of the table, Wingate on the other, his elbows propped on a map of North Carolina.

"What brings you here, of all places?"

"We have information," Kate began, "concerning the threat to President Lincoln I told you about."

"I'm listening." Wingate leaned back in his chair as Kate recounted their meeting with Robert Standiford, explaining how he had set his deadly scheme in motion and sought their help to escape Washington.

Skepticism was etched on Wingate's face. "Hundreds of ex-Rebels are roaming the streets now. I passed three gray uniforms this morning."

"How many of them served in the Confederate Congress?" Jack countered.

"Point taken," Wingate shot back. "But I can't say as I blame him for fleeing to Canada. If I were in his shoes I'd be running as fast as they could carry me."

Kate stared intently at the ceiling. Jack and Wingate stared at her, then looked up to see what might be drawing her attention. "Of course!" Her eyes filled with excitement. "If Lincoln is killed there will be a massive manhunt for whoever is responsible. Standiford wants us to whisk him away before the Federal authorities can connect him to the murder."

"With all due respect," Wingate said softly, "that's a bit far-fetched."

Kate's back stiffened. "For four years, Confederate agents regularly moved from Montreal to Richmond. And you never caught one. Standiford could be safely in Montreal by week's end and you wouldn't even know he'd left town."

"How would a law-abiding subject of the British crown know about that?"

"That's not important."

"It is to me." Wingate spoke through gritted teeth. "It's my duty to find people who smuggle Rebels out of the country."

"I know all about duty," Jack interjected. "I also know it can blind you to reality."

Wingate's eyes darted to Jack. "You're a soldier, aren't you?"

"Richmond Provost Marshal's Office."

Wingate raked his fingernails through his beard. "So you've seen this Standiford character close up."

Jack shrugged. "Enough to know who he is. Enough to have seen his handiwork."

"What's that supposed to mean?"

Jack looked toward Kate. She gave a small nod. He launched into the story from the beginning—from Harry Kincaid to his confrontation with Tarleton and finding Felix's body.

"That's quite a tale," Wingate said. "If it's true."

"For God's sake!" Jack exploded. "What do I gain by lying? The war is over. You won. We've admitted enough for you to toss us into Old Capitol Prison. The president, your president, could be killed any moment. What more do you want?"

"Relax. I happen to believe you." Wingate spread his palms on the map before him. "I have information, too, and it fits with what you've told me. An incident some weeks back convinced me your old friend John Surratt is up to no good and Booth is in it up to his neck. They've been consorting with this Tarleton, so he's mixed up in it, too." He ran a hand through his hair. "Standiford's arrival surely signals bad news."

Jack was surprised at the sudden change in the Yankee major. He tried to keep it from showing on his face. His eyes shifted toward Kate. She sat still, betraying no emotion.

"For the record," Wingate continued, "I have no plans to toss either of you into Old Capitol or any other prison. I know things that can help you. You know things that can help me. If we work together, we have a better chance of protecting President Lincoln."

Wingate leaned against the table, crunching the map beneath his arms. "Let me be frank. I don't know where any of these men are. Do you?"

"Booth has a room at the National Hotel," Kate began, "but he's hardly ever there. As for Standiford, he kept his cards close to his vest. Wouldn't tell us where he's staying."

"Then," Wingate grumbled, "we'll have to hope for a lucky break. I know how to find you. And you obviously know how to find me. Next time you want to get in touch, send a message. Not everyone in this building would look kindly on two Confederates roaming the War Department."

Tuesday, April 11, 1865
Evening

Throngs of people celebrating the Union victory clogged Pennsylvania Avenue. Tarleton and Booth shouldered their way through the crowd. They spotted Davey Herold, standing with Lewis Paine in front of Willard's Hotel.

"Half of Washington is here," Herold bubbled as Booth and Tarleton joined them.

"The other half hasn't sobered up yet," Booth groused. "Let's go."

The carnival atmosphere intensified as they approached the White House gates. A brass band was playing. "The Battle Hymn of the Republic" floated on the evening breeze. "Oh, Lord. That dreadful song," Booth groaned.

Torches and lanterns carried by the crowd turned the Executive Mansion's walls a soft yellow. It looked like a gigantic firefly in the dark spring night. People laughed and sang as they jockeyed for position near the front.

"Look at them," Booth whispered to Tarleton. "I wouldn't be surprised to see Mrs. Abe out here selling lemonade."

A single word floated above the noise, passing through the crowd. "Look!"

A butler appeared at a window in the portico, shouting, "The President of the United States!"

The crowd roared a cheer so deafening Herold put his hands over his ears. Lincoln's tall, thin frame filled the window. The cheering grew even louder.

Booth spat in front of his feet.

Torchlight bathed Lincoln in a pale glow. Tarleton couldn't make out his face, just the fringes of his black hair and beard. The president dipped his head formally to the crowd, setting off more cheering.

Booth turned to Tarleton, his mouth twisted in an ugly snarl, his face flushed, veins throbbing on his neck. Tarleton grabbed his arm and squeezed, a silent reminder to be quiet. Booth drew back from the unspoken rebuke and looked up at the man he wanted to kill.

Lincoln motioned for quiet. "Sssshhhh!" people at the front hissed, the admonition passing through the crowd until it sounded like a colony of snakes.

The butler stood behind the president, holding a lamp over his shoulder. Lincoln looked down at a sheaf of papers. "We meet this evening," he began, "not in sorrow, but in gladness of heart."

Booth, Tarleton, and all around them leaned forward, straining to hear the high-pitched, nasal voice. Unsatisfied cries came from behind. "What's he saying?" "We can't hear!" "Speak up!"

Lincoln laid out his vision for the nation's postwar path, spelling out policies better suited for a cabinet meeting. After several uninspiring moments, the crowd began rustling. People looked around. They whispered as the reedy voice droned on.

"The colored man, too," the president proclaimed, "is inspired with vigilance, energy, and daring. Should he not receive the elective franchise?"

"My God!" Booth seethed through clenched teeth. "He's talking about nigger voting!" His face glowed red.

People were now talking openly among themselves. Tarleton noticed not so much disagreement as disinterest. Lincoln had lost them.

The speech eventually ended and received polite applause. Lincoln stood as if frozen in marble. Then cheers returned, not for his words, nor for even for Lincoln himself, but for victory and for the nation he had kept intact.

The band struck up "The Star-Spangled Banner." Lincoln disappeared into the White House.

"A whole lot of nothing if you ask me," Herold griped as they left the grounds.

"What do you think, Cap?" Paine asked.

Booth's hands closed into fists. "That," he said in a voice burning with rage, "was the last speech he'll ever give. I'll make sure of it."

Wednesday, April 12, 1865
Morning

During his weeks in Washington, Jack had made a point of avoiding Murder Bay. But when morning came and Sam hadn't returned to the hotel, he set off for the south side of Pennsylvania Avenue.

In the dirt street before him, a scrawny dog licked at dried vomit. Nearby, a black man lay facedown, an empty bottle still in his hand. Jack began asking for word of Sam, describing his pale blond hair, his lanky frame. He was answered by bowed heads, eyes staring at feet, a mumbled, "No, suh."

He drifted from block to block, poking his head between shacks, asking anyone he found, hoping the worry gnawing his insides was groundless. He saw a small group of men gathered along a stone wall. The increasingly disgusting odor told him it bordered the Washington Canal. The men were staring into the waterway.

"What's going on?" he asked a policeman holding a red handkerchief to his nose.

"Pulling a body out." His words were muffled. "A darkie found it floating this morning."

A dog's leg stiff with rigor mortis stuck above the surface of the water. Behind it, Jack saw a corpse floating facedown, muck and mire matting the hair. Two black men used poles to pull it to them. When it came within reach, a dozen black hands fought to pull it out of the fetid slag.

"City pays a bounty to anyone who hauls out a body." The policeman shook his head. "Pretty sorry way to make a living."

They laid the corpse on the grass, then turned it on its back. Jack drew back as Sam's face rolled into view. His skin was drained of color; his eyes and mouth bulged open. A stretch of rope was tied around his neck.

Jack staggered as if he had been shot. He had seen terrible things in the war, horrible things that lived in his nightmares. But this was more than he could stand.

"Well, now." The policeman grimaced. "A hanging. Don't see many of them wind up in the canal. A shooting or stabbing maybe, but this here is a horse of a different color."

A crowd gathered, gawking at Sam's lifeless body. Jack backed away blindly, bumping into a tree. He slumped down and put his head in his hands.

The policeman stood over him. "You knew this fellow?"

"He was my friend."

"Maybe you'd better come along with me."

Jack looked up. "I didn't do it, if that's what you're thinking."

The policeman's fleshy face softened. "Friend, I've been toting this badge for twelve years. I ain't never found a killer standing beside the canal when they fished out his victim's body. No, sir, I don't think you did it."

Jack nodded his appreciation.

"We'll take him to an undertaker. Give me his name, next of kin, any particulars you have. Then you can claim him." The policeman helped Jack to his feet. "Awful sorry, mister."

Jack looked at the curiosity seekers. "So am I."

"Wait here." The policeman patted Jack's shoulder. "Now listen up!" he shouted. "Anybody see what happened to this boy?"

There was a chorus of half-spoken "No, suh's" and shaking heads. A man crouching over Sam's body straightened up. "I seen something. A white boy was running down the street last night, lickety-split, with a Yankee soldier on his heels." He pointed to the body. "It was this white boy."

Jack's ears perked up.

"Do you know who the soldier was?" the policeman asked.

"No, suh. But he showed up later at the old church," the man said. "He was ringing the bell. Said Lee had surrendered, then told us to go home right away."

Jack called over. "What did the soldier look like?"

"Tall. No beard. An officer, I think."

"What color was his hair?"

"Blond."

"You're sure?"

"I'm sure. You don't see much blond hair in this neighborhood." The men around him laughed.

"Did you see his eyes?" Jack asked.

"It was mighty dark by then, suh. I only saw his hair."

"Know who it might have been?" the policeman asked Jack.

"I don't know any blond soldiers," Jack answered.

In time, a wagon arrived and left with the body. Jack went to the police station and shared the few facts he knew about the short life of Sam Jenkins. As he was leaving, Kate showed up. She didn't explain how she knew. She didn't question Jack about the circumstances of Sam's death. She simply took him in her arms and held him.

"Do you have any doubt who did it?" she asked.

"None."

"We need to tell Wingate. I'll arrange a meeting."

"Tell Wingate anything you like," Jack said. "But he needn't worry himself with getting Tarleton. I will."

Wednesday, April 12, 1865
Evening

Wingate stretched his arms and surrendered to a hearty yawn. The Intelligence Office was empty. Eight o'clock and everyone had already gone home. What a difference peace made.

He got up and walked around. Unlike his colleagues, he was stuck there, working on a report Secretary Stanton wanted to see in the morning. Looking out a window, he saw people celebrating in the street.

Wingate longed to join them. He had spent the afternoon

checking leads. Now, much as he dreaded any lengthy encounter with a pen, he had to write his report. He settled into the chair and dipped the nib in a bottle of black ink.

It was a long task, for he did not write well, which made it all the more miserable. Finally he penned the words "Respectfully submitted," and scrawled his name. Only as the ink dried did he realize how tired he was. Weeks of working day and night were wearing him down. He rubbed his eyes, stood up, and buttoned his coat. He headed to the secretary's office to drop off his report before going home.

Wingate was surprised to see two men in black suits standing in front of Stanton's door. He recognized the potbellied Congressman Ambrose Houghton, a Radical Republican from Pennsylvania, but not the other man.

Houghton waved his hands as he spoke.

"Sounds promising," the stranger drawled. "But can Stanton be trusted?"

Alarm bells rang in Wingate's mind. Why was Houghton hanging around the secretary's office with a Southerner? The men set off down the corridor. He followed at a discreet distance.

"Don't worry about Stanton," the congressman assured his companion. "He'll be with us when the time comes. With his backing we can be rid of the whole sorry mess."

The other man frowned. "What you propose is nothing short of a coup d'état."

Houghton's head fluttered in agreement. "Some very important people in this government fear for the future of our Union. They—we—are convinced there's no other way."

The men stopped. Wingate ducked into an open doorway.

"It's murder," the stranger noted. "No other word for it."

"Call it what you will. The man must be dealt with."

"Are you sure this is the best way?"

"The only way." Houghton hooked his thumbs in his plaid waistcoat. "You'll be rewarded, I assure you. How's this—'Robert Standiford, Military Governor of Georgia'? How would your pals back home like them apples?"

"Not a bit. But it'd keep my neck from being stretched."

Houghton chuckled. "All those years in the Rebel Congress will finally pay off. So, you're with us?"

"Of course I am."

"Good." Houghton laid a hand on Standiford's shoulder. "I need to introduce you to the rest of our little band. How about Friday night? We can meet at my home."

Standiford shook his head. "It's not wise for me to be seen around town. Why don't you bring them to my room, number 218. It's safer there."

"Suit yourself. Say around ten?"

"I look forward to meeting them. I'd best be going now."

Houghton gave Standiford's hand a shake. "I'll see you Friday night at Willard's."

Standiford disappeared down the vacant corridor. Houghton turned the other way and walked off.

As their footsteps faded, Wingate's heart was racing wildly. The man Jack and Kate had warned him about was right here, in the War Department. He had to do something.

Tell Stanton? No, they had talked about Stanton's cooperation. Good Lord, was Stanton involved in a conspiracy to murder Lincoln? The thought chilled his blood. He looked at the report in his hand, then slowly tore it to bits.

Friday night. Willard's Hotel. They would all be there. And so would he. And that would be the end of it. Lincoln would be safe, the case would be closed, and finally he could go home early.

Thursday, April 13, 1865
Afternoon

"He could have come up with a better place to meet," Jack griped. He took off his battered hat and wiped his brow as they walked across Lafayette Park. The day was unseasonably warm.

Kate twirled a white parasol above her head. "It seems an ideal location to me. Besides, it was my idea."

"That figures," Jack muttered as they approached a Greek Revival building north of the park. For fifty years, St. John's Episcopal Church had been the unofficial White House chapel. Presidents, senators, and cabinet members worshipped there.

"We can slip into a Holy Week service without drawing attention," Kate said as Jack led her across the street. "It certainly wouldn't harm you to go to church."

They passed between white Doric columns and entered the sanctuary. Wingate sat alone in a back corner pew. "Good afternoon, Major." Kate slid in beside him. Jack followed.

Wingate looked straight ahead. "They're going to strike."

"Who might *they* be?" Jack asked.

"Sssh!" An elderly woman two pews ahead gave them a cold look.

"Sorry, ma'am," Jack whispered.

"Standiford's bunch." Wingate's face flushed. "And their supporters inside the U.S. government." He described his chance encounter.

"You're certain it was Standiford?" Kate insisted.

"Houghton called him by name."

"Do you think Stanton's mixed up with them?" Jack asked.

"I don't know what to think anymore," Wingate said. "Lincoln has enemies everywhere. Maybe even in his own cabinet."

"We have news of our own," Kate said sadly. Jack bowed his head as she told of Sam's murder.

"Tarleton?" Wingate asked.

"I'd bet my soul on it," Jack replied.

"It's all fitting together," Kate said. "Tarleton lurking about. Standiford wanting to get out of the country fast. This meeting at Willard's. Whatever they've got planned is going to happen tomorrow."

The old woman ahead cast an annoyed look their way. Kate smiled an apology.

"Tomorrow night," Wingate whispered, "I'll arrest Standiford, Houghton, and whoever else is with them."

"You don't know who'll be on the other side of that hotel room door," Jack cautioned.

"That door might open Pandora's box." Wingate spread his hands helplessly. "But I see no alternative. Better to get them all at once than chase them all over the city. Which leads to your role."

"Find Tarleton and Booth," Jack offered.

"Precisely. I want you to track their every movement tomorrow. The moment the brains of this operation are in custody, I'll seize their minions. With any luck, by midnight the whole lot will be inside Old Capitol Prison."

"A fine plan," Kate agreed through a diplomatic smile. "But don't you think arresting a famous actor, a congressman, a former Confederate congressman, and Lord only knows who else, might draw just a wee bit of attention?"

"The newspapers will have a field day," Jack chipped in.

"That is precisely the point." Wingate poked the air with his forefinger. "When such high-profile arrests are publicized, it'll make anyone else think twice before harming the president."

"Can't argue with your reasoning," Jack said.

"Good. Keep an eye on them. I'll need the latest on Booth's and Tarleton's whereabouts." Wingate stood up. "I'll attend to them after I've rounded up the men at Willard's."

"What if we need to reach you before then?" Kate asked.

"I'll be at my office until sunset." He shook their hands. "I just thought of something." A thin smile curled his lips. "Tomorrow is Good Friday."

Kate chuckled. "Ironic, isn't it? Saving Lincoln's life on the very day the Savior lost His."

"No one ever said the Lord doesn't have a sense of humor."

Thursday, April 13, 1865
Evening

Booth and Tarleton found Lewis Paine and George Atzerodt and Davey Herold in Paine's room at the boardinghouse. "The hour of action is upon us, gentlemen," Booth solemnly announced. "Our mission has changed. There is no longer any need to kidnap The Ape. We must now eliminate him." He looked into the faces gathered around him. "And the rest of his tyrannical government, as well.

"At the appointed time," he went on, "we shall all strike simultaneously. My target is Lincoln, of course." His words were met with nods of assent. "George and Basil will take Vice President Johnson at his lodgings in the Kirkwood House. Lewis, you will strike Secretary of State Seward, an easy target as he lies recovering in his sickbed."

Tarleton watched the men intently. They sat in silence, eyes fastened on Booth.

"Lincoln, Johnson, Seward." The actor ticked them off on his fingers. "President, vice president, secretary of state. Gone. The government will be plunged into crisis. Then panic. While the Yankee potentates squabble, we'll make our way south. With a good head start, we shouldn't have any trouble reaching General Joe Johnston in North Carolina. That, gentlemen, will be the end of our nation's misery." Booth's eyes gleamed. "And the beginning of our glory."

Herold piped up. "What about me?"

"You have an important job, Davey. You'll get everyone to the Navy Yard Bridge. We'll need a steady hand with a gun to make sure we get across."

Herold radiated satisfaction.

"When we gonna get 'em, Cap?" Paine asked.

"The moment I learn of an opportunity I shall summon you. You must be ready to spring into action at an instant's notice."

Booth circled the room, pausing to lay a hand on each man's shoulder. "We have reached the point of no return. Can any among you say he's not up to the commission I have given him?"

The room was silent. They sat frozen, mesmerized by Booth's words.

"Then let us leave here and do what must be done. The next time you hear from me, it will be to rid the world of . . ." He smiled sweetly at some thought he didn't share, then concluded with painfully plain hatred, *"Him."*

Ten

THE FINAL ACT

Friday, April 14, 1865
11:00 A.M.

Scissors snipped Jack's dark brown locks, restoring order to his unruly hair. While looking for Tarleton that morning, he had caught his shaggy and stubbled reflection in a barbershop window and gone inside. He settled down for a haircut and shave. After a few minutes of efficient snipping, the barber draped a hot towel over Jack's face.

The shop door rattled open. "A fine good morning to you, Charles," a cheerful voice boomed. There was something familiar about the tone, but Jack couldn't place it. The leather chair next to him creaked as the newcomer slid into place.

"Time to look handsome once more."

"That won't be hard, Mr. Booth."

Jack stifled an urge to sit up. Now he recognized the voice that had recited Shakespeare on command a few nights earlier. He wanted to rip the towel from his face, grab the actor and shake him until he revealed Tarleton's whereabouts.

"Ready for a good spring shearing?" the barber asked Booth.

"Not too much. We have to leave something for the ladies to run their fingers through." The two men chuckled.

When the towel came off Jack's face, he shot a sidelong glance at Booth. A brush heavy with shaving cream obstructed his view. "Sit back, please." The barber behind him lathered his face and scraped off his beard.

Jack listened intently as Booth and the other barber exchanged small talk. They swapped ribald jokes, discussed the weather, and gossiped about the theater world. Booth finally stood up, dusting stray clumps of hair off his chest.

The barber hurried over with a whisk brush and completed the job. "Do you have a big role coming up?"

"Yes, I do." Booth handed the man a half dollar. "The biggest role of my career." He picked up a freshly cut black curl from the floor. "Save this, Charles. Your children will be glad you did." He set it on the chair and walked out the door.

Jack tore the white sheet from his neck, spots of shaving cream still clinging to his face.

"I'm not finished, sir!" his barber insisted.

"I am." Jack tossed the man two quarters, put on his hat, and hurried after Booth. He kept a safe distance—close enough to keep the actor in sight but far enough not to be seen.

Booth turned onto Tenth Street and walked into Ford's Theatre. As Jack hurried after him, a door flew open and two men came out. Each clutched tickets in his hand.

"As soon as I heard the Lincolns and the Grants would be here tonight," one said, "I knew the good seats would go fast."

Jack stepped toward them. "Excuse me."

The men gave him a puzzled look. Jack self-consciously put a hand to his face and felt the shaving cream. "Pardon the mess." He wiped it with his sleeve. "Who did you say would be here tonight?"

"President and Mrs. Lincoln, plus General and Mrs. Grant."

"Tonight?" Jack repeated.

"They're doing *Our American Cousin,*" the man continued. "I've seen it at least five times. Hell, I've seen Old Abe that many times, too. But I've never seen the man who won the war. General Grant in the flesh is worth the two dollars." He jerked a thumb toward the door. "If you want good seats, you'd best hurry."

Jack tipped his hat. "Much obliged," he said as the men walked off.

Lincoln and Grant together. Jack now knew Tarleton would strike tonight. He had to tell Kate. She had mentioned she was meeting Lucy Hale for tea that afternoon.

Some time for a tea party, Jack thought.

1:00 P.M.

Wingate bent over his desk, filling out a requisition for a squad of soldiers to help break up the meeting of conspirators that night. A man cleared his throat. Wingate looked up into the fleshy face of Louis Weichmann.

"Am I disturbing you, Major?"

Wingate put his pen aside. "Not at all."

"There's something you need to know." Weichmann leaned over the desk. "Tuesday, Mrs. Surratt asked me to take her on some errands over in Maryland. We came upon the fellow who rents the Surratt Tavern. Mrs. Surratt said something that struck me as odd." Weichmann lowered his voice. "She told him, 'Those shooting irons will be needed soon.' "

"She said 'shooting irons'?"

"Yes, sir."

Wingate rubbed his jaw. "That's very interesting."

"There's more. Today, she asked me to ride with her out to the tavern. She says she must deliver something that someone will be calling for tonight." Weichmann pulled a handkerchief from his pocket and mopped his brow. "I don't mind telling you, sir, I'm scared."

Wingate sat back in his chair. Guns. Surratt. Friday night. It all fit. "You were right to bring this to my attention. I'll look into it at once."

Weichmann stuck the handkerchief back in his pocket. "What do you think it means?"

"Thank you, Mr. Weichmann." Wingate rose. "I'll take it from here."

"Of course." Weichmann nodded a farewell.

Wingate grabbed his pen, dipped it in ink, and finished the requisition as fast as his fingers would fly.

5:00 P.M.

"Are you ready for Madrid?" Kate said as a black waiter served tea in the National Hotel's "Ladies' Salon."

"Not in the least." Lucy Hale sighed. Her father, the former senator, had just been appointed ambassador to Spain.

"When do you leave?" Kate sipped her tea.

"Papa is waiting for the paperwork, then we're off."

"It must be hard saying good-bye to your friends."

Lucy nodded. "One in particular."

Kate gave a sly smile. "A certain dashing actor, perhaps?"

A giggle erupted. "Of course, you silly goose! I saw him here at the hotel earlier today. It was the oddest thing—he asked if I was going to Ford's Theatre tonight. When I said I had other plans, he told me to change them. Wilkes said I could see something no one would ever see again."

"What did that mean?" Kate stirred her tea.

"Papa says President and Mrs. Lincoln are going to Ford's tonight. It's probably a special show for them."

Kate's hand froze in midstir. Terror ran down her spine. "You're sure he said Ford's?"

Lucy nodded. "General and Mrs. Grant are going, too. I think *Our American Cousin* is playing. You know how Mr. Lincoln loves a comedy."

Kate plastered a smile to her face as Lucy prattled on. Her mind was focused on a single, inescapable conclusion—Booth and Tarleton were going to kill Lincoln at Ford's Theatre that night. She grabbed her handbag. "I must leave."

"Is something wrong? You're as white as a ghost."

"I feel ill," Kate said truthfully. "I had some beef for lunch that's not settling well."

"Oh, dear!" Lucy covered her mouth with a gloved hand. "A neighbor of ours before the war—her husband was a congressman from Alabama—she had some bad beef for dinner one night and—"

"Forgive me." Kate raced into the street. She had to find Jack.

She began running as fast as her hoop skirt would allow.

As fast as she ran, her fears ran ahead of her.

She didn't have to go far. One block later she saw Jack coming toward her.

"I just came from Lucy Hale," she told him.

"I saw Booth this morning," he countered.

"It's going to happen tonight—"

"At Ford's Theatre."

6:00 P.M.

"Everything is at the ready." Booth's voice was filled with self-assurance.

Tarleton was impressed by the actor's display of self-control. Now that the big moment was at hand, he was focused entirely on the night's mission. Booth strode across Tarleton's hotel room, dressed in riding breeches and shirtsleeves, nursing a whiskey instead of his usual brandy. Even his drinking seemed under control.

"I went to Ford's again this afternoon," Booth continued. "I drilled a small peephole that will let me see into the Ape's box and took care of a few other tasks. There will be no problems tonight."

Tarleton nodded his approval.

"I gave Mrs. Surratt a pair of field glasses that might come in handy when we head south. She's leaving them at her tavern for us, along with guns and other supplies."

"Does she know what's happening tonight?"

"Of course not."

"Good." Tarleton stretched out on the bed. "Let's go over the plan one more time."

Booth flashed his famous smile. "You would have made a fine director."

"This show runs one night only. It must be a perfect production."

"I'll meet with everyone individually before the curtain rises." Booth put aside his drink. "Atzerodt has already checked into the Kirkwood House where Andrew Johnson rooms. I left a note for the vice president." A look of delight wreathed his features. "That should cause some confusion when this is all over." He pointed at Tarleton. "I need you with George. His will is weak."

"I know my part, Wilkes."

Booth began pacing. "I'm sending Davey Herold with Lewis Paine. We can't risk Lewis getting lost again. He'll pretend he's delivering medicine to the poor, wounded secretary of state."

The actor pounded a fist into his open hand. "Davey is the key. He has to make sure Lewis gets away from Seward's house. Then he can collect you and George and it's off to the Navy Yard Bridge."

"Everyone knows what time to strike?"

Booth nodded. "As close to ten-fifteen as possible." He retrieved his whiskey. "Lincoln. Grant. Johnson. Seward." He took a sip. "When we're through, it will take the Yankees a month to sort out who's in charge."

"By which time we'll be long gone."

Booth hoisted his glass. "To Dixie—and freedom!"

8:00 P.M.

It was the third time Jack and Kate had gone to the War Department that evening. At first, Wingate's office was empty. A clerk told them he was at dinner. They paced around Lafayette Park for an hour, then returned. Still no Wingate. Too anxious to eat, too worried to sit still, they paced the park again.

As darkness fell, they returned to Wingate's office once more, finding him at his desk. "They're going to strike tonight," Kate cried as they hurried into his office.

Wingate, immaculate in his dress uniform, leapt up. "For God's sake, lower your voice."

"But it's tonight!" Kate repeated.

"I know." Wingate ducked his head into the corridor, looked briskly around, then pushed the door closed. "And if you keep shouting, the rest of the building will know, too."

"You know?" Jack asked.

"My sources confirm everything is in motion for tonight. I've requisitioned a squad to help me arrest the villains at Willard's Hotel."

"You mean Ford's Theatre," Kate corrected.

Confusion clouded Wingate's features. "What are you talking about?"

Jack and Kate related what they had both learned.

"My God." Wingate gritted his teeth. "We'll have to get them, every one of them, all at the same time."

"Just how do we do that?" Kate demanded.

"I'll take half the soldiers to Willard's and have the rest report to you at Ford's. Between us, we can keep Tarleton from Lincoln *and* round up all the conspirators in one fell swoop."

Jack fished a watch from his pocket. "It's after eight o'clock. The play has already started."

"Do you think it can work?" Kate asked Wingate.

"It has to."

8:15 P.M.

Tarleton stood before a mirror in his hotel room, studying his reflection. He buckled on a thick black belt, feeling the sword hanging against his left leg. You would have made a fine officer, he told himself.

But would a military career have been as satisfying, as rewarding? Could anything?

Birds sing because they are birds, he thought as he dabbed cologne on his neck. I do what I do because of who I am.

One last look in the mirror, taking in the reflection from his neatly combed hair down to his brightly polished boots. And I am damned good at it.

It was dark when he reached the street. To his left, the Capitol's new dome glowed in the distance, lit, as it had been all week, in triumphant celebration. He turned right and began walking.

8:30 P.M.

Typically, it took only a few moments to cover the six blocks between the War Department and Tenth Street. But this night was far from typical. The free-flowing, wholesale revelry that had filled the city all week was reaching a crescendo. Jack and Kate were trapped in the middle of it.

"It's as if the whole county has come to town for market day," Jack grumbled.

People jammed in all around them. Women in their finest silks and brightest bonnets laughed off the river of misery that had washed over them all for the past four years. Men held flaming torches aloft, their orange tongues brilliantly shining in store windows. Some carried placards. A GRATEFUL NATION HAILS ITS HEROES, one proclaimed. Another read, simply, PEACE.

Jack tried to clear a path. A stray hand thrust a whiskey bottle at him. He brushed it aside.

Kate folded her arms over her handbag, pressing it close to her. Jack felt her shiver. "I wish I'd brought my shawl," she said as a damp breeze swept over them. Low clouds hid the moon. She craned her neck. "I'm not even sure where we are."

"I think that's Fourteenth Street."

"Four blocks to go." Kate pushed against the people ahead of them. "We *have* to make it in time."

9:00 P.M.

Wingate had stomped all around the War Department looking for the dozen soldiers he had requisitioned. They were nowhere to be found. His boots echoed through empty hallways as he rushed to the requisition office. A lone gangly corporal stood at a window, watching the throng pass outside.

"I'm looking for a detachment of men I requested," Wingate announced.

"They ain't here," the corporal answered in a nasal Hoosier twang.

"Where are they?"

"Don't know, but they ain't gonna be here tonight. Nobody is. They've canceled all troop requisitions."

"Why, in heaven's name?" Wingate exploded.

"Couple of boys from a New Jersey regiment got liquored up and had their way with some local gals. Now everybody's got to stay in camp till things settle down."

"I must have those men!" Wingate thundered.

"Well, sir," the corporal replied without bothering to turn around, "you're free to go to any camp you please and get 'em. But there ain't no men here tonight."

Wingate fought down the urge to grab the kid's scrawny neck. It might make him feel better, but it wouldn't produce any soldiers. He darted out of the building and sprinted across the White House grounds. It was faster than fighting his way through the crowded street. Willard's Hotel was two blocks up Pennsylvania Avenue. With luck, he might still reach Room 218 in time.

9:30 P.M.

Jack and Kate finally saw the lighted façade of Ford's Theatre to their left. The jubilant crowd moved on to the Capitol, allowing them to break free. They hurried to the theater.

"Everything seems normal." Jack nodded to a sleek black carriage parked at the curb. "That's not a bad sign."

"It's Lincoln's," Kate agreed. "At least we know he made it here."

Jack opened a door and they hurried to the box office. "Two tickets, please," he told a pudgy man behind the counter.

"In the orchestra," Kate added.

The man shook his head. "Only have seats upstairs. Everything down front is sold out."

"That's fine." Jack produced some crumpled bills and handed them over.

The man gave him two tickets. "Enjoy the show."

9:45 P.M.

The entrance to Willard's was clogged with celebrants trying to get in and guests trying to get out. Wingate clawed his way to the door and looked inside. The lobby was as crowded as the street. A wall of people blocked the main staircase. No point trying to go that way.

He made his way around the corner to a service entrance. He pushed on the door and said a silent prayer of thanks when it swung open. He bounded up a back staircase. At the second-floor landing, he stepped into a carpeted hallway. Gas lamps burned on both walls, their glow reflecting on the brass numbers attached to each door. Number 226 was directly before him. Standiford's room was eight doors down.

He moved cautiously, silently. His heartbeat quickened as he crept closer to Room 218. He pressed an ear to the door. Men's voices were engaged in a heated discussion. He reached for the doorknob.

"Pardon me, Major, do you know—"

Wingate swung around and saw a man walking toward him. He drew his revolver.

"Don't shoot!" The man raised his hands above his head.

Wingate cocked the hammer. "Identify yourself!"

"I'm, I'm, uh, Jim Bennington," he stuttered.

"What do you want?"

"I was . . . I was just wondering if you knew where I could get a bite to eat at this hour."

The door swung open behind Wingate. "What's going on out here?"

Wingate wheeled around, pointing his gun at Congressman Ambrose Houghton. He looked over his shoulder at the man in the hallway. "Are you with them?"

"What is the meaning of this?" Houghton fumed.

"I . . . I don't know what you're talking about," the man in the hall stammered.

"Get!" Wingate snapped, sending the man running.

"See here!" Houghton bellowed. "I demand to know—"

"Shut up!" Wingate ordered. "Back in the room."

Houghton stepped backward. Wingate followed, revolver still drawn, closing the door behind him.

"Who is this?" Robert Standiford demanded.

A half-dozen other men stood around him. Wingate recognized several Republican members of Congress.

"I'm Major Drake Wingate of the United States Army. You are all under arrest."

There was a stunned pause, then a collective, "What?"

He waved the gun. "Everyone sit down." The men exchanged questioning glances as they took seats.

"I demand to know on what charge we are being arrested," Houghton barked, "and by whose authority."

"The charge is conspiracy to murder the President of the United States." There were gasps all around. "On the authority of Edwin Stanton," Wingate continued, "United States Secretary of War."

"Do you know who I am?" Houghton huffed.

"I do, Congressman. What I don't know is why you want President Lincoln dead."

"If this is some kind of joke . . . ," Standiford murmured.

Wingate turned the revolver toward the Confederate congressman. "You'll find out how funny it is soon enough, when I take you off in irons. Right now, I want you to tell me about your plot to assassinate President Lincoln."

"I don't know what lunatic asylum you've escaped from," Houghton exploded, "but I'll make sure you're sent back there. This is a political meeting."

"I heard you myself in the War Department, talking with this Rebel." Wingate nodded at Standiford. "He used the word 'murder.' " Wingate trained the revolver on the Confederate. "Where can I find Basil Tarleton?" Standiford's face went ashen.

"Who?" Houghton looked at the others in the room. All shrugged and shook their heads, except Standiford, who sat silent.

"I want answers." Wingate raised his pistol for emphasis. "Now."

"This nonsense is over, Major." There was steel in Houghton's voice. "And so is your military career." He pointed to a man seated at a table. "That is Charles Felton, assistant to the secretary of war."

Wingate lowered his gun. For the first time he felt his resolve slip.

"Tomorrow morning, Mr. Felton will notify his boss—your boss—about this episode. Come tomorrow night, we won't be in prison," Houghton shrieked. "You will!"

The magnitude of Wingate's miscalculation was sinking in.

Jack and Kate were right.

The threat wasn't at Willard's Hotel.

It was at Ford's Theatre.

He whirled around, flung the door open, and flew down the hall.

Houghton's voice followed. "You'll hang for this, Wingate!"

9:55 P.M.

Laughter rang inside the theater. Kate and Jack went to the closed doors that led into the auditorium.

"Our tickets are up there." Jack pointed to a staircase at the far end of the lobby.

"I want a good look down here first."

"But—" His protest was cut off by a burst of laughter flowing through the door as she opened it. Jack followed her inside.

Colorfully costumed actors promenaded on the stage, which was decorated to resemble an English manor. The gaslights illuminating them washed over the audience.

"Tickets, please," a young usher whispered.

"Of course." Kate gave him a flirtatious smile. "My husband has them. Isn't it exciting? President Lincoln and General Grant, here together. What a glorious night!"

"Just President Lincoln, ma'am," the usher whispered. "General Grant didn't come."

Kate's astonished look was genuine. "Really? What a shame. So where does the president sit?"

"If I can just see your tickets—"

"They're here someplace," Jack whispered as he patted his coat.

The usher looked nervous. "I can't—"

Kate took the young man's arm. "My husband would lose his head if it weren't fastened on. Now, where did you say the Lincolns are sitting?"

The usher pointed to the right. "Up there, in the box with the flags and picture of George Washington."

Kate stood on her toes. "I can't see him."

"No, ma'am. Not from here. Only the folks on stage can see him. Now, I really must see those tickets."

"Ah, here they are." Jack passed them to the young man.

He squinted. "These are for the dress circle upstairs."

Kate's hand flew to her mouth. "I am so dreadfully embarrassed! Please excuse us."

They returned to the lobby. Jack let out a long breath. "Nothing seems out of order."

"I'm still worried." Kate's eyes wandered around the lobby as more laughter roared through the doors. "I've got to see inside that box." She started toward the curved staircase.

Jack hurried after her, clutching her elbow as she reached the stairs. "Wait. Maybe we should look around for Booth and Tarleton."

"You go ahead, then meet me upstairs."

"All right." He kissed her cheek. "Be careful."

Kate lifted her skirt and darted up the stairs. It grew darker as she neared the balcony. An army officer stood on the top step blocking her way. Light from the stage surrounded his head like a halo. "What a pleasant surprise," he said as she reached him. "Enjoying the show, Mrs. St. Claire?"

"Excuse me, Colonel," she said. She was about to step around him when she realized he had said her name. Then she caught the icy blue glint in his eyes. Her breath stuck in her throat. "You."

"What do you think of my costume?" Tarleton smirked. "This is a playhouse, after all."

"I know why you're here." Kate stiffened her neck. "It isn't going to happen. I won't let it happen."

The audience erupted in laughter again.

"This is hardly the place to talk." Tarleton seized her wrist. "I know a more private spot."

His hand felt as cold as a dead man's. Pangs of fear stabbed her stomach. She glanced at the stage. The play was nearly over. If she could occupy him for a few more minutes, Lincoln might leave the theater alive.

"I'll go," she whispered. "But if you so much as breathe the wrong way I'll scream 'rape.' "

"You wouldn't be the first." He pulled her along the back wall of the dress circle.

A small lounge opened off the far side of the balcony. He yanked her inside and closed its double doors, then shoved her toward a settee. "Sit down."

Kate rubbed her aching wrist as she looked around the room for another exit. She saw only gold-papered walls, more settees, a long table, and several brass cuspidors. Tarleton braced a chair against the doors, blocking them. With a reptilian grin he reached up to the gas lamp on the wall and shut it off.

Darkness enveloped the room. She heard a scratching sound, caught a whiff of sulfur, saw a small burst of yellow light.

Tarleton clutched a match in one hand. His predatory blue eyes held her in an unblinking gaze as he touched the match to a candle stub.

"What are you going to do?" she demanded.

"To you? Or to Lincoln? Not that it matters. You'll both be dead by the end of the play."

"You'll never get away." She shifted her skirt to hide the purse at her side. Her hand inched into it. "They'll hunt you down like the dog you are."

"Just the idea!" he mocked. "My dear Kate, they will never even look for me. I'll be free to savor my accomplishment for the rest of my life." His face sobered as he bent over her. "Killing you, however, is another matter. There's no pleasure in it for me, just necessity."

Kate's fingers closed on a small derringer in her bag. She slid it into her palm and in one swift movement pointed it at Tarleton's face. "You're not killing anyone."

He smiled again, a cold, cunning grin. "Oh yes, I am."

The candle went out. Kate jabbed the gun where Tarleton's face should have been. She encountered only air. A powerful blow struck the base of her neck. She crumpled to the floor.

Uneven light flickered on her closed eyelids. His hand was stroking her. She wanted to crawl away, but didn't have the strength.

There was a soft clicking, as if he had opened a pocket watch, followed by a grumbled oath. Then he was gone and she sank into darkness.

10:00 P.M.

Jack ran out onto Tenth Street. Two drunks wobbled in front of the saloon next door. Black coachmen stood beside carriages. Stragglers from the roaming victory celebration wandered by. Everything was quiet, orderly, safe.

He noticed a small alley on the south side of the theater. Jack ran toward it.

10:05 P.M.

Tarleton stepped out of the lounge. With the play building to its climax, laughter was growing louder by the minute. He walked along the dress circle to a closed door. A man was seated beside it. Tarleton gestured to the State Box. The man looked at his uniform, then nodded approval.

Tarleton entered a vestibule perhaps six feet long. A door stood open at the far end. Walking toward it, he passed a glimmer of light. It was the hole Booth had drilled. He peeked through it.

Lincoln sat in a rocker. His wife was in a low chair beside him, a hand on his knee. There seemed to be other people in the box, though he couldn't make them out.

Tarleton noiselessly slipped through the doorway and eased toward Lincoln. He stood motionless, taking in his surroundings. Light from the stage spilled into the box. It was decorated with a deep red carpet and matching wallpaper. A young woman sat on a chair beyond Mrs. Lincoln. There was a couch with a young man in uniform perched on one end. A wooden partition stood against the wall behind them.

The president was barely three paces in front of Tarleton. He wore a heavy black overcoat and rocked absently in his chair. On stage, an actor's speech provoked howls from the audience. Lincoln smiled mechanically, barely stretching a face that looked as old as parchment.

The young woman stirred. Tarleton's heart beat more wildly than he ever remembered. Her gaze remained fixed on the performance. Lincoln leaned forward, propping his chin in his right hand, the other resting on the flag-draped railing.

Tarleton caught a motion in the corner of his eye. John Wilkes Booth stepped into the box. His eyes swept around, eventually resting on Tarleton. The actor froze.

Tarleton pulled out the derringer he had retrieved after his tussle with Kate. Booth's mouth fell open. Tarleton stepped forward.

The audience exploded in the loudest laughter of the night. Tarleton took a deep breath. He raised the derringer and pulled the trigger.

The little gun's report was lost amid the roar of the crowd. Lincoln's arms jerked up. He swayed, then his head sagged to his chest.

Thin, sulfurous smoke filled the box. Tarleton turned to Booth. "A little gift from Kate St. Claire." He tossed the derringer at the actor, who shrank back from it. "Take a bow, Wilkes. You're on." He ducked out the door.

Behind him, he heard sounds of a scuffle, then a bloodcurdling scream. Tarleton rushed through the vestibule and pulled on the door leading to the balcony.

It didn't budge.

Jack stepped carefully on the uneven paving stones of the alley. In an open space behind the theater, he saw a man holding a horse. A door flew open and another man charged out, snatched the reins, and jumped into the saddle. The horse clattered away, leaving only echoes of hooves beating against masonry.

Jack recognized the horseman. It was John Wilkes Booth.

He heard screams. Sounds of a great commotion drifted out the open door.

Something had happened.

Terror gripped his heart. He had to find Kate.

Jack ran back the way he had come.

Tarleton gave the door another try. Then another. He swore. Something was blocking it. Booth's handiwork, he concluded grimly.

"They've shot the president!" a woman cried from the box.

Tarleton's blood turned to ice. He reeled about, expecting a pursuer. There was no one. He crept back to the box and looked inside. The young officer was pointing to the stage as blood streamed from a long gash down his arm. Lincoln's wife was crying hysterically. The blood-soaked young woman stared at the limp body in the rocker with tears pouring from her eyes. Booth was gone.

Shouts roared in from the dress circle. It was just a matter of time until someone burst into the vestibule. Tarleton retreated into the box and pressed himself into the space behind the door.

Fists pounded on the vestibule entry. Minutes passed. There was a loud crash, then footsteps rushed down the passage. Soon, the box was filled with voices. "Put him on the floor," someone ordered.

A quavering voice moaned, "Will my husband die? Save him, please save him!"

Several men held a shouted conference.

"We must get him to the White House."

"He'll never survive the carriage ride. The Star Saloon is next door."

"For God's sake, we can't let the President of the United States die in a barroom!"

"Well, we've got to get him out of here. Find something to carry him on."

Tarleton spotted the wooden partition against the wall next to his hiding place. "Put him on this," he called as he stepped out from behind the door.

"Good." A doctor bent over the stricken president. "Come help us."

For the first time since the shooting, Tarleton saw Lincoln up close. There was surprisingly little blood. His breathing was slow and jagged, his color gray. It didn't take a doctor to tell he wouldn't last.

Tarleton helped prepare the partition for use as a litter. He stepped back, trying to blend into the crowd. "Give us a hand, Colonel," the doctor implored. "Every second counts."

Tarleton joined the men lifting Lincoln. They started moving, creeping inches at a time, slower even than pallbearers in a funeral. Soldiers cleared a path through the dress circle and down the stairs.

Tarleton stared at Lincoln's eyes, already dark and swollen. It took everything within him to suppress his utter joy. He wanted to shout, "I did this! Basil Tarleton has just claimed the ultimate prize. And you don't even know the killer is here among you!"

They stepped into the murky night. Street lamps cast yellow blurs of light. An officer brandished his sword to part the crowd clogging the street. "Clear the way!"

"Bring him in here!" someone shouted from a brick town house across the street.

They slowly carried Lincoln away from the scene of the shooting, away from the madness.

And away from a familiar face Tarleton had spotted in the crowd. As he helped move Lincoln across the street, he passed within a few feet of Jack Tanner.

Of all the pushing and shoving Jack had done that night, nothing compared to this. As word of what happened spread, people who had tramped through Washington's streets all evening descended on Ford's. They grew sullen, angry, fearful. Hundreds of others who had been in the theater during the shooting streamed outside. Tenth Street was a sea of humanity.

An old woman looked up at Jack, tears flowing down wrinkled cheeks. "Why'd they have to shoot him?" Her wailing weaved into a tapestry of voices.

"I was lookin' up at the box when it happened. My God! It was John Wilkes Booth!"

"Hanging isn't good enough for the likes of him."

"The Rebels are behind this. You'll see. Richmond's fine hand is in this foul business."

A small child's voice pierced the wall of sound. "Ma, are they gonna finish the play?"

Jack elbowed forward. He had to keep moving, keep fighting. If he didn't, he might succumb to the anguish that was threatening to overwhelm him. He thought over all that had happened during the past six weeks, thought back to how absurd Harry Kincaid's first warning had sounded. Now Kincaid was dead, and likely Lincoln, too. And Sam and Felix. For what? Tarleton had triumphed.

For the first time in his life, Jack felt total failure.

When he reached the corner of Tenth and E Streets, his eyes caught the ruffle of a skirt on a stone step before a darkened store. A woman crouched in the shadows, dark red hair covering her face.

"Kate!" Jack screamed. She looked up, then ran to him. Her hair was in wild disarray. Dried blood coated her chin. They flew into each other's arms in the middle of the crowd, hugging and kissing and crying as if they were all alone. They held each other for a long time.

"I couldn't stop him, Jack." Her head was buried deep in his shoulder. "I tried, but I just couldn't stop him."

"It's all right," Jack repeated over and over as she sobbed freely.

"He took me into the lounge and said he was going to kill Lincoln. He said he was going to kill me. Then he hit me and I blacked out." She sniffed back a fresh sob. "When I came to, my gun was gone and everyone was screaming." A fresh cascade of tears began flowing. "I was the last person who could have kept Tarleton from reaching him."

"Tarleton?"

"He showed up in a Yankee colonel's uniform right after you left."

"Tarleton tried to kill you?"

Kate sniffled, nodded.

"Everyone in the theater saw Booth. They're all convinced he shot Lincoln. I watched him ride away."

Kate shook her head. "All I know is Tarleton was there. He said he was going to kill Lincoln. And I couldn't stop him."

Jack gathered her tightly in his arms. The sense of failure that had filled him earlier now gave way to a raw burning rage.

The crowd had parted down the middle of Tenth Street. Half took up vigil outside the house where Lincoln lay, the other half stayed planted in front of the theater. There was just enough space to pass between them. Jack felt a hand on his shoulder.

"Thank God I found you!" Wingate shouted. "I've been looking everywhere. You were right. About Booth, about Tarleton, about everything."

"Did you catch the conspirators?" Kate asked. "Did you break up their meeting?"

"There was a meeting all right. A bunch of congressmen who are all furious at me. My military career will probably be finished by daybreak. While I still have some authority left, I want to help you find Booth and Tarleton."

"What have you heard?" Jack said.

"Seward was attacked in his house tonight."

"My God," Kate said.

"Stabbed in his bed about the time Lincoln was shot. He may not make it. The attacker got away. Folks are saying Vice President Johnson was killed, but I ran into a general who told me that's not true."

"What about Booth?" Jack asked.

"A man matching his description crossed the Navy Yard Bridge on horseback right after the shooting, before the guards had orders to close it. A few minutes later, another rider passed."

"Tarleton?" Kate asked.

Wingate shook his head. "A guard reported he was a young kid."

"What about the other bridges?" Jack wanted to know.

"Locked down tighter than a drum. Stanton's got people at the train stations. The whole city is crawling with soldiers. All the major avenues of escape are covered."

Jack thought for a moment. "Booth fled over the Navy Yard Bridge, then someone else did. Tarleton will try to escape that way, too. We can get him there."

"But how can you be sure—"

"Major," Kate interrupted. "Remember what happened the last time you ignored our warnings?"

Wingate opened his mouth, then closed it and looked down sheepishly. "We'll take F Street. It's the quickest way."

It was a most unceremonious room for a president to spend his final hours. Barely five strides across and full of people. Tarleton stood in a corner, his back against gold-striped wallpaper. Lincoln lay on a spool bed, his body at an angle so his feet wouldn't hang over the footboard.

His oldest son, Robert, stood at the head of the bed, sobbing on a senator's shoulder. Members of Congress and cabinet officers, military commanders, and doctors crowded in. The room was hot, the air foul with the stench of drying blood and sweat.

One sound kept everyone's attention riveted to the unconscious figure on the bed—the slow, labored struggle of Lincoln's breathing. Doctors continuously checked his pulse and heartbeat, but were powerless to stop the inevitable.

Outside the room, somebody shouted, "Here she comes."

Skirts rustled as Mary Lincoln and another woman entered. The men stepped back from the bed. She fell down and moaned, "Father, speak to us! Say just one word, my beloved!" The only response was his agonized effort to breathe. "Take me with you, please!" She hurled herself onto his chest. A doctor gently pulled her to her feet. Her son led her out the door, her hysterical sobs leaving an audible trail behind her.

Tarleton took a final look at the inert figure on the bed, suppressed a satisfied smile, and made his way out of the room.

In a parlor a few steps down the hall, a portly bearded man was barking orders and dictating telegrams to a stream of military orderlies. "For General Dix in New York City," he snapped. "'President's condition unchanged. No hope entertained for his survival. Put troops at all rail stations in the city. Search every incoming train for the actor John Wilkes Booth.' Got that?"

"Yes, Secretary Stanton," the man responded.

Stanton spotted Tarleton. "Colonel!"

It took a moment for Tarleton to realize the man was speaking to him. "Yes, sir?"

"What is your command?"

Tarleton blurted the first name that came to mind. "Second Rhode Island Infantry."

"Take this to the War Department and have it telegraphed immediately to New York." Stanton thrust a paper at him. "Then ride over to the Navy Yard Bridge. Make absolutely sure they stop anyone from crossing. It's bad enough Booth got away. I don't want any more Rebels using it to mosey down to Richmond."

Stanton moved on. "Send this order to—"

Tarleton recognized his ticket out of the city. He tucked the order inside his coat and hurried from the house. Light but steady rain was falling. Despite the weather, Tenth Street remained filled with people awaiting word of Lincoln's condition.

A man touched Tarleton's sleeve. "Any change, sir?"

"None," Tarleton said tersely as he rushed past, trotting up the street and around the corner. He darted through the open door of a small livery stable. A black man sitting by a lantern turned a tearstained face. "Oh, sir, is there any news?"

"I'm afraid he's a goner."

Without the least trace of shame, tears flowed freely down the man's face.

"I'm Colonel Taylor. Saddle my horse."

"Yes, sir," the man sniffed. He walked down a row of stalls and soon returned, handing over the reins of a magnificent bay. Tarleton mounted. Drizzle beat against his face as he galloped down F Street toward the Navy Yard Bridge.

The long, low wooden span was the most direct route from Washington into Maryland. Jack and Kate huddled under a clump of trees as Wingate spoke to the three soldiers on duty at the bridge. A shamefaced sergeant was explaining how he and his men had allowed two riders to pass. They had heard nothing about events at Ford's Theatre until much later.

Wingate motioned for Jack and Kate to join them on the rain-splattered ramp. "They have orders not to let anyone pass before daybreak," he explained. "If Tarleton comes this way, we'll stop him here."

Jack looked at the bridge. Tendrils of mist rose from the river, obscuring the far end. "Let him pass," he said quietly.

Wingate's face screwed up in protest. Jack continued, "He'll be on his guard until he steps onto the bridge. He won't be expecting anyone to challenge him out there."

He could see Wingate's thoughts playing out on his face. After a moment, the major nodded. He turned to the sentries. "We're expecting a man to show up at any moment. He's tall, and wearing an officer's uniform."

"A colonel," Kate interjected.

"Right. Once he passes your position," Wingate told the sergeant, "close the gate and guard it. If he returns, kill him."

The sergeant blinked raindrops out of his eyes. "Yes, sir."

Wingate turned to Jack. "Come along."

"I'm not going out there unarmed, Major."

Wingate looked at the soldiers. "One of you men have a sidearm?" A pimple-faced private handed over a revolver. Wingate passed it to Jack. "Ready now?"

"Just a moment." Jack took Kate's arm and led her back to the trees. "You stay here."

"Jack . . ."

He laid a finger on her lips. "You can identify Tarleton. Stay out of sight and give the sergeant a signal if there's any question it's him. Will you do that for me?"

Her lower lip quivered, then she set her mouth firmly and nodded. "Be careful," she whispered.

He kissed her cheek and walked toward Wingate. "Let's go."

They mounted the ramp, skirted the gate, and strode onto the bridge. Mist rising from the river completely enveloped them.

They walked in silence. At the midway point, Jack stopped. "Go on ahead."

Wingate whirled toward him. "Why?"

"I'm going to take him here." Jack gestured at the haze enshrouding them. "I'll hear him coming long before he can see me. I'll have the element of surprise."

"You're right. This is a good spot for an ambush."

"Go to the other end of the bridge," Jack continued. "If he gets past me, you'll be our final line of defense." His eyes narrowed. "Kill him, or die trying."

Their gazes locked, exchanging the unspoken oath of warriors preparing to put their lives on the line. Wingate extended his hand. "Good luck, Rebel."

Jack gripped it firmly. "Thanks, Yank."

Tarleton reined his horse when he spotted the soldiers at the bridge. He looked around, but made out very little in the gathering fog.

A sergeant stepped forward. "Halt and identify yourself!"

"Colonel Ira Taylor, Second Rhode Island Infantry."

"State your business, sir."

"I've just come from the city. Secretary Stanton has ordered me to take a dispatch to a detachment over in Charles County."

The sergeant stepped back and saluted. "You may pass, sir. Open the gate!"

Two soldiers lifted the wooden barrier. Tarleton returned the salute, then spurred his horse. It sauntered onto the bridge, hooves clomping loudly on the damp wooden planks.

Jack heard the hoofbeats from a long way off. They rang out over the sound of the Anacostia River rushing beneath his feet, carried on the rising wind that lashed his face.

"Get on," he heard Tarleton urge his mount.

Jack clutched the revolver, slowly drawing back the hammer. There was a faint click. Jack squeezed the walnut handgrip, never taking his eyes off the swirling mist.

The steady clip-clop grew louder, each step echoing the pounding in his chest. The horse was panting now.

A hoof penetrated the foggy veil, followed by a foreleg. Jack slid silently to the center of the bridge. He aimed the revolver at the shadowy outline of the rider.

"Stop right there!"

The horse whinnied, rearing up.

"Get down, Tarleton. Now."

The horse lowered its front legs. A shot rang out. Splinters from the planking just to the right of Jack's foot showered onto his boots.

"Heeyah!" Tarleton yelled, and the big animal charged straight toward Jack. He jumped back as it sped past, lost his balance and fell down hard.

Jack raised the revolver, aimed at the spectral image in the saddle, and pulled the trigger. The horse gave a terrible cry and fell face forward onto the wet planking. It tumbled, shrieking in pain, taking Tarleton down with it.

Jack rose. He kept the gun trained as he limped over to Tarleton, who was lying beside the wounded horse. "Get up."

"Can't." Tarleton grimaced. "My leg is under the saddle."

Jack approached cautiously, his gun still aimed at the assassin. "Are you hurt?"

"I think I broke it. Feels like the bone is jutting out of the skin."

"Don't worry. They'll have you patched up in plenty of time to walk to the gallows."

"I'm not going to make it to the gallows," Tarleton groaned. "I'll bleed to death before you can get this horse off me."

Jack's gun stayed in place. "You'd better not be lying."

"I'm dying. This is no time for lies."

Jack stood over him, studying the prey he had pursued so long and so far. "Why did you do it?" he finally asked.

"Lincoln?"

Jack was surprised by the admission. Perhaps Tarleton really was dying. "How much did Standiford pay you?"

"Not enough, I assure you. But I didn't kill Lincoln for money."

"What was it?"

"You of all men should understand." Jack could hear a smile creeping into Tarleton's voice. "I did it for Kate St. Claire."

Jack stepped back. "What?"

"She's quite a woman, our Kate. Planned the whole thing."

"You're a damned liar!"

"I'm a dead man." Tarleton paused, his voice growing weaker. "Who do you think introduced me to Booth? And when Richmond alerted us that you were on our trail, Kate kept you occupied." He gave a sharp laugh that broke off in a yelp of pain. "Kate is very good at keeping men occupied."

"That's a lie!"

"She even made sure I shot Lincoln with her very own gun."

Jack wiped the rain from his eyes with a sodden sleeve. "You haven't said a word of truth. I know what you did to her tonight before you went into Lincoln's box."

Tarleton gave a laugh so weak it sounded as if his strength might give out at any moment. "Part of the plan. Kate got rid of you first, then met me for one last tryst. She even mussed herself up like she'd been attacked. That way, if she saw any police or soldiers, she'd have a reason for sending them after an imaginary assailant, keeping the path clear for me to reach Lincoln."

Jack stood frozen, unsure of Tarleton's story.

"Well, friend, you win after all." Tarleton grunted. "You didn't stop me from doing my duty, but now you've fulfilled yours. I have one last request."

"What's that?"

"I'll be damned if I want to go in this position." His hand stretched over the back of the prostrate horse. "Pull me free. Let me die like a man."

Jack looked at the dark, pathetic form beneath him. "You don't deserve to die like a man."

"That's true," Tarleton whispered. "But you do."

He jumped up, butting his head into Jack's stomach with full force. The revolver flew from Jack's hand, splashing into the river below. Tarleton, obviously uninjured, moved with the power of a possessed man, throwing himself at Jack, knocking him down and pinning him against the slick planks. "You've been a fool every step of the way," Tarleton sneered.

"Not fool enough to believe that swill about Kate."

"Here's a nugget of truth for you. I enjoyed ravishing her after I knocked her senseless. I did things to her that sailors would never dream about. And you know what I'm going to do after I kill you? I'll find her and have seconds."

Jack channeled all his mounting fury into his muscles. He heaved Tarleton off him with a thrust so powerful it sent the killer sprawling. Jack fell on top of him. They rolled, grabbed and pushed, each somehow making it to his feet. They swung and punched, each giving, each taking blows that would have sent lesser men collapsing in surrender.

Jack's fist connected with Tarleton's chin, driving him backward. Tarleton reached into his boot and pulled out a long knife.

Jack danced back as Tarleton got up, inching toward him, blade first.

"This is quite a night," Tarleton panted. "First, I have Kate. Then I kill Lincoln. Now I kill . . . you!" He lunged forward. Jack jumped aside at the last instant.

Tarleton lost his balance on the wet span. His feet flew out from under him and he landed hard on his backside, sliding off the side of the bridge. Just as his body was going over, his hand grasped the wet surface, his fingers desperately gripping the slippery wood.

Jack stood over the dark figure struggling to keep from falling into the rushing water below. "Tell me you're sorry," he demanded. "Say you're sorry for what you did to Kate, what you did to Lincoln. For what you did to Sam and Felix and heaven only knows who else. Give me a reason to believe there's a trace of a soul inside your miserable body, and I'll pull you up."

Tarleton looked up, mustered a wide smile, and said in a proud voice, "I swear before God . . . I loved everything I did."

Jack lifted his right foot and stomped the heel onto Tarleton's fingers, grinding and crunching them with all his might. Tarleton screamed. His grip gave way. Jack watched him plummet into the darkness, then heard a loud splash. He peered down at the rushing water. It swirled and raged, washing away all the hatred Tarleton had aroused in him.

Footsteps pounded behind him. Wingate rushed up. "What happened?" Jack raised a hand to ward off the questions, but Wingate kept asking. "Where's Tarleton? I heard shots."

Jack nodded wearily toward the river. Wingate looked down. "Did he say anything?"

"He admitted shooting Lincoln. And he said he enjoyed doing it. That was all." Jack left Wingate staring into the water.

Summoning all his strength, he forced himself to move. The farther he went, the weaker he felt.

"Jack!" Kate's voice cut through the mist. It gave him the will to push on, to fall at last into her embrace.

She kissed his face and ran her fingers through his soaked hair. He leaned on her, his arms wrapped tightly around her. He rested his cheek on the top of her head.

"It's over," Jack said. "Now, and for always, it's over."

He took Kate's hand and led her away, away from the scene of the last killing, away from all the deaths and sorrow. They walked off the bridge and headed west.

Cedar Branch, Colorado Territory
June 1866

Jack put the mules in the lean-to barn for the night, then went into the one-room sod cabin.

"Know what I was just thinking?" Kate stirred a pot over an open fire. "Blue curtains would look lovely in the front window. Next time I'm in town I'll buy some material."

Jack poured water into a washbowl and scrubbed his hands. "I'll sew them if you finish plowing the back field."

"Just the idea!" Kate laughed. "Come and eat."

There was a sharp knock on the door. "Who could that be?"

"One way to find out," Jack said as he crossed the room.

A man in a scraggly dark beard and a dusty black suit stood at the door. "Am I too late for supper?"

Jack stared at the wind-burned face. "Major Wingate?"

Kate rushed to greet him. "What a delightful surprise! Please come in. If you don't mind stew, a pone of corn bread, and a cup of buttermilk, then you're just in time."

"Best offer I've had all day." Wingate settled into a handmade chair at the handmade dining table. "You folks are sure hard to find. I've been looking for nearly a year now."

"We've been right here," Jack explained. "Busting sod and trying to make a crop."

"And what about you, Major?" Kate handed him a steaming bowl and a spoon.

"Ex-major." He scooped up a mouthful of stew and washed it down with a swig of milk. "The boys in Washington eventually got me cashiered from the service."

"That's a shame," Jack said.

Wingate shrugged. "With the war over, I'd have mustered out anyway. And I wanted to track you two down."

"However did you find us?" Kate asked.

"Ran into a fellow down in Texas." Wingate took another bite of stew. "I mentioned I'd been in Washington, and he said he lived there during the war. He asked what I was doing out this way, and I told him I was looking for two friends. And he did the damnedest thing." He sipped his buttermilk. "Told me, 'Jack and Kate are up in Colorado Territory.' Without another word, he walked away."

"Rufus," Kate whispered.

"Who?" Wingate asked.

"An old friend," Jack answered. "Why were you looking for us?"

"I had one last adventure before they kicked me out of the army." Wingate wolfed down more stew. "I was assigned to the search for Booth. I was there when he was shot."

"We read about his death in the papers," Jack said.

"The papers didn't say we found his diary. I was the first person to read it." Wingate scraped a piece of meat from his tooth. "Funny thing. When it reached Washington, several pages were missing. No one knows what was on them or what happened to them." He removed a small envelope from his coat and dropped it on the table.

Jack and Kate stared at the packet as Wingate resumed eating. "You tried to warn me," he mumbled between bites, "but I didn't listen. I'll regret that as long as I live. I figure this might even the score between us."

He dropped his spoon into the empty bowl. "That was wonderful. Now, if you folks will excuse me, I've got to be heading on to Denver." He rose.

"Night's coming on," Jack pointed out. "Stay here with us."

"I appreciate the offer." Wingate placed his hand on Jack's shoulder. "Truth is, I like riding at night. It's better than facing my nightmares."

They said their good-byes. Jack and Kate watched Wingate ride off until he was nothing but a blur against the prairie sunset. They returned to the table, each staring at the envelope he had left them.

"Do you want to open it, or should I?"

"I will," Kate said hoarsely. She removed three small pages and read Booth's scribbled words. They fell to the table as her hands flew to her mouth.

"What's wrong?"

"R-r-read it," she stuttered.

Jack picked up the papers. It was like hearing Booth speak from beyond the grave. He could imagine the actor's voice, filled with bravado, bragging about Lincoln's murder, bemoaning his life as a fugitive, blaming others for the lowly state to which he had fallen.

Then he came to the passage that had so shaken his wife.

Of all the cruel ironies which have befallen me, the cruelest of all is knowing that I didn't commit the deed for which I am now persecuted. I am betrayed not by failure of resolve or inadequacy of design. I am betrayed by the hand of a man I believed true to our Cause. I am betrayed by the hand that struck the blow I had intended to strike myself. The blessed bullet was actually fired by a man calling himself Basil Tarleton. As he handed the weapon to me, he told me it was a gift from our acquaintance, Mrs. Kate Saint Claire. Surely the misery I now face, and the fate soon to be visited upon me, should be shared by her. And by him, may he burn in perdition.

"My God," Jack whispered.

The color drained from Kate's face. "The diary would have implicated me as a conspirator."

"Wingate saved your life."

"It was my gun," Kate said slowly. "I must live with that forever."

"You tried to save Lincoln, not kill him."

A tear trickled down her cheek. Jack gently brushed it away. Then he stuffed the diary pages back into the envelope and walked to the fireplace. He dropped it into the flames and watched it curl into black ashes. When there was nothing left, he returned to the table.

"If we get enough rain this summer," he told her, "our first corn crop should do nicely."

She nodded and sniffed. "You know, blue curtains would look lovely in the front window."

AUTHORS' NOTE

When fiction is woven into history, one question always arises: How much is true?

We have tried hard to remain faithful to the characters of historical figures. That said, their personalities, and events themselves, are open to interpretation.

Was Lucy Hale secretly engaged to Booth? We strongly doubt it, though he likely made her *believe* they were engaged. Was Richmond involved in Booth's conspiracy and Lincoln's murder? Cases can be made both ways, but we lean against it. Did the conspirators actually attempt to kidnap Lincoln on March 17? Details are so vague and based entirely on recollected accounts, almost anything may have happened—or not happened. Even the date is disputed.

Most of the characters in this story are fictitious. There were no Basil Tarleton (thank goodness), Congressman Robert Standiford or Ambrose Houghton, or Assistant Secretary of War Charles Felton. Jack Tanner is a composite of various real soldiers. There was no Confederate espionage queen named Kate St. Claire, though she is based on a woman one of the authors once loved. History might have been richer had Rufus really existed, but he did not. Drake Wingate, Sam, Felix, Professor Beeler's Minstrels, and even Maguire's Theater are products of our imaginations.

There is no evidence Booth ever visited Surratt Tavern before midnight on April 14, 1865. We also took the liberty of transferring John Lloyd's "shooting irons" testimony to Louis Weichmann.

The events surrounding Lincoln's assassination remain remarkably murky nearly 150 years later. In most cases, we have tried to take a middle ground. Was Mrs. Surratt involved? (She may have been aware something was being plotted under her roof, but she probably did what many people in that troubled time did: She chose to look the other way.) Was Edwin Stanton part of an anti-Lincoln conspiracy? (The idea grows more absurd with the passing of time, though we had fun creating a scenario suggesting he might have been.)

One thing can be said with complete confidence: John Wilkes Booth alone murdered Abraham Lincoln.

J. Mark Powell and L. D. Meagher
Atlanta, Georgia
September 2004